Thinking 9
With

SAMHAIN AWAKENING

THE FALL OF THE VEIL

SABBAT SERIES
BOOK TWO

DEANN BELL

To Rachel,

Sending you lots of
luck, energy, and light
on this next Part of your
journey. Blessed Be!
DeAnn Bell

G Publishing Partners, LLC

BLURB

From Crafted Spells to Ageless Ties: When History Bites, Love Never Dies.

In the heart of Boston, Phoebe Pierce is more than just a witch at The Craft Shop; she's a fervent believer in the authentic magic of aligning personal energies. Yet, with Samhain's approach and eerie supernatural reports flooding in worldwide, she's tempted to double down on her protections and keep a low profile. But when an impromptu reading of an enchanted tome sweeps her off her feet—quite literally—she finds herself amidst ancient stones and face-to-face with the enigmatic vampire, January *ap Ionawr*.

Hailing from Deganwy, Wales, 1240 AD, January isn't just any vampire. On Lammas, in search of his destined mate, he summons an Unguided witch—enter Phoebe. She's the enchanting answer to his age-old wishes. Yet, shadows from January's distant past aren't just lurking; they're hunting, hell-bent on destroying her to thwart an ominous prophecy: the fall of the Veil.

The twist? Phoebe is intrinsically linked to a sudden surge of the Unguided in Boston. As the two navigate this web of power and prophecy, a love like no other kindles. But with the October air thick with spirits and intrigue, they must not only vindicate Phoebe but also confront bygone sins, and carve a shared path through the chaos of the Veil's descent.

ALSO BY DEANN BELL

Yule Moon

Samhain Awakening

Beltane Ash

Samhain Awakening
Fall of the Veil
Sabbat Series Book 2
COPYRIGHT©2023
DeAnn Bell
Cover Design by Wren Taylor

Published in the United States of America by:

DLG Publishing Partners

San Antonio, TX 78217

www.DLGPublishingPartners.com

The publisher does not have any control over and does not assume any responsibility for the author or third-party websites or their content.

CONTENTS

1. The Craft Shop   1
2. Lock and Key   14
3. Horns and All   29
4. Twilight Zone Moments   44
5. The Unseelie Court   52
6. Lammas Blessings   56
7. The Way You Are   67
8. Vampire Restaurants   77
9. Broken Promises   90
10. Shadow Curse   94
11. A Shape in the Darkness   98
12. Falling in Love   108
13. Mabon Magic   121
14. Magic and Divination   143
15. Echoes of the Future   151
16. The Mabon Council Meeting   163
17. A Family Affair   176
18. Old Vampires and New tricks   186
19. Lovers and True Companions   194
20. The Summons of Enir   204
21. The Witch's Ball   215
22. Samhain Curse   232
23. Larkshead or Die   246
24. How to Catch a Demon   254
25. The Witch's Ladder   272
26. Augusta Recovery Center   283
27. The Circle is Cast   292
28. Witch Hunt   306
29. Samhain Blessings   312

Acknowledgments   317
About the Author   319

This is for my wonderful husband, Rob Bell, and our feline family Swt, Cinder, and Ella. Also for my witchy Halloween loving sister, Jennifer DuBerry. I carry you always in my heart.

THE CRAFT SHOP

"Damn it, Olivia," Phoebe growled looking around at the mess left in her office.

Her beautifully organized desk was covered in crumpled receipts, open books, scribbled post-it notes, powdery dust that must have been the remains of incense, some packaged herbs, and a half-eaten tube of Oreo cookies.

No amount of warding her office or positive visualization could keep the shop owner, Olivia Clay, from treating the entire place like it was her personal potions storeroom. Technically it was. She owned the store, the brand, and the contents. About once a month she whirled into the store in a flurry of red shoes and purple scarves just long enough to drop off receipts and stock purchases, wreck Phoebe's well-organized world, and pocket whatever struck her fancy in the store.

Olivia's lack of basic organization was both the reason Phoebe had a job and the reason she often wished she had a different job. She promised Phoebe that once things were "settled" here in Boston, she would open a new branch of The Craft Shop in Larkshead, Maine, where Phoebe would be completely in charge. What exactly needed to be settled here was never clear.

She supposed normal people just shook their head at these types of situations and went about their day. What she really needed to do was to look Olivia straight in the eye and say stop making a mess. Unfortunately, she hated conflict more than she hated cleaning up, so she chose to silently seethe.

Separating what she could identify as relevant receipts from what appeared to be notes scribbled on the back of any old receipt, Phoebe began a calming mantra.

"This is no big deal. Olivia doesn't do it on purpose. This is a necessary step in your…"

Her affirmations trailed off. The next words were supposed to be *This is a necessary step in my journey,* but why bother saying them? This was a crossroad she'd been standing at for quite some time. It was time to choose. Either make her place here or walk away.

This job paid her bills, gave her time to study her magic and help other people learn, she got a great discount, she could walk to work from her apartment. In the grand scheme of things this was a good life. Scraping the incense dust carefully into the trash, she separated the herbs, the receipts, and put the Oreos in her top drawer. Finders keepers. It didn't help her feel better about the situation.

Lammas was on the horizon, it was time to do a stock take at the store so she could let her hyper organization fetish go wild today, and she could already smell the pumpkin spice coffee her colleague, Melissa, was brewing in the staff kitchen. Other than the complete mess in her office, today had all the ingredients of being a perfect day. Hadn't she always said all she really wanted to be was happy? What was happy anyway?

If her feelings right now were any indication, it wasn't

this. She'd created a regimented ridiculous predictable existence where her biggest decisions were whether to eat frozen pizza three nights in a row. It was time to make a change.

The delivery man, Sean, showed up before the store opened with several large boxes marked fragile. Phoebe just waved him through the door. Lugging them down the basement stairs into the storeroom, she placed them in the white circle with the other supplies waiting to be smudged and checked in.

"I hope those boxes are from Candle-Lit," Melissa said following Phoebe down the stairs carrying two mugs filled with pumpkin spice coffee, extra sugar, and whipped cream. Like a gothic Rainbow Bright, her black pigtails were decorated with an array of autumn-colored ribbons. "The Sisters of the Sun called every hour on the hour yesterday to see if they were here yet."

Phoebe took a mug and sipped the spicy sweet drink carefully. "Why don't they just order them online like everyone else?"

Melissa clinked her glass against Phoebe's narrowly avoiding slopping whipped cream onto the floor. "Apparently because we cleanse them better than anyone else. Also, word on the Witchy scene is that the candle maker, Emily Rollins, is holding back stock to try her hand at the Larkshead Christmas Market. This Lammas delivery might be the last one we get until after Christmas."

"I've always wanted to go to the Christmas Market or to the Yule celebration. It's supposed to be the best on the East coast."

"Well, when Olivia finally lets you open your own store there, you'll get to go every year." Melissa cradled her coffee close. Looking on the bright side was her super-power. "Then you can find some random excuse for why I need to be there for the holidays too."

Phoebe grinned. "Sure. We'll let Olivia run the store on her own during the busiest seasons we have. I don't even want to imagine what this place would look like when you got back."

"Ahh, you saw your office."

"What was she doing in there? It looks like she was burgling the place."

"Apparently looking for a fancy green book that she ordered and can't find."

Phoebe went to the supplies cupboard placing her coffee on a coaster. In a dark wooden box was a cedar and sage smudge stick and a lighter long enough not to singe fingers. Because supplies came in from all sorts of places, Olivia insisted that each be smudged to clear out disruptive energy. The cleansing ritual was one of the first that Phoebe learned, and it was still her favorite.

Lighting the blackened fronds of the stick, she quickly drew circles of smoke around herself, Melissa, and then the objects in the circle. The salty green smell immediately helped her relax and shake off some of her earlier anger.

"Better?"

"Much."

"I'm sure the Mabon blessing candles are in one of those boxes. Find them and put them on the system first so I can sell them and get the Sisters off my back, and I will let you use your Lammas present in the stockroom."

Phoebe laughed. "Lammas present? Lammas is about celebrating the first harvest, not presents."

"So, you don't want this?" Melissa walked back to the bathroom door and pulled out an industrial sized Shop-Vac.

Phoebe squealed balancing her sage stick on the rim of her coffee cup and rushed over. "You are a goddess. Is this the one with the extended crevice tool attachments?"

"Yep." Melissa picked up the sage stick balancing it on the edge of a nearby shelf and handed Phoebe her coffee. "I made sure it had all the weird and wonderful attachments that you love so much. Drink this first or it will be cold by the time you finish."

"How did you get permission to buy this? Olivia says vacuums suck up all her wards."

Melissa shrugged. "She also says that she can read minds, but she didn't see this coming."

They both laughed until tears were in their eyes.

"Come on Phoebe, Lammas includes gifts to honor the God and Goddess to ensure an easy winter. Nothing will make my winter easier than not hearing you moan about the dust. Olivia resets the wards after a major sabbat. Technically, we're saving her a job."

Phoebe didn't have to be asked twice. By the time she'd finished hovering the last of the dust from behind the shelves of the stockroom, her heart was happier, and the store upstairs was heaving with customers.

Inventory list in one hand and pen in the other, she began to open the new boxes, check items off the list, and try and find somewhere to put them. Candles from Candle-Lit filled most of the first two boxes which delighted both Melissa and the Sisters of the Sun. Without ceremony, Melissa hauled a fat green candle out of the box called "Enlightenment" and lit it. The candle filled the storeroom with scents of sweet, dried hay, wildflowers, and something that reminded Melissa of a moonlit beach and Phoebe of dark forests.

The scents from the Candle-Lit candles were always a treat but today Phoebe could almost feel the light of this candle burn away the last of her gloom. Taking one deep breath and then another, she pulled the scent through her lungs as she worked. With her second cup of coffee, she looked into the flame of the green candle.

"I'm lost," she whispered to the glowing flame in the sparkling clean stockroom.

The scent of dark forest filled the room and even though all the windows and doors were shut, the candle flickered in an invisible wind that danced along her skin.

Shivering, she opened the third box which was a mixture of what appeared to be new books and old singing bowls. For all that Olivia got on her nerves, she was kind. If she felt another witchcraft shop was struggling, she purchased a portion of their back-stock to help them out. Phoebe began checking the items off her list with the satisfaction only a true neat freak understands. *Love Spells for the Recently Divorced*. Three books; check. *Controlling Your Life through Meditation*. Two books; check. *Witchcraft with Vampires and other Enlightened Beings*.

She read the title a second time sure she'd misread it. Yep. Witchcraft with Vampires. She looked at her list again noting that all the items in this box were on the inventory except for this one. The volume was nicer than most of the other stock; hardbound in green leather for one thing, with the title engraved in gold writing. Probably the book Olivia was looking for this morning. Unfortunately, the list for the new acquisitions was still in her office.

She stepped outside the white circle placing the book on the top of one of the other boxes to retrieve the other list. No sooner had she set the book down and turned to leave when she heard it drop to the floor.

Turning, she was struck by the sheer beauty of the illustrations and calligraphy inside. Picking it up gently, she ran her fingers over the illuminated words and read the incantation aloud. As a witch and a person who watched too many scary movies, she should have known better.

"My body standing on this plane,
dissolve and become whole again.
By Earth, Air, Water, Fire
bring me to my heart's desire."

A sudden flash of light hit her like a fist in the chest. Blinded, she opened her mouth to scream but there was no air in her lungs and then there were no lungs. She dissolved into light, into pure being, and for one heart stopping second, she understood how and why she was connected to everything and everyone in every time that had, or would, ever exist. It was soul breaking in its magnificence. Then, as if the moment had never been, she was standing in the middle of a stone circle surrounded by a dense forest.

Falling to her knees she clutched the green book to her chest like a shield and then shoved it away from her scrambling back. The circle itself was like something from a dream. Twelve large slabs of standing white stone spaced equidistant from each other created an enclosure for the emerald grass beneath her. The ground outside the circle was covered in thick red, gold, and brown leaves but the circle itself was clear. Something like dandelion fluff hung suspended in the sunlight that slanted through the twisted branches of the huge surrounding trees.

Through her panic she felt both the power and the serenity of the place seep into her. A physical tangible magic like she had never felt before made its way up her arms and through her body untangling knots of muscle, self-doubt, and worry before making its way down her legs and back into the ground.

Grounding, cleansing, these were words she knew but

this wasn't the personal magic that Phoebe had always believed in, this was a primal thrumming of energy all around her that she hadn't known existed. Not only was the energy traveling through her, but she found if she closed her eyes and concentrated, she could sink into the ground with the energy twisting through the dense roots of grass and recapture the connection she lost. It was incredible.

"Are you alright?"

The gruff voice surprised her, and her eyes snapped open. Her consciousness slammed back into her body knocking the breath from her for a second time. Only then did she realize the warm tears making their way down her face. A white man sat just outside the circle beside the largest of the stone slabs. It wasn't just that his skin was pale; it lacked all but the barest trace of color; like he was made from the same stone as the circle.

How she'd missed him she had no idea. He was wearing dark jeans that outlined powerful legs and a grey long-sleeved shirt rolled up muscled arms. His hair was white and pulled back into a ponytail, but there were only the barest of lines around his eyes and mouth. Not an old man. Albino? She looked into his eyes; they were the grey blue of a winter ocean. He was as wild and as beautiful as the forest surrounding them.

If he was surprised to see her materialize in front of him, he didn't show it. They watched each other for a long minute and Phoebe became aware of her breathing, and then of a stirring in the back of her mind that felt curiously like attraction. She shifted forward to sit on her knees and looked around again trying to identify something familiar.

"This can't be happening." She said it carefully, more to herself than to the man across from her. "This is some kind of dream."

The man before her smiled slowly as if the expression

didn't come naturally to his face revealing a set of long canine teeth. "I would not consider myself to be anyone's dream."

Phoebe snorted. "Then you don't look in enough mirrors." She stood up dusting herself off. "You are too beautiful to be real and I am too rational to believe in vampires or teleportation."

She believed in magic. Magic could help you believe in yourself, its main power was to help you focus on what you wanted to achieve, to connect to the world around you. The kind of magic that could physically transport you places where incredibly sexy vampires were waiting for you only happened in movies. She closed her eyes and tilted her face toward the sun.

"Wake up Phoebe. This is just a dream."

January watched the sun sparkle in the moisture left behind by the woman's tears, her auburn curls drinking in the fiery warmth of the afternoon sun, and he wanted to destroy whoever had made her weep. The feeling should have disturbed him, but 800 years of being undead had taught him to accept his emotions rather than question them.

The autumn leaves fell around her creating a perfect picture of earth magic. In jeans and a green cowl-necked sweater that hugged her rounded breasts and hips, she wasn't dressed for a formal Lammas ritual. That she was able to appear here in his personal place for magic without an invitation meant that she was both practicing magic and powerful.

He had brought his own offering of honey, bread, milk and the last of the summer flowers to the White Stone Circle this Lammas Eve to ask for a blessing. Not just for the air to move in and out of his lungs and the blood to flow through his veins, but to feel alive. What he needed more than anything right now was a companion. To have the circle suddenly provide him with someone stunned him on a level that he'd never known. Could it truly be that easy? To wish for someone and then have them? His rational mind rejected the scenario, but he couldn't deny that he felt drawn to her.

"Phoebe?" He repeated her name slowly, tasting it. "You look a little confused. What spell were you trying to cast?"

Moving slowly to his feet, he was aware of the furious beat of her heart. Something here was terrifying her. He might have thought it was himself, but her eyes wondered over his face and body with nothing short of sexual hunger. She desired him. He moved toward her.

She held up her hand as if to shoo him off. "Inventory. I was doing inventory and inventory is boring. Okay, I like it but to most people it's boring. I'm asleep in the store-room at The Craft Shop. This…," she made a sweeping motion with her hand, "…is a dream. I mean, vampires, really? How sexually repressed teenage angst is that for a fantasy?"

January laughed not sure if he should be flattered or insulted. There were a couple of his kind who had a bit of a Count Dracula thing going, but he wasn't one of them. He smiled at her letting her see his fangs clearly. Rather than stepping back in fear her pupils dilated and she took in a sharp breath.

"All right," he said willing to humor her. "If you're asleep and this is a fantasy, what do we do next?"

The smile she gave him was pure temptation. "If I wasn't at work there are several things I'd like to try with you, but since I am at work, I need to wake up."

She looked around for a minute as if weighing her options and then closed her eyes and slowed down her breathing. "When I open my eyes on the count of three, I will be back in the storeroom. One, Two, Three…Phoebe wake up!"

January watched quietly but nothing happened. She opened her eyes and then met his gaze with a frown that looked determined rather than defeated. She stood up biting her lower lip and brushing her palms against her jeans.

"Okay, lucid dreaming books say I should take an action in the dream that signifies waking to the subconscious."

January felt the subtle thrum of magic in the circle. She was fascinating. He had no idea what was going on, but he was enjoying the hell out of it. He moved toward her again. "What would you suggest?"

She shrugged. "This dream is some sort of romantic fantasy or fairy tale. So maybe a kiss? That's what wakes Sleeping Beauty up, right?"

"You want me to kiss you?" He didn't even pretend he wasn't flirting. The way she watched him move made him feel sexier than he'd ever felt in his life. She crossed her arms over her chest, her green eyes narrowing. He held up his hands. "I'm just making sure I get this right. Strangers don't normally ask me to kiss them."

"Do you have a better idea?"

"Not at all. I would love to kiss you. But if I'm not a dream, then when we finish kissing, maybe we kiss some more, and then we go get a drink?"

She laughed rubbing her forehead. "I thought vampires only drank blood."

January shrugged again moving slowly, almost casually toward her. Enlightened beings typically avoided stepping into a circle with an unknown witch because it was a place witches had absolute power, but January was too interested to care that she might be trying to control him.

He crossed the circle boundary and for the first time

since his Enlightenment, he felt the stirrings of Earth magic in his blood. Stopping when he was close enough to smell incense and dried herbs on her skin, he waited for her to make the next move.

"I didn't specify what each of us would be drinking. I would make sure that you enjoyed it either way."

She rolled her eyes. "That's a bit cliché. Come on then, Dracula Prince Charming, I have work to do. If Olivia catches me asleep in the stockroom after I vacuumed, I am in deep trouble."

Like she'd done it a hundred times before, she wrapped her arms around his neck standing on tip toe to kiss him. Once, twice, her lips feathered across his as if she were asking his permission. He bent closer and angled his head to give her full access to his mouth. She took his offering expertly stepping further into his embrace and deepening the kiss. He pushed his fingers through her thick warm hair and used his other hand to mould her soft body to his.

Curiosity turned to pure desire when she moved willingly into his arms. It felt like an eternity since he'd been accepted for what he was without fear. Even his own people tended to give him a wide berth.

She moaned in pleasure bringing her hands up to untie his hair. Caressing the back of his neck and his scalp, she grabbed him close as if she could not breathe without him. He lost track of time consumed by her kiss until he felt her pull her head back to whisper against his lips, "Phoebe, wake up."

There was a burst of raw power and blue light, and then she was gone. He was dizzy with the sudden loss of her. The only evidence that she'd been there was the light smell of her on his skin, the taste of her on his lips, and a green leather-bound book she'd dropped when she got here.

Crouching down he touched the earth inside the circle

and whispered his thanks for the blessing. Whatever else the witch was, she was a blessing to him today. He walked over and plucked her book from the ground reading the title with interest. So that was her game? Witchcraft with Vampires tended to focus on sex and blood magic. He enjoyed both. It would not matter where she went, he would find her and finish what they started.

2

LOCK AND KEY

January used every bit of his supernatural speed to catch Phoebe as she fainted. It was a skill he hadn't utilized since the days of tight corsets. He lowered her carefully to the floor cradling her close. Her head lulled back a moment, but her eyes were closed. The intensity of the relief he felt tore the breath from his lungs. If she were shutting down, her eyes would be open. He glared at James.

"Tell me what's going on here?"

Melissa knelt down beside him brushing the hair from Phoebe's face and fanning her. "She's okay. She just fainted. Not surprised with you two Neanderthals pushing her so hard. How long has she been Awakened?"

"I don't know," they said in unison.

James reached towards Phoebe's arm to check her pulse and January bared his teeth and growled. He hadn't known he was going to do it but once it was done, he knew he meant it. Both Melissa and James jumped back with their hands in the air. He waited a second trying to regain his calm.

"I will care for her until she is well enough to make her choice."

James cleared his throat. "If the cases of the Unguided are spreading in Boston, then I need to take her to the recovery center for questioning. She might be able to tell us who brought her through the Veil."

Melissa crossed her arms over her chest and shook her head. "If either of you two thinks I'm going to let you take her anywhere unconscious and without her permission you have another thing coming. Olivia told me to watch her. Phoebe hasn't made any choices yet. We're damn lucky she hasn't shut down already."

Logically what Melissa said made sense, but he cradled Phoebe to his chest knowing he wasn't going to leave her here. Someone close to her was responsible for forcing her through the Veil. It could be this Melissa or Olivia. If James wanted to guide Phoebe, the person responsible might be someone much more powerful.

"I appreciate what you're saying but are you strong enough to protect her if you're attacked?"

Melissa opened her mouth, but James interrupted her.

"Then do as the witch asked and leave her in the shop. Let the Recovery Unit pick her up from here." James clicked his wings again. "The wards are strong here. Or let me take her in to the Recovery Unit myself. You know I can protect her. This is my job."

January scooped Phoebe up off the floor and stood. It felt right to hold her. "You both mistake me. I'm not asking for your permission. I'm telling you what is going to happen. I am taking Phoebe somewhere safe. When she's awake, she can decide what she wants to do next. You will not interfere."

"Compulsion doesn't work on me, hot shot," Melissa moved between him and the door. "And if you think I am going to let anyone walk out the door with my unconscious friend you have another thing coming." She snapped her fingers twice and said, "*Salutem!*"

Brilliant wards wove tightly around the shop. James backed away from the exits.

January looked around appreciatively. "Your ward word means safety. If I meant to hurt her in any way, I could not carry her through your ward."

Melissa crossed her arms over her chest but didn't say anything. James looked at her with respect. The ward pattern was complicated even for an experienced witch.

January carried Phoebe around the witch and to the front of the store. He pushed the door open with his hip. He stood with Phoebe in his arms half inside and half outside the wards. The golden light glittered but did not restrain him.

"I mean her no harm. She is under my care until she says otherwise." He stared directly at James. "I will not tolerate any more interference."

With that, he carried Phoebe out the door and into a new world.

A burning prickling sensation in her nostrils yanked Phoebe from a deep and dreamless sleep. She woke with her eyes watering and her lungs sputtering for air.

"It's all right," a soft feminine voice said. "It's just smelling salts. January gave them to me. You fainted."

She sat up in a bed dashing tears from her eyes and looking around. Rather than being in The Craft Shop with Melissa, a vampire, and an actual demon, she was in what appeared to be a luxury bedroom straight out of Arabian Nights with an angel. Could this day get any weirder?

The most beautiful woman Phoebe had ever seen in her life tucked hawk-colored wings beneath her long black hair, but it was her eyes that held Phoebe captive. Wide but not innocent, eyes so dark brown that they were almost black. They looked at her with so much kindness and understanding that Phoebe felt a lump of emotion form in her throat.

"Am I dead?"

The woman put her cool slender hand on Phoebe's brow with a twinkle in her eye. "Definitely not. I'm Doctor Loftin, you can call me Rosalind, and you are very much alive. How are you feeling?"

Waves of reassurance and love flowed over Phoebe washing the knots of fear from her brow and shoulders. She sat up slowly swinging her legs over the side of a very plush bed thinking that the impression that Dr. Loftin had wings would go away if she changed angles. They didn't.

"I'm losing my mind. This morning my biggest concerns were not getting caught vacuuming upwards and whether I should really eat frozen pizza three nights in a row. Tonight, I thought I had a date with a vampire, I think I saw a demon, and you look like an angel."

The woman laughed a deep hearty sound. She gently smoothed Phoebe's blouse and whispered something in a language Phoebe didn't understand.

"Sounds like a complex story. Perhaps you should start at the beginning?"

Rosalind started to speak but Phoebe held up her hand.

"No. Never mind. I don't want to know. I just want it to stop. I'm going home and I'm going to take a long hot shower and go to bed. Tomorrow I'm going to wake up and find out I was running a really high fever today and I hallucinated all of this because I watch too much television. I'm probably in my bed right now."

Phoebe lay back in the bed picturing her own bed, the details of her pillow and duvet, the light scent of cupcakes that came from her bedside candle. Before she understood what she was doing she felt the power gather around her like it had in the circle. If she went back toward the power, maybe she could find her way back to her own reality.

She closed her eyes and whispered, "Wake up, Phoebe."

January came through the door carrying a bag of take-away just as the blue light flashed through the room. Rosalind stood staring at the empty bed with a look of pure disbelief on her face. He stifled a laugh. Apparently, angels could be surprised.

"She's really good at that."

He sat the take-away by the door and came calmly into the room even though his inner demons were screaming at him to follow her. Luckily self-control was something he'd been good at even before he'd turned vampire.

"Did you get a chance to make sure she was okay before she disappeared?"

Rosalind stood up smoothing her hands over her jeans. "Yes. Medically she's fine. Magically she's incredible. Mentally she's close to shut down. If I'm not mistaken, that disappearing trick she just pulled was probably her subconsciously using her magic to keep herself sane."

"I agree. Do you know where she went?" He regulated his voice as much as he could to disguise his desire, but Rosalind wasn't fooled.

"She needs time and space to think about what's happening."

"Alex is in the kitchen. You now have a very nice bag of expensive food that must be eaten. I'm sure that you can think of something to do while I make sure Phoebe is safe."

"Alex is here? Wait." Rosalind shook her head crossing her arms. "This is bribery. That woman is fighting for her sanity. Understand?"

"And I am currently fighting for mine. I can't explain why but I need to know where she is and that she's safe. If you won't tell me, I'll find another way to find her tonight.

Meanwhile your food will be getting cold, and your date is growing impatient."

Rosalind didn't budge. "You told me you met this woman this morning. I know you've always had some Chivalric hang-ups but I'm hearing worry not duty in your voice. What's this woman to you?"

Her question stopped him in his tracks. Honesty with himself was a trait that had kept him alive through the centuries. He wanted her. It was as simple and as complicated as that.

"I don't know. When I saw her this morning I was intrigued. I'd asked the Stone Circle for a Lammas blessing, to find a companion, and she appeared. When I saw her this afternoon, the attraction was stronger. I needed to touch her. When James reached out to take her pulse this evening, I was possessive, not protective."

Rosalind dropped her tough stance and put her hand across her heart. "James was there?"

"He was and I didn't care. I was glad to see him but that's it. I was so focused on finding Phoebe I barely noticed him." He ushered Rosalind towards the kitchen stopping to hand her the takeaway. Alex was making as much noise as he could to let January know that he could hear them. Werewolf hearing was exceptional and so were their manners.

"That should bother you," Rosalind said but her attention was already moving toward the kitchen. "If you were a smart man, you'd stay away from her until you figured out what was going on."

"We both know I'm not that smart."

She opened the bag and peeked inside. "You're a good man but if you hurt her, I will personally make sure that you spend an eternity alone in a stone box on the underside of a mountain somewhere."

"You have my word, Aingael, she will be safe with me."

19

Rosalind laid a hand on January's arm just before they entered the kitchen. "She's the first Unguided we've been able to identify in this territory. She might be the key to understanding what's happening to the Veil. She needs to be brought before the Mabon Council."

January's jaw tightened. The thought of anyone having authority over Phoebe made his teeth lengthen in his mouth.

"This is bigger than both of us." Rosalind cupped his chin meeting his eyes with understanding, but her message was clear. She was his friend, but she would do what was best for the Enlightened.

"I understand. Will you help me find her?"

"Only if you promise not to rush back." She winked at him and then shut her eyes. The room filled with whispering in a thousand languages, some that January hadn't heard since he was a child. Rosalind chuckled. "She's safe at home asleep in her own bed."

January arched his brow at her. "I can't leave you to entertain if I have nowhere to go."

Rosalind opened her eyes and the voices disappeared. "211 Washington Park street, Apt 3. My sources say her door is locked and warded and her keys are in her handbag at her workplace."

January hugged her. "You're a good woman."

She sighed and returned his embrace. "No, I'm not or I wouldn't still be here."

The Washington Park apartment must have been a large family home at one point in its history. He parked his car on the curb in front of the house catching site of a hitching ring in the sidewalk. When it was finally clear in the 1970's that cars would become the main source of transport, he'd reluctantly learned to drive one. As a vampire from the 13th Century, he missed horses.

Like many other buildings of its kind, the mustard-colored home was divided into four apartments. One of the top ones was Phoebe's. The outer doors required a key, but he'd taken the time to return to The Craft Shop and collect her handbag.

Although the shop was closed, locked, and warded, being a vampire had its advantages. He'd climbed the outdoor fire escape to a second-floor window and forced it open. When no alarm sounded, he'd simply walked in. The bag was on the counter next to the place Phoebe had fainted. Not only did it smell like her but a quick shake revealed a set of keys with a ridiculous number of keychains at the bottom, one of which said Phoebe.

Glancing through the darkened windows close to her apartment he admitted that he wasn't as familiar with this part of town as he should have been. When he lived in a city, he walked every street at least once a year. It kept him aware of what was going on and gave him an early warning when it was time to go. Boredom was dangerous for his kind. It led to depression and unnecessary risk taking. When he lost interest in exploring a town, he knew it was time to move on. Only the recent outbreak of unsanctioned Awakenings and a matching spike in the number of werewolves in Boston had given him reason to delay his departure. If he'd gone, he might not have found Phoebe.

After trying a couple of keys in the apartment building lock, he unlocked the door and walked up the generous stairs making notes of the names and scents of the current occupants. As someone who regularly removed recently Enlightened people from unsuitable guides, he had no shortage of enemies. That was one of the reasons he'd offered himself as a companion rather than a guide. As a potential companion, Phoebe would be protected by all vampires. Companions were sacred to his people.

He acknowledged to himself that taking her out of The Craft Shop was unnecessary. In fact, they would probably still be in the Recovery Center together had he simply waited with her. In the dark quiet night, he gave himself permission to admit that he didn't care if what he was feeling was a spell or an answer to his prayers. He just wanted a chance to know her.

Finding her door was as easy as following her scent. The apartment across from hers was empty and he made a note to himself to keep it that way. The wards set around the entrance of her home were impressive. Wards were walls of energy around objects and spaces that were charged with a frequency that allowed some things to pass through and others not to. Even with a key, he doubted he would have been able to simply walk through the door without a direct invitation. Vampires didn't typically need an invitation to come inside like they did in stories. Only the Unseelie, specifically demons, needed a direct invite.

"Revelare," January whispered the command for the wards to reveal themselves. As his breath hit the doorway, colors flashed and moved across the threshold. Phoebe's wards allowed anything that did not directly or indirectly mean her harm to enter. They inspired a sense of neighborly goodwill. He almost opened the door and stepped inside to check on her but a series of small purple threads in the ward stopped him. Without a direct invitation to come inside, the ward was set to make you forget why you'd come. It was an odd combination, but that last ward firmly kept him outside her door. He wasn't sure she was powerful enough to make him forget her entirely, but he wasn't about to take the chance.

Now that he was standing outside her door with her safely inside the truth of Rosalind's words filtered through his mind. Phoebe was a woman standing on the brink of a complete and permanent shut down. If he pushed her too hard, he might never have a chance to learn anything about her. He'd seen people shut down before, their minds gone, eyes staring sightlessly. Both alive and dead. It was the reason unsanctioned Awakenings were punishable by true death rather than soul banishment. The old eye for an eye was the only punishment bad enough to discourage the Unseelie.

January used the key to open the door. Rather than going inside himself he swung the handbag around the door frame and let it drop to the floor so she would have it in the morning. He looked through the entrance noting the long living room filled with bookcases, a small dining area, and what appeared to be a half open bedroom door. The smell of vanilla, lemon, and sage kept him from being able to know for sure if she was in there. He waited silently in the doorway another couple of moments hoping that she snored or talked in her sleep but other than the soft hum of the refrigerator, the apartment was frustratingly silent.

Locking the door, he strode downstairs and then out the front door of the building into the cool night air. Staying here until dawn was an option but what he needed was a watch cat. He whistled softly and slightly off key four times and then waited. If he was lucky, he'd catch a local in a friendly mood. January got into his car, made himself comfortable, and waited. Almost an hour later a very lanky looking one-eyed calico colored bundle of feline pride walked purposely down the street. She approached with a slight limp and sat down beside the car with her tail twitching.

Getting out quickly, he gave her a short bow and then sat down on the street so that he could converse with her on her level. Cats detested being talked down to.

"Thank you for coming." She stared at him expectantly. "What should I call you?"

"Honey."

She said it so low that a passer-by would assume she merely yawned. It wasn't her real name. Cats, like the Fey and necromancers, were very careful with their real names.

"Honey. Thank you for coming. I need a favor for a favor."

Her ears twitched back and forth. "Maybe. What do you want?"

"There is a new witch in this building. She is Unguided. I need you to watch her door and tell me immediately if another Enlightened approaches her or if she leaves before I can return."

"Boring," Honey said with another yawn. "What do you trade?" she asked perking her ears forward.

January bowed. "Name your price."

Her smile put the Cheshire cat to shame.

"New litter and a young mother not far from here. Find her and her young ones a safe place to complete their lives. Bring me food since you disturb my hunt. I will do this favor."

January bowed again. "It's a deal. What should I get you to eat?"

January came through his door in the middle of the night with a cat carrier full of cats just in time to see Rosalind sneak out of Alex's room.

He frowned at her knowing before he said anything that there was nothing he could do about it.

"If you leave before he wakes up, he will think he's done something wrong."

Rosalind gasped and jumped-up hovering for a second

over the floor before setting down with a thump. "Presumptuous of you. For your information, it has to be like this."

"It doesn't. You're making a choice." He motioned for her to follow him into the kitchen placing the cats gently on the counter. Four pairs of suspicious eyes looked back and forth between them.

Rosalind walked forward on quiet feet. She patted January's shoulder, her dark brown eyes looking sad and torn. "I wasn't here for him."

She lifted the cat carrier from the counter.

January grabbed her wrist. "You can't. I made a promise."

"I know. A promise you would find a place where they could complete their lives. I will take them to that place."

January put his hand on the carrier and returned it to the counter. "It will be their choice."

He opened the door guiding three orange kittens and one very suspicious mother out. He bent close to the mother.

"I offer you a choice. I will find you and your family a home or provide one myself. You may also go with Rosalind who says she has a home for you. If these options do not suit, I will take you somewhere safe to make your own way."

The kittens looked at him intently, but he doubted they knew much about speaking to vampires yet. He stroked their downy heads gently. Their mother blinked slowly in thanks and then headed back to the carrier and for Rosalind. Her little family followed her. It didn't surprise him. An angel, even a fallen one, tended to lead to good fortune."

Rosalind grinned. "Tell Alex I will see him for dinner tonight. Tell Honey her friends are safe with me. I need their help. She'll understand."

With that, she picked up the carrier and walked out the door. January found himself for the first time in a long time at loose ends. Alex and Phoebe sleeping peacefully, no cats to settle, he made his way to bed propping the window open in case Honey sent word. It was getting close to the time when he needed to sleep and feed but in his current state of agitation, he doubted he could. There was only one human he craved and until she offered to satisfy his hunger, he would just have to wait. He settled for a long bath and an early night.

Although his mind felt restless sleep came to him almost instantly. He was plunged into a nightmare he'd not seen in over 40 years. He was sitting on a hilltop watching a beautiful golden headed woman in a black dress move over a battlefield going from dead soldier to dead soldier. At first, he thought she was a mourner, a wife or sister come to claim the body of her fallen, but she lifted each of the freshly dead to her mouth and appeared to suck from their throats. Something in him screamed in horror.

He pulled his sword from its sheath and rode toward her determined to stop the desecration of the dead. His horse reared over her, he raised his sword, she looked up with blood dripping from her mouth and hissed viciously. His sword struck true cleaving her head from her shoulders. There was a shriek in the distance. The memory of it, the rage of it, caused fear to crawl through his body even now. He looked up to see another woman, some sort of noble woman, atop a large black horse, on the same hill behind. She rode toward him and although he knew it was useless, he turned and fled from her.

This was the home of his Lord. He knew every trail and track like the back of his hand, but she caught him as easily as if he were standing still. Her strength was incredible. She plucked him from his horse as if he were a child and pulled him face down across her lap.

She snarled, "You deprive me of my companion, you will follow her to the next life."

They rode a short distance from the field, and she threw him to the ground. The impact knocked the breath out of him and before he could raise his arms to defend himself, she was on top of him. She broke both of his arms as if they were twigs and then yanked his head back. He thought that she would kill him; it felt like she was killing him. Sharp teeth ripped a chunk out of his throat. Never in his life before or since had he felt such pain. His eyes began to drift closed, and he was glad for it to end. Then there was nothing but darkness.

He was never sure how long he was unconscious but when he woke, both his arms were healed. He was laying on the ground where she'd attacked him but now the sun shone brightly overhead. Dizzy and disoriented he headed for higher ground trying to recognize where he was. Sun glinted off a small stream some distance away and he understood that he was no more than half a league from the battlefield.

Moving towards the water he rubbed his hands up and down his arms and then his throat but there was no sign of any wounds other than sticky dried blood on his hands and clothes. The distance disappeared under his feet as if he were running even though he felt as though he were barely moving. Water tumbled over beautiful moss-covered stones, and he knelt beside it and cried. Cried for the dead and for himself for not joining them.

Reaching for the water he splashed his face washing the dried blood and dirt from his hands, and throat. He put the water in his mouth and drank deeply. It went down like swallowing blades and he wretched it up almost instantly. Crawling back to the water's edge he caught the first look at himself and saw a monster. He screamed.

In all the dreams he'd had before that was where he

woke up alone. When he screamed this time, arms came around him, not the crushing arms of his maker but gentle arms. A smell, her smell, lemon with sage, filled his nostrils. He opened his eyes with a start, and she was there. Phoebe was in his bed, her head on his chest as if she'd always slept there, her hand tucked under his shoulder pulling him close. He froze unable to separate dream from reality.

"Phoebe?"

She snuggled in closer tucking her face under his chin so that her soft breath warmed his skin. Unsure of what to do, he gathered her close allowing the feel of her to chase the nightmare away. As soon as he relaxed, his mind was filled with curiosity. What was she doing here? Did she even know she was here?

She was still fully dressed, and he wondered if Honey had guessed what happened. Gently stroking her back, he allowed his fingers to learn the shapes of her face, her shoulders, and the texture of her hair. She made a sound somewhere between a sigh and a purr that made him smile. He didn't allow himself to explore further without her consent but settled her more comfortably against himself tucking the blankets around them. He closed his eyes and waited for her to wake them.

3

HORNS AND ALL

Phoebe was leaning against the stockroom door looking at a man with horns. Not overly spiked hair, not plastic horns you could buy for Halloween, but curly goat horns that came right out of his forehead. This was not good.

"Do you guys carry Valerian?" Goat man asked and Phoebe pointed towards the section of the store that held loose herbs. That was what she'd done for the woman with the pig nose, the man with no eyes, and the guy with the lizard tongue. She'd politely pointed in the direction of whatever they were looking for and pretended to be mute. She was pretty sure if she opened her mouth at all that she would start screaming.

Huddling deeper into her sweater, she wondered if anyone would notice if she pulled the cowl neck over her head...probably not. Melissa continued blithely sweeping the artifact section of the magic shop. She had not commented at all about these people, not even when the lizard boy licked his eyebrow while asking her to compare patchouli-scented candles. First, her vampire hallucination, and now this. This was not good.

"Phoebe?" Melissa came to stand beside her.

"I'm here," she said watching the door in a kind of morbid fascination.

Melissa touched Phoebe's long, cold coffee cup with a frown. "Are you sick? You never leave coffee. Was your vacuum not good? Did the stockroom finally defeat you?"

"I'm fine." The bell above the door rang again announcing another customer, and she shut her eyes. When she opened them again, it would be fine. Everything would be fine. She rubbed her forehead, trying to understand what was going on today.

Melissa followed her gaze. "Ahh. Are you having one of my I-hate-people days? I can cover the front if you want to go back to the storeroom."

Phoebe actually gave it a thought but not even lizard boy could make her think that going back down there alone was a good idea. That's where this mess started. When she'd opened her eyes in the stock room a couple of hours ago, she was standing right where she'd been previously. It was easy to believe the kiss, the book, and the circle had been a wonderful daydream. The candle Melissa lit earlier was still lit, the stockroom was freshly vacuumed, and there was no green book anywhere.

Unfortunately, there were damp grass stains on her jeans where she had knelt in the stone circle and a taste on her lips that no lip gloss could mimic. It was absolutely impossible. She'd come out to get some fresh air and that's when goat man had arrived. Her mind was clinging desperately to the edges of logic. She believed in magic, she really did. But magic was subtle adjustments of personal energies and intentions that helped you connect with your higher self. There was no such thing as vampires...okay, there were energy vampires, but not sexy suck-your-blood and make you wish for a ball gown type of vampires.

She opened her eyes slowly and looked around Melissa towards the door and saw a woman with an eye right in the middle of her forehead walking towards the tarot cards. Phoebe took a deep breath to keep her coffee safely inside her stomach. Dehydration or exhaustion could cause hallucinations, right?

"Phoebe?" Melissa stood directly in front of her looking intently into her eyes. "What's going on? You look like you're going to faint."

"I'm okay. Maybe just more tired than I thought. Overdid it in the stockroom. I'm just going to go wash my face and get some water. I'll be out in a moment."

It took only a couple of minutes on his phone to find The Craft Shop in town. It wasn't a shop he'd ever visited. Olivia, the shop owner, was both Enlightened and in the business of helping newly Enlightened witches come to terms with their powers. That did a lot to help explain Phoebe's disbelief even if it did somewhat counter his original hope that she'd been sent to him to grant his wish. Witches tended to be half in and half outside the Enlightened world all the time.

The Veil that kept humans from seeing the Enlightened in their true form was thinner for witches. It allowed them to see shadows and glimpses of the real world. Those shadows of truth tended to scare those witches into avoiding a path that would truly Awaken them but that didn't mean they didn't occasionally pop through on their own. He hoped that was the case. The alternative was that she was an unsanctioned Awakening.

Unsanctioned Awakenings happened when a human was forced through the Veil by being exposed to an Enlightened event that could not be "reasoned" away. Humans went to extraordinary lengths to ignore the supernatural world. A goblin opening a door in the house was the wind, a form in the woods was just imagination.

Unsanctioned Awakenings were even more rare than witches pulling themselves through the Veil. Yet there were an unprecedented number of these Awakenings being reported across the world.

One of January's many jobs was to help the newly Enlightened vampires understand their choices when they crossed into their true lives. His Awakening was forced, and his guide Enir had ensured it was filled with lies, blood, manipulation, and violence. Stopping the abuse, misinformation, and violence was why the Recovery Units existed and why he used to be the person they came to when someone broke the laws. He'd stepped out of that role because the violence was too much for him.

The Boston Recovery Center wanted him to return and help them track the unsanctioned Awakenings to their source. He'd said he would keep an eye out and report anything unusual. He even picked up the phone to make the call but stopped because he wanted to get to Phoebe first.

When she appeared in the circle, she'd been afraid, but her magic appeared strong and controlled. She'd grounded the excess power after her teleportation as if she'd always done it. Even as he thought it, he knew he was wrong. She didn't believe in vampires. Thought he was just a dream. If she had recently Awakened herself, he would make sure she had a guide.

Not himself. Sex was discouraged between guides and their guided because it tended to confuse things. The kiss they shared assured he was going to do his best to be her lover. He placed the green book under his arm. Giving thanks to the circle and to the fates one more time, he turned towards the path to go home.

.   .   .

The drive into Boston took him just under an hour. Walking up the long row of brownstone shops near Newberry Street, he caught sight of Phoebe from just outside the main store window. The wealth of curly red hair alone made her hard to miss. Her distress was clear, even from where he was standing. She watched each Enlightened being with a mixture of fascination and fear.

A guide as experienced as Olivia Clay should never leave her charge alone in such a situation or allow their guided to practice a teleportation spell. There was no telling where a witch could end up or if she would be able to get back. Not to mention some of the Enlightened, the Unseelie court, for one, could be very dangerous if you didn't know exactly how to treat them.

Phoebe disappeared out of sight, and January opened the door to The Craft Shop, intending to have a harsh word with Olivia. He felt the wards of the place shimmer over his skin, but these were different than the power he'd encountered in the stone circle. His eyes moved over the store, establishing where the exits were and what weapons were available to him if this was some sort of trap. What he found was a perfectly ordinary magic shop and no sign of an experienced guide. An overly friendly dark-headed witch approached him with a smile.

"Welcome to The Craft Shop. I'm Melissa. Can I help you find something?"

Phoebe came out of the bathroom feeling grounded and determined to put her hallucinations behind her and get through the rest of the day. Unfortunately, the man from her dream was strolling around the shop absently picking things up. Melissa followed him politely pointing out new stock and tools for beginners. Phoebe could see why she was trying so hard to have a conversation. He was tall, broad shouldered, pale, mysterious, and incredibly grace-ful; everything a goth Rainbow Bright could want.

Vampire.

The thought ran involuntarily through her head. Maybe her dream was some sort of premonition of his coming in today? Olivia told her all the time not to ignore her dreams and visions. Why the vision hadn't been polite enough to tell her what he wanted was beyond her understanding. With the way things were going today she was just waiting for him to sprout wings and fly off.

Forcing herself back onto the shop floor, she smiled as he turned to look at her. There was no mistaking the recognition in his eyes or the sexy grin that tugged at the corners of his mouth. She licked her lips remembering the taste of him. The door chime rang again.

Phoebe looked up to see Olivia breeze in. She was wearing every conceivable shade of purple except for her shoes which were always bright red. Her smile was bright and airy until she caught site of the guy. Then her eyes narrowed and her voice became clipped and professional. She made what looked to be a formal bow in his direction with her arms crossed over her chest.

"Welcome. We are in the circle."

It was not the way she normally greeted customers, or anyone else for that matter. Melissa shot Phoebe an odd look and then went about tidying an immaculate shelf full of herbs.

He nodded and responded, "And the light protects us all." The man's lips turned down in a frown so menacing that Olivia's chin went up in defense. "Your guided is afraid, and you left her unprotected today. You will surrender her contract to me."

Olivia's eyebrows almost met above her eyes as she glanced at Melissa. "My guided appears calm and has almost completed her contract. She doesn't need my formal protection any longer."

He gestured towards Phoebe with his chin. His eyes were blue, was Phoebe's first thought. The second was that she must remember how to breathe. She had no idea what was going on here, but she could sense that it was important. Melissa moved to Olivia's side.

Olivia put a hand on Melissa's arm. "You're mistaken. Melissa is my guide. There are no others here."

"She has been Awakened. Are you telling me it was unintentional?"

His eyes swung towards Phoebe with an interest and intensity that made the blood rush to her cheeks. He turned his back on Olivia and Melissa and walked straight to her.

"Hello again, Phoebe."

He stood close enough that she had to look up to make eye contact. Normally, that would have made her feel crowded, but instead, she wanted to move closer, to put her hands on him. The need to touch him was almost irresistible. She opened her mouth to respond, but no words came out.

"I wasn't finished when you left."

Before she could clearly understand his intent, he bent down and kissed her with an intensity that left them both breathless. No other part of his body touched hers, but she felt claimed just the same.

He moved away, whispering against her lips, "My name is January, *Ionawr* in my mother's tongue. I am not a dream."

"January," she repeated a little breathlessly.

He brushed the hair away from her face tenderly. "You're safe now. Just relax and take it in. What you're seeing is real."

Senses still buzzing from his kiss, the soft rhythm of his

words began to unknot some of the fear in her chest. It was real. He was real. She took a deep, calming breath and then another.

"You were awake in the circle. I think that means I owe you a drink. What time do you get off work?"

His accent was more pronounced than it was in the circle, but the teasing tone of his invitation was unmistakable. "Six."

He handed her the green book from under his arm.

"You dropped this."

She took the book back, looking down at the cover. *Witchcraft with Vampires*. "Are you a Vampire?"

"Yes. Can I come back for you at six? Then we can have our drink, and I'll start explaining what's going on here."

All the little hairs on the back of her neck stood straight up and yet she couldn't make herself tell him no. In fact, she didn't want to.

"I would like that."

His sexy smile revealed a set of sharp white fangs. Her world tilted around the edges, and he reached forward to steady her with one large, warm hand. Vampires were supposed to be cold, right?

"Don't fight what's happening," he said softly. "Just breathe and observe. Pretend it's Halloween, and there isn't really anything to be afraid of."

He stepped back to give her some space. "If you start feeling overwhelmed. Head home. Your boss will understand." He turned to Olivia. "I'm declaring Phoebe as Unguided. If I find that your carelessness is responsible for it, there will be consequences. She is in your charge until I return from the council."

With that, he gave Phoebe a wink. "I'll be right back." He left the building like a man on a mission.

Melissa let out a low wolf whistle as the door chimed shut behind him.

Olivia nodded. "You can say that again."

Ten minutes till six, the door chime rang. Phoebe ignored it, walking back to the stockroom with an armful of Yule merchandise that Olivia seemed to have produced out of nowhere. If it was January, he would just have to wait. Olivia had left about a hundred tasks for Phoebe to do, which included strict instructions that she wasn't to leave the store without Melissa. Then, she'd flown out the door in a tizzy. Phoebe tried to ask her what was going on, but she'd only gotten more tasks for her questions. Melissa was equally closed-lipped, saying only that it would be sorted out soon. In the end, Phoebe picked the inventory book up and tried to stay out of the way.

Melissa popped her head through the office door, grinning. "Girl, what spell did you cast and why didn't you include me?"

"What?"

"The guy this morning was hot, the guy this afternoon was even hotter, and the guy standing out at the counter looking for you is about to burst into flames. You know I love, *Love* spells. What spell did you cast and why didn't you include me?"

"What guy this morning?" Phoebe demanded trying to think back.

"The guy who was asking me about the Patchouli candles," Melissa said as if it was perfectly obvious.

Phoebe peeked around the office door towards the register at what had obviously stirred Melissa's interest. The devil was standing at the counter. His skin was a darkish red, no scales, but not smooth like skin should be. Sculpted muscles that spoke of power were barely contained by his tight black t-shirt and equally tight black jeans. His thick black hair trailed down his back to his waist through a pair of red bat-like wings. He turned his head to look out the large display window a moment, and though Phoebe could not see horns, the man's movements were agitation in its purest form.

"He's waiting for me?" Phoebe squeaked. "Tell him I'm not here."

"Are you crazy? Look at him! He's gorgeous." Melissa crossed her arms, looking back toward the devil with obvious appreciation.

"The guy at the counter?" She asked with her eyes riveted on the man's claws that were tapping out his displeasure on the counter.

"Uhh, yeah. Or do you see some other Adonis?"

Phoebe started backing away, "Tell him I'm not here."

James could feel his heart beating with excitement. Olivia Clay had flown into the White Witch Council and demanded a contract for an Unguided witch named Phoebe Elizabeth Pierce. Ten steps in front of her, the only creature that James had ever really loved in his long life, January *ap Ionawr*, had reported Phoebe as Unguided. On the heels of that report, he'd put in a request to protect her until she could choose a guide. If January wanted to protect Phoebe Pierce, then she was an asset worth having. There were not many people on the East coast who didn't owe him something, including James, meaning if you wanted something done you came to January. What James wanted was a second chance.

Unguided cases had to be investigated by Recovery Units before a guide could be assigned. Normally James would have avoided extra work, but he made it a point to be assigned this case. It was the only way he could get close to January again. It was January who convinced James to become a Recovery Unit enforcer. It was a job that made demon existence bearable in a city ruled by white magic. About a century ago he'd repaid that kindness by publicly humiliating and then dumping January. At the time he believed that it would make him powerful in the Unseelie court. He'd been stupid enough to believe their interest was in him and not his vampire lover. It was a mistake he was still paying for. Ironically, if he hadn't been working for the Boston Recovery unit, the Unseelie would have already discarded him.

Werewolves, vampires, Fey, Selkie, and all the other Enlightened had only one body of law, and that was the Recovery Units. The Enlightened worked with, were married to, and obeyed the laws of the Unenlightened who just didn't see them. Not couldn't; didn't. No one was sure why. Occasionally, and for reasons that were highly debated, an Unenlightened person would push through the Veil. In normal circumstances this was caused by the Unenlightened encountering a situation that could not be rationally explained as natural. If they were too rigid in their views, the information overwhelmed them, and they shut down. They almost never recovered.

If by some miracle they came through intact, the Recovery Unit closest was responsible for retrieving that person and making sure that they had someone to guide them through the complex social rules of the Enlightened. Contracts were immediately put into place by the White Witch Council who wanted to assure that guidance was fairly compensated for, and guides were held accountable for the health and safety of their guided.

About two years ago the Recovery Unit around Metropolis Illinois had come across some cases of what they thought were missing guides. Then they thought it was a rogue forcing Unenlightened people through the Veil, but the cases kept expanding and it seemed unlikely that the phenomena could be attributed to a single person. What was so unusual about these cases was that the Unguided were coming through without any memory of contact with an Enlightened person. They were shocked and afraid of the unknown but otherwise mentally sound.

James requested to oversee the Unguided investigation unit in Boston for two reasons, the first was that he was good at getting answers, the second was he'd been ordered by the Unseelie Queen herself to register and track Unguided witches. It was easier to do so with the White Witch Council blessings. As a double agent, his investigation was leading him back to January. Could it be fate? He hoped so.

He'd come here to persuade Phoebe to exchange contracts with him first. As her guide, he could trade her contract back to January for what he truly desired. Time. Their relationship had been short and intense. James ended it to have some freedom. Without January's protection or favor, the Unseelie court had made short work of his so-called freedom. He wanted January and that freedom back. Who would have thought that feelings could remain so strong for so long?

The woman with the autumn ribbons in her hair smiled at him kindly. He wasn't surprised. The witch who cursed him to eternal temptation for breaking her heart was thorough. The innocent flocked to him determined to save his soul. He loved each one of them for their goodness but eventually they would see him as he truly was and leave. Cursed to love but never really be loved. The Unseelie knew just what to do to destroy a soul.

The dark headed witch shrugged as she came around the counter. "Phoebe said to tell you she wasn't here."

He smiled trying to use what was left of his charm. "It will only take a minute. Can you ask her again?"

"She's got a date tonight."

The witch said it softly, almost like she was trying to cushion the blow. She must think he was a potential suitor. He put on what he hoped was a hurt expression. There was more than one way to get the information he needed.

"She said she wasn't seeing anyone seriously."

"Well, it looked serious to me. At least it looked pretty physical. You know what, I'll let Phoebe explain."

She disappeared towards the back rooms again. James smirked taking a moment to roll his stiff shoulders. The shop bell rang behind him sending a shiver through his body. The woodsy scent of January wrapped around his senses like a glove. He turned and met his former lover's grey-blue gaze. Regret and shame for what he was doing, what he'd become, and what he'd agreed to do twisted in his gut.

"James!" January said coming up to wrap him in a hug. "My god, man, I haven't seen you in ages. What are you doing here?"

"He's here to talk to Phoebe." The dark headed assistant seemed to come out of nowhere. "I tried to tell him that you guys had a date tonight but he wanted to hear it from her.

January's expression grew serious. "Is she in some sort of trouble?"

"No. Of course not," James said quickly. A little too quickly.

January stepped back from their embrace, his eyes narrowing. "Then tell me why you're here."

The compulsion in January's words took James by surprise, but even if it hadn't, he would not have been able to resist it. Before January's Awakening he'd been a witch, not powerful but very persuasive. Although traditional witchcraft was impossible for most Vampires, January's mortal death changed rather than destroyed his magic.

"I've been ordered to track the Unguided witches in the area."

The words were true. It was the only reason January's compulsion eased. As a rule, Demons didn't lie. They could only hold back portions of the truth when it suited them. Normally this sort of answer would have prompted January to investigate further but the woman in question chose that moment to make an appearance.

He clicked his wings in irritation, and she looked up at them. James forgot his embarrassment. This Phoebe could see him, what he really was. Not the enchantment. She knew what he was. He needed to move fast.

"Phoebe my name is James. I'm here from the Boston Recovery Unit. I'd like to offer you my guidance in the Enlightened world."

January's eyes narrowed as he looked a James, the promise of retribution so clear in his expression that James almost wished he hadn't been so hasty.

January turned to Phoebe with a half-smile. "I am also offering guidance, but as a protector and perhaps later, a companion."

Melissa stepped forward with a shrug. "What the hell. I'll throw my two cents in. Phoebe, I offer you my guidance in the Enlightened world. I don't fully understand it myself and I'm not sure I'm allowed to guide anyone yet, but if I was, the first thing I would tell you is that you don't have to make the choice now. A fact that I believe your other two potential guides were just going to gloss over."

She made a tsking sound with her tongue.

"The second thing I will tell you is that I don't want to sleep with you like your vampire does. Sleeping with your guide isn't against any rules, but it tends to cause compli-cations." January frowned but didn't deny what Melissa said. "The third thing I'm going to say on the subject is not to bargain with demons." She pointed at James. "They never give anything away for free, and they always get more out of a bargain then you do. The last thing I'm going to say to all of you is that it is twenty-five minutes till seven, and you guys are making me late for yoga."

The redheaded woman looked at all three of them for a moment as if they were crazy, and then her eyes rolled back in her head, and she dropped towards the floor like a stone.

4

TWILIGHT ZONE MOMENTS

Phoebe woke up in the early morning light fully dressed, shoes and all, in her own bed with a crick in her neck like she'd been sleeping at a funny angle. The last thing she remembered was talking to an angel but in the bright light of day in her own bedroom, the idea felt silly. What day was it? Had she simply fallen asleep again after she'd dressed for work and had the most elaborate dream of her life? Or had she really made a date with a vampire, seen monsters with mortgages, and teleported herself home from an unknown bedroom?

"Right Phoebe. Follow the yellow brick road back to reality and see how late you are for work." She rubbed her hands against her face trying to chase away the dream of being cuddled all night.

More than a little disappointed, she went through the dream symbols one at a time like Olivia taught her. The vacuum was an easy one for her. A desire for order. The stone circle was a symbol of respected power. The vampire, sexual desire. The monsters argued with Melissa over who would…guide her. She shook her head. No idea, but she could guess it had something to do with the podcast she'd been listening to. Voices from the Void. The podcaster, Ben Linzy, was tracking what he referred to as Twilight Zone Moments.

For about three months this podcast tracked supernatural movement across the USA. People seeing mermaids, ghosts, monsters straight out of a horror film doing things like driving cars and crossing streets. It made sense that her brain would translate that type of information into a dream about the supernatural shopping at The Craft Shop.

At first, she thought the podcast was all a big scam. That maybe it was some War of the Worlds type Halloween prank, but she had to admit she was addicted and beginning to believe that some of these people believed what they saw was true.

Her logical explanation of the events made her feel more in control. The first thing to do was to find her phone and figure out what time it was. As she leaned forward to stretch her neck and back, she spotted dried grass stains on the knees of her jeans. *From when you fell in the stone circle.*

"Impossible," she muttered walking to her living room to grab her handbag from its usual place beside the sofa. It wasn't there. In fact, it was sitting just a little left of her front door. Where had she seen it last? At the shop. She'd had it over her shoulder when she'd seen Melissa arguing with…No. Shaking her head furiously, she scooped her handbag from the floor and dug for her phone. If her vampire was a dream, it would be Thursday, the day before Lammas. If he wasn't, it would be Lammas and she would…

Her phone was almost dead and as she swiped the screen to wake it up she could almost hear her heart beating in panic. The screen opened with a cheery chime and a pre-programmed message.

Happy Lammas! Today is going to be a magical day."

Her handbag and her phone slipped from her hands and her head swam in circles until her apartment looked like it was underwater. Putting her head between her knees, she took several long deep breaths. A faint scratching at the front door kept her from giving into temptation and passing out…again. Since when was she a swooning maiden?

"Get a grip, Phoebe."

Going to the door she tested the handle to find it locked. She opened the deadbolt and carefully drew open the door to find a very skinny one-eyed calico cat eating what appeared to be the remains of a very large lobster on her doorstep. The cat looked up at her, stretched, and then went inside her apartment as if it had been waiting for her all night. Phoebe looked down the hall to see if maybe she had a new neighbor but the building was completely quiet. Turning back to her living room she saw the cat sniffing her dropped handbag with a swishing tail. She reached her hand out for the cat to sniff.

"Umm. Hello. Are you lost? You don't live here."

The cat looked back over her shoulder then proceeded to search each of the rooms of the apartment. She followed the cat intending to scoop her up and set her back outside when she noticed how her skin hung over her thin hips and the slight limp in her front paw. If she did have a home, someone wasn't taking very good care of her.

After completing the inspection of the entire apartment, the cat jumped up on Phoebe's couch and laid down. Phoebe laughed hunching down to cat level and held her hand out again for inspection. A soft pink nose tapped the back of her hand more out of politeness than interest. Phoebe stroked her gently.

"Hello beautiful. Poor sweet girl." The cat purred with approval. A surge of energy almost like a small breeze travelled up Phoebe's arm to whisper in her ear. A name formed on the back of her tongue.

"Honey?"

She spoke it out loud and the cat looked up at her obviously answering to her name. Phoebe tried to remember if she'd seen her somewhere around the apartment building. "Hello Honey. It's all right. I'll find out where you're supposed to be." The cat blinked back at her with what she thought was approval and then put her head down on the couch and began to snooze. Phoebe stroked her for a moment longer feeling suddenly calm and protected. Honey purred peeking through her half-closed eye.

Safe.

Again, the word seemed to travel on an invisible breeze. She'd get Honey settled, change clothes, and call Melissa and see what was going on. No sooner had the decision finalized in her brain when there was a knock at the door. Honey picked up her head alert. Phoebe opened the door slowly to find Melissa holding a bag of Union Square donuts.

"Why is there lobster on your front step?" She looked over Phoebe's shoulder and squealed in delight. "When did you get a cat?"

Melissa pushed past Phoebe on a one-track cat snuggling mission.

"Hello most gorgeous girl in the whole world. Aren't you beautiful?"

Phoebe watched Melissa pick Honey up and sit down on the sofa with her. At first, Honey tensed up as if to smack Melissa and then she relaxed into the full body, two-handed, strokes, and gave a slow blink of approval. She stood in the abundance of affection for another couple of minutes before pushing away to get down.

Melissa released her reluctantly and then looked

around the apartment. "Where is the vampire who carried you over the threshold last night?"

"Vampire?"

"Yeah, about 6 foot tall, looked like Geralt of Rivia's sexy younger brother, kissed you like a long-lost lover yesterday afternoon? His demon friend called him January. Olivia and I have been crying like mad trying to locate you two, but we didn't get a hit until this morning."

"January," Phoebe said his name remembering the feel of it against her lips. She felt a little dizzy again and sat down hard beside Melissa.

"Ooh. Don't faint again. Take deep breaths," Melissa said pounding Phoebe's back as if she were choking. "I remember that feeling. Like someone dropped me into an alternate universe. You can't let it overwhelm you. Take a deep breath and just repeat the things you know for sure. Your name, where you work, your favorite song. It seems stupid but Olivia says it gives you something to focus on when things get weird."

Phoebe leaned forward putting her head between her knees. "What if I don't want things to be weird? What if I want them to be exactly like I know they should be?"

Melissa stopped pounding Phoebe's back and smirked. "Then you're not very adventurous."

A soft bony purring body rubbed against her side. Phoebe took another deep breath allowing Honey to force her way into her lap. The cat smelled like old fish but the rumbly purr and the feeling of her course hair sliding through Phoebe's fingers was soothing.

Melissa petted them both. "Come on. Let's have some donuts, I'll make some coffee, we will walk to work like this is any other day, and Olivia can start explaining it all to you."

"Explain what?"

Melissa beamed. "Your Awakening. Coming into the

Enlightened world. It's a whole different ball game from here on out."

"What about Honey?"

Melissa frowned. "I guess you can have honey in your coffee if you want."

"Honey the cat," Phoebe clarified.

Honey looked at them for a moment and then jumped off the couch and went into Phoebe's room.

"Umm. My guess is that she lives here until you can put some found signs up. Although judging by the state of her, whoever had her before she got here doesn't deserve to have her back. We can go down to the store and get what she needs. I'll call Olivia and let her know where we are.

It was about 8:30 am when the yowl of a cat startled him awake. He sat up slowly waiting for the morning's deep lethargy to pass. Looking around he noted that his bed was empty, and the bedroom door was still closed but Phoebe's scent was mixed deliciously with his on his skin. The cat yowled again impatiently. January stumbled to his window pushing it open. A large orange tom cat from the house down the road looked up at him and then jumped on to the windowsill. The cat leaned close enough to brush January's face with his whiskers.

"Honey say she's awake. Someone safe come. Rest. Safe. Both safe. You not needed now. Come later. Bring dinner, more lobster." The cat looked up and waited.

January bowed his head in respect. "I understand. Thank you."

The cat bobbed his head in acknowledgement and then jumped back out the window. As cat messengers went, he was very polite. Most cats didn't wait for acknowledgement and almost all asked for something in exchange for a message. Whoever Honey was, she must have some clout.

January got up feeling lost for a moment. He walked into the kitchen to find a very hung-over but annoyingly cheerful Alex nursing a cup of coffee.

"Good morning for both of us, I guess. Does your guest want a cup of coffee or is she a blood drinker like you?"

"My guest?"

"The absolutely stunning red head sprawled across you this morning? Surprised the hell out of me. I thought you were some sort of monk."

"You came into my room this morning?"

"I smelled someone different. I'm a bit paranoid after…" Alex stopped, his smile dropping, and he looked at January with the same vulnerable look that had prompted January to offer to guide him. Then, like slipping on a mask, his smile returned ear to ear. "Being a good friend, I smelled someone unusual and came to see if you were okay. Do I even want to know what you two got up to last night?" Alex waggled his brows up and down. "I don't think I've ever seen you sleep so deep. I opened and closed the door without either of you moving."

"Is she still here?"

Alex frowned. "She's not out here. I assumed she was still with you."

"Trust me, if she was with me, I would still be in my bedroom not chatting with you."

Alex hooted with laughter. "She snuck out?"

January arched an amused brow. "What time did Rosalind leave last night?"

Alex raised his coffee cup in a mock salute. "Touché. She said I could come to her place about half past seven tonight."

"As your guide, I must tell you to be careful. Angels are very easy to fall in love with and hard to stay in love with. Their path is solitary."

Alex sipped his coffee slowly. "You think I shouldn't go?"

"Go if you want to. Just know what you're walking into. Rosalind is earning her forgiveness so that she can return to her heaven. When her task is complete, she can't take you with her or stay until you can go. One way or another, she will leave you."

"She's an angel. What could she possibly need forgiveness for?"

"Only she can tell you that."

5

THE UNSEELIE COURT

James approached the elementary school playground with his head bowed low and his wings tucked behind him. The Albuquerque sun was partially blocked by scattered clouds holding no promise of rain. Sat on a bench under a tree reading to a circle of children was one of the most unimposing and yet powerful Fey in the world. In a court filled with Fey who constantly worked the system for their own gain, Isla Wildwood created a powerful place for herself by being neutral. She delivered messages between major houses both Seelie and Unseelie stripping away the veiled threats, empty promises, and flattery so that both parties were confident that what was being said was crystal clear.

She directly reported to both parties any attempts at deception or bribery. James secretly believed that she was Seelie, but her honesty was worth enough to all parties involved not to challenge her. When she caught sight of him over the top of her book, she stood up dusting invisible sand from her dress, and walked over to him. The children around her scattered into the nearby playground and didn't even cast a glance toward him. He held his breath hoping he hadn't overstepped himself.

Approaching her when she hadn't given permission, and he hadn't made an appointment, was normally out of the question but the information he had was vital to the Unseelie Queen and he feared her more than he feared anyone else. Bowing his head low, he waited to be acknowledged.

"James. You are a long way from home, and you are intruding on my time. Make an appointment and I will see you later."

"I'm sorry. My message is for our Queen, and I was instructed that delaying the information would be at my own peril. It can't wait for an appointment."

"Rise and speak her common name and the code word she has given you."

James stood up without meeting Isla's gaze. It was pointless. She would deliver his real message regardless of the words that came from his mouth. "*Banrigh*, Unguided."

Isla nodded. "What is your message?"

"The first Unguided witch in Boston is Phoebe Pierce. I've applied to guide her to finish the task I was given, but I need help to get my application accepted."

"*Banrigh, Búsqueda del corazón.*"

Isla's response startled him. The Queen had left a message for him. A cold shiver went through him. "Go ahead."

"January will come to you soon with a request. Agree to it even though it appears to be against everything you desire."

He handed Isla a USB stick. "This is a list of all the Unguided witches that have been reported to East Coast recovery Centers in the last six months."

Isla took the stick slipping it into her pocket. "After the Mabon celebration and before Yule, you are instructed to shut down all Unguided witches in your area. This includes Phoebe Pierce."

"After Mabon? Why the delay? The longer we wait, the harder it is to make it happen."

Isla looked at him sharply and he stopped talking. Her look was a warning that she would repeat his doubts to their queen, a creature who would rather burn down the world than have her authority challenged. For a moment his gratitude for her kindness almost caused him to over-step his rank and kiss her hands. "I understand. It will be as she commands."

Isla nodded again. "Now words of my own. If you disturb me without an appointment again, I will never carry another message for you or to you. I swear it's on my line."

He bowed low. Isla was the only Fey the Queen trusted right now. To refuse to carry his messages would mean he would be completely cut off from the court. His current rank was too low to even think about applying directly for an audience and even if he could, she was the queen of deception. He would never know if what she said was what she meant. "I understand. I'm sorry. It won't happen again."

Isla caught his eye for a moment and instead of icy calm or disdain, he thought he saw pity there. Not the kind his curse often caused but something deeper and more sinister.

"See that it doesn't."

She walked away and whistled, a soft joyful sound that caused all the children on the playground to stop what they were doing and line up behind her. He bowed low understanding that he'd been dismissed. He stayed low until the last patter of small feet disappeared into the school.

With a heavy heart, he returned to his car. He loved to drive but now the return journey would be haunted with questions rather than answers. Shut down the Unguided. The instruction was clear.

It made him sick to even think about it. He'd done many things he wasn't proud of in his long life, but he had never directly attacked the innocent. The Unseelie were inherently selfish, and this was a test of his selfishness. Would he destroy a stranger's life for his own happiness?

Had he already been doing just that by providing the Queen with the names of the Unguided? By Mabon January's relationship with Phoebe would be firmly established and with it, January's protection would be in place. James wanted to be January's companion, not his enemy.

Did the Queen know something he didn't, or had she discarded his desires in order to fulfill her own? Was that what Isla was trying to tell him with her sad gaze? He put the car into gear and turned towards the freeway rather than the airport. Time. He needed time and space to think.

6

LAMMAS BLESSINGS

After her second Yum-Yum doughnut and her third cup of coffee, Phoebe walked into The Craft Shop with Melissa feeling almost in control of herself. Her house keys appeared to be missing but Melissa pointed out that she'd left her handbag at the shop. Given that it was in her living room this morning, Phoebe assumed January had tossed it inside and taken the keys with him in order to lock the door. She used Melissa's spare key to lock up.

After the initial shock of seeing people that were not entirely human, she found that she could almost cope if she pretended it was Halloween like January suggested. Melissa called the non-humans Enlightened because they could see both sides of the Veil, i.e., the supernatural and the mundane world.

The Enlightened treated Phoebe as if she were unaware. Melissa explained that it was difficult to know who was and wasn't Enlightened because the Enlightened were not supposed to chat to the Unenlightened about the supernatural.

Unlike the Unenlightened, being different was the normal rather than the exception in the Enlightened world so they didn't feel it necessary to acknowledge the differences in each other. Only the newly Awakened did that and they were mostly treated like uneducated children. Phoebe did admire a fox woman's tail which got her an appreciative look rather than scorn. She was doing fine. Okay, she was still freaking out and trying not to gape and stare because that was rude no matter who you were, but she didn't feel like fainting or screaming anymore which was an improvement.

They came into The Craft Shop just after opening and as Phoebe stepped through the door, she saw a shimmer of gold. It was so beautiful that she walked back and forth through the door a couple of times just to see the shimmer again. She was frowning up at the frame trying to figure out what was causing the glow when she heard a chuckle behind her.

"So, it's true?"

Olivia's voice was gentle and soothing. It was so unlike the tone she typically used in the shop that both she and Melissa turned around. She was standing behind the counter with a book clutched to her chest, the same green book that January had brought back to the store yesterday. Phoebe also noticed that for the first time since they knew each other, Olivia wasn't standing in the middle of a self-made mess. Rather than her normal purples and reds, she was dressed head to toe in shades of orange and brown for Lammas. The chaos around her was calm.

Phoebe smoothed her own clothing self-consciously. "What's true?"

"You've Awakened. I thought you might, but I didn't expect it to be so soon. It's what we've been waiting for."

Melissa went to stand beside Olivia with a slightly guilty smile. "You were so close to being Awakened when we met you that we've been watching out for you just in case."

Olivia came around the counter setting the book down on a random shelf and wrapping Phoebe in a hug. "Welcome to the Enlightened world, witchy sister. What happened? I had the worst feeling yesterday. Like you'd been snatched straight through my wards. I came as quickly as I could, but by the time I got here it was too late."

"The wards!" Melissa slapped her forehead. "Phoebe, we vacuumed up the wards! I'm so stupid. I told you to do it. I even bought the vacuum!"

"Vacuumed?" Olivia hissed the word towards Melissa.

"It's Lammas today. You always reset the wards on Sabbats. I thought...kill two birds with one stone. Stop Phoebe from constantly bitching about the mess in the basement and help you prepare for the ritual today.

"I don't bitch," Phoebe grumbled.

"There is no mess," Olivia said indignantly.

They spoke simultaneously. Olivia waved her hand. "Start again. First Melissa, then you Phoebe. Don't leave anything out. It's important that we get the story straight before we speak to the Recovery Unit."

"What is a Recovery Unit?" Phoebe asked collecting the book Olivia sat down.

Olivia frowned and then reached out to take the book from Phoebe. She stepped back to retain it. She wasn't sure why, but she didn't want to let go of it.

"Phoebe, let me see that book. I ordered it for a customer, and its warded. Even with my own wards vacuumed up, and yourself Awakened, you shouldn't be able to see it much less read it. It's a rare and dangerous text."

Phoebe looked down at the book in her hands. "I've read it already. That's how all of this started. The book was in the stock I was putting away. It wasn't on the list, so I went to get the list of second hand books from upstairs."

Olivia and Melissa looked at one another with a frown.

"Think hard," Olivia said gently. "Were you inside or outside the circle when you read the spell?"

Phoebe pulled the image up in her mind again. The woodsy sent of the green candle, the feeling of accomplishment thanks to the newly vacuumed space. "The whole area was smudged, but I carried it out of the circle. I sat it on a shelf and it fell open."

"Open to the spell you read?" Melissa asked softly.

"Yes." Phoebe rubbed her brow. "I don't normally read random spells out loud but this one was so beautiful."

"Can you show me which spell it was?" Olivia came around behind her.

Phoebe opened the book and began to flip through the pages, but they were all suddenly blank. "I don't understand. The spell was here."

"A ward laced with a compulsion spell," Olivia said tsking her tongue. "I'm getting lazy. I should have seen that from a mile away." She took the book from Phoebe and blew gently on the pages. A sound like hundreds of shards of glass rolling over one another filled the shop and then the blank pages were again filled with spells. "Do you remember what it said?"

"Not exactly. Something about dissolving and going to my heart's desire."

Olivia flipped a couple of more pages but the words and images in the book wavered and became blank again. "Damn. The ward is too strong to hold it open for long. I'll call the customer tonight and tell her that it's here, and that she better explain what it's for, or I'll take it directly to the council."

"It's just a harmless book," Phoebe replied but even as she said it, she knew it wasn't true. There was a feeling, deep in her chest, like panic. It was a feeling she recognized as bad energy. Watching Olivia close it she ignored her impulse to snatch it back again. If there was one thing she knew for sure about magic, it was best to know exactly what you were getting yourself in to. She wrapped her arms around herself. "You know, there was a moment between disappearing from here and showing up in the circle when I felt like I knew how I was connected to everything. Now everything feels different. I don't know what to do."

Olivia tucked the book under one arm and put the other arm around Phoebe. "I can't think of a single person, witch or not, who can wake up in a new world and not feel a little lost. I can't explain what happened, but I can trust that it happened for a reason."

"What do I do now?"

"Decorate the shop for autumn, like you love to do every Lammas even though it's August and it's boiling outside. If anyone Enlightened comes in, be polite and act natural. In the meantime, you can help Melissa and I to reset the shop wards. I'll put this book somewhere safe until I know what it wants."

Phoebe loved to decorate for the sabbats but today brought a new level of understanding to the process. The three harvest festivals Lammas, Mabon, and Samhain always made her feel like magic was a real tangible thing. As she slid a collection of stones in place or set the autumn foliage bundles across a doorway, she understood that she was also blessing the place in her own way. The carnelian shimmer of Olivia's wards mixed with the gold of Melissa's and finally the bright green of her own energy. Olivia and Melissa worked well past lunchtime setting each ward with care, by which time the shop was filled with customers.

Every nook and cranny was filled with orange, brown, gold, and green fall foliage. At Mabon, they would add dried corn, apples, and fancy gourds to symbolize the Autumn Equinox and the second harvest. At Samhain, they added photos and messages for the dead and honored the cutting of the last grain and the Pagan New Year.

The decorations were a reminder of the movement of time. To set them out and rearrange them until every time you looked at them you felt peace was a type of meditation. These were things that Phoebe knew and had always known, but she recognized today that she'd been holding just a little bit of herself back. She'd been afraid to believe because she didn't want that belief snatched away.

In the gaps between customers, Melisa gave her a hand with the decorations and little bits of fascinating information. There were ways to peek through the Veil such as a spirit summons, spell work, shapeshifting, and divination. Almost every action an Unenlightened witch involved herself in was an attempt to reach across the Veil. A foot in both worlds is what Melissa called it.

Phoebe sat a box of new stock on the counter and they both began to sort and price it. Shelf space was always at a premium here, and it usually took a couple of days to figure out how to cram new stuff in. Without knowing why, Phoebe found herself at the windows looking for January. She had his first name but no phone number or address, no plans to meet up later, just a feeling that he would come. She handed Melissa a box full of incense cones trying to keep her attention focused on her job. "Is it rude to ask how long you've been Awakened?"

Melissa priced the boxes and put them into stacks. "You wouldn't ask a complete stranger, but the question is considered small talk in most Enlightened social situations. I came here, to The Craft Shop about 5 years ago because I did something stupid. I wanted to see magic, to prove to myself it was there, so on Samhain I went into the woods alone and I summoned a spirit."

Although Melissa said it casually all the hair on Phoebe's arms stood up.

"I was so amazed that my spell worked that I didn't have the sense to be terrified." Melissa rubbed the smooth black stone of the hematite ring she always wore on her thumb. "It demanded to be returned to where it came from, but I didn't know how to send it back. It fed on fear, and it made sure I was scared all the time. I honestly wasn't sure if what I was seeing and feeling was real. It made me doubt everything."

The afternoon light was giving way and the whole shop had a lovely warm orange glow but there was a chill in Melissa's voice that made Phoebe want to reach out and hug her. "How did it scare you?"

"Shadows moving too quickly or not fast enough. Things moving around when I wasn't looking and then when I was. The worst was that when I looked into a mirror, I would catch a glimpse of a little boy with completely black eyes standing right beside me. I'd jump, he'd laugh, and then it was like it never happened."

"That sounds like a horror story."

"It was. I came here because I had to use the bathroom but as soon as I stepped through the door, I knew it couldn't follow me in."

"The wards," Phoebe said glancing back at the door.

Melissa nodded. "Exactly. I stayed here until the shop was closing. When Olivia finally suggested I come back tomorrow, I burst into tears and told her what was happening. Instead of calling the cops or a psychiatrist, she walked to the shop door, opened it wide and summoned the spirit to her."

Phoebe's mouth dropped open. "You must have been terrified."

"I seriously almost peed my pants but then I saw what had been chasing me. I thought it was a little boy, but when it came to Olivia it was a full-sized man's shadow. She asked where it was trying to get back to and it didn't say anything but somehow, I knew, it was angry because I brought it to me and it didn't know how to get back home. It was lost. That's my gift. I draw things and people who are lost."

"Do you see spirits all the time?"

"Not really. Most spirits know exactly where to go."

"What happened to the spirit that you summoned?"

"Olivia called this necromancer from Maine, a guy called Cicero, and within a couple of minutes, it was gone. Olivia asked to be my guide, I said yes, started working here, and my whole life started again."

"Is it really that easy?" Phoebe arranged the last couple of oak branches across the front of the counter for prosperity. "You just throw what you know about life out the window and start again?"

Melissa placed the boxes on the shelves under the till. "What's the alternative? Count yourself lucky. At least you Awakened as a witch. Awakening as a werewolf or something undead comes with a much steeper learning curve."

Phoebe counted to 10 while the world swam around her and then asked the question she'd been wanting to ask all day. "Do you know anything about vampires."

Melissa clasped a hand over her heart with a dreamy sigh. "I don't know a whole lot about them, but I'd love to. Whatever makes them a vampire kills them first and then brings them back. They must hypnotize their donors because none of the Enlightened I know have ever seen one feed or fed one themselves."

"That's pure gossip."

Melissa and Phoebe swung around to see January standing in the doorway. He was wearing dark jeans and t-shirt much like the first time she saw him, but for the first time she noticed the silver acorn and oak leaf that hung from a leather thong around his neck. Like some sort of silly schoolgirl, she felt her mouth go dry, her head go empty, and her heart flutter.

"Happy Lammas to you both," he said with a smile that didn't bother to disguise his extended canine teeth. "A quick lesson on vampires." He moved across the store at an incredible speed swooping Phoebe up, swinging her around, and setting her down again. "We do drink blood, but we don't take more than can be replaced without consequences to our companion. We prefer to take blood from a trusted lover or companion but will drink it from a bottle which comes from a donor bank if we need to. Feeding can be quick and painless, or it can be slow and sensual. The offer of blood is sacred to most of us."

He leaned forward to tuck a piece of Phoebe's hair behind her ear. "Ask me anything you want to know. I have nothing to hide from you. I hope you decide to feed me one day, but if it happens, it will be with your knowledge and consent."

Drawn to him was an understatement. Without understanding why, she caught his hand and pressed her cheek to his palm nuzzling it in a movement that felt more intimate than a kiss. Blushing, she let go of him wondering if vampires had compulsions on them like the book had.

He cupped her chin, the smile on his face full of wonder. "I feel it to. The attraction. The need to touch you. It isn't normal for me either." Bringing her lips to his he kissed her gently, almost reverently. "In fact, I've been absolutely useless all day because I was counting the minutes until 6 p.m. As you can see, I wasn't even able to wait that long."

Phoebe placed her hand over his heart feeling the slow steady beat. "What do you think is happening?"

Olivia cleared her throat. "January *ap Ionawr*, blood son of Enir the Norn, that is a good question. What does an

800-year-old vampire want with a newly Awakened human witch? I was informed by the Mabon council this morning that you didn't put your name forward as Phoebe's guide."

He swept Phoebe under his arm. "No. Your name, your guided's name, and apparently my former boyfriend James have put their names forward as a guide. I would be happy with anyone but James."

"Because he's a demon?" Melissa asked.

"No, because his taste in women and mine are very similar." January looked at Phoebe directly. "I don't want the competition."

That little flutter in her chest happened again. She could feel herself blushing which was ridiculous. She took a deep breath and looked at January. "You don't want to guide me?"

January threaded his fingers through hers and kissed the back of her hand. "You're a witch and I'm a vampire. I'd love to guide you as my vampire companion, but if you're going to remain a witch what you really need is another witch. You can spend time with the people who put their name forward or choose someone yourself. The Mabon Council wants to talk to you about your Awakening. I would suggest you choose your own guide by then."

He took her other hand and pulled her playfully towards the front door. "Not tonight, though. Tonight, the August moon is full, the first harvest festival has started, and you and I made plans yesterday which I hope to revive today."

Phoebe looked at Melissa for guidance, but Melissa was looking at January.

"I have to take care of my new cat first. She's been home alone all day."

January laughed. "Honey. Yes. You're right. We'd better see to her first. We'll start at your place."

She drew her hands back in surprise. "How did you know her name was Honey?"

He shrugged with a bashful grin. "She told me. I asked her to watch over you while I wasn't there."

Phoebe recognized she was playing way outside of her league. She dated shy boy-next-door type of guys who always expected her to make the first move. His absolute confidence made her suddenly wary. What did she really know about vampires?

He reached for her hand again and placed it over his heart. "On my honor and on the blood of my house, I vow to you in front of witnesses that I will not force your compliance on any matter. You can trust me, Phoebe."

Olivia drew in a sharp breath. "Your vow is witnessed."

January nodded looking Phoebe straight in the eye. "If I break that promise, then my maker will be called to destroy me. Will you celebrate Lammas with me?" He rummaged through his pocket and held the keys to her house out to her as if they did this all the time.

The moment so full of symbols that it would take a lifetime to figure them all out. She took the keys and smiled. "I'd love to. I'll get my bag."

7

THE WAY YOU ARE

January walked beside Phoebe still holding her hand as they made their way to her apartment. Her question about what was happening between them weighed on his mind. He'd gone to the stone circle and asked for a companion. The woman beside him was better than anything he could have hoped for. He knew his attraction was strong and genuine but he didn't know whether his spell was compelling Phoebe.

Walking beside her in the growing darkness he recognized that even their most casual touches sent desire racing through his body. If their attraction was an unintended compulsion, he would remedy it first and replace it with genuine desire. She walked close enough to brush her arm against his and he relaxed a little.

The last thing he wanted was for her to be afraid now that she knew what he was. Knowing he was a vampire and understanding what that meant were different. He'd shown her his speed and a little of his strength, but the first feeding was normally the deciding factor. Even though there wasn't much blood involved in feeding, it took a special kind of person to accept the reality of the situation. To see the mark healing on their body, to know their blood had been taken and would be taken again, was a lot to ask of any partner.

While Phoebe was collecting her bag from the shop, he'd ordered his car and Honey's second lobster to be delivered to her apartment. Alex hadn't been thrilled with the request, but werewolf pack ranks and vampire house ranks were similar, when your Elder asked for something, compliance was in your best interest.

Alex was parked in front of her apartment leaning against January's car by the time they arrived. Smiling at Phoebe with frank appreciation, he pitched the keys to January.

"Hello, boss. Lobster and car delivery man at your service." He held a hand out to Phoebe. "I'm Alex, January's delivery man. He's my guide."

Phoebe reached forward with a beautiful smile and January found himself suddenly taking her hand and standing between them. He looked down at Alex not sure who was more surprised. Shaking his head, he stepped out of the way releasing her.

"Apologies. Apparently, I've lost my manners today. Alex Kimbos, werewolf, my current guided and roommate, applicant to the House of Norn this is Phoebe…" He paused realizing that although he'd kissed this woman and spent the night holding her while they slept, he didn't know her whole name.

"Pierce," she said stepping forward with a wry grin to shake Alex's hands.

"Nice to meet you awake, Phoebe." He turned to January. "I made you a reservation at The Sailor's Catch."

She frowned confused confirming January's suspicions.

"Awake?" She looked at January and then back at Alex. "You must have me confused with someone else."

January gave a slight shake of his head to tell Alex to drop the subject which Alex completely ignored.

"Werewolves don't make those kinds of mistakes. I would know your smell anywhere. I spotted you in January's room this morning. Not going to lie, I was a little jealous of him. Feel free to invite me into the action next time."

Phoebe's mouth hung open for a moment and then she looked up at January horrified. "What's he talking about?"

January could have kicked him. "Don't you have somewhere to be, Alex? If not, I have several tedious and painful things you can do tonight."

Alex threw his hands in the air and laughed. "I'm going now. If I hear you come in tonight, I will make myself scarce."

"Make yourself scarce now," January growled.

Alex turned on heel and trotted off down the street.

Phoebe watched Alex Kimbos jog down the lane. He was the kind of perfect sculpted beauty you expected to find in New York supermodels. Standing next to January, he seemed like a golden retriever standing next to a Siberian tiger. A tiger whom she was about to lead straight into her apartment.

She directed January up the stairs. At least with her back to him, she could ask the question she was afraid she already knew the answer to. "What happened last night?"

"Nothing to be embarrassed about. After you fainted yesterday in the store, I was concerned. I brought you to my home to make sure you were okay. You met Rosalind there."

"Rosalind the angel," she said feeling a bit dizzy. Angels were real.

His hand came up to the small of her back to steady her

but he continued as if nothing unusual had taken place. "Yes. She's a doctor. I asked her to make sure you hadn't shut down. She said that you woke up in my room and then teleported yourself back to your own home."

"Teleported?"

"Yes." There was absolutely no indication in his voice that this was unusual. "I followed you here but I...didn't want to invade your privacy by going into your place without your permission. I asked Honey to watch over you until I could come back."

She turned to stare at him a moment hoping he was teasing. "Honey the cat?" She could hear the disbelief in her own voice. Looking at him was a mistake. His face was the perfect picture of reasonableness. Sexy reasonableness. She found herself looking at the way his lips formed increasingly ludicrous answers to her questions rather than really listening to his answers.

"Yes," he said stepping up to be closer to her. The stairs put them at eye level with one another.

"Okay. That explains how I got home. How did we end up..."

"In bed together?"

His teasing grin combined with just the slightest waggle of his brow packed his statement with so much innuendo that Phoebe had to laugh.

"You're enjoying this aren't you?"

"So much." He kissed the tip of her nose. "To answer your question, I'm not sure how you ended up back in my bed. I left you safe at home last night in Honey's care. I went to bed alone and had a nightmare. I was...distressed. When I woke up from the dream, you were with me. I didn't question why you were there; I was just grateful. I went back to sleep with you in my arms. I woke up alone."

"With you how?"

"You were asleep on my chest with your hand tucked

around my shoulder."

She rubbed the back of her neck suddenly. She'd had this type of crick in her neck before. Not in a very long time, but she recognized it. "Did we have clothes on?" She wasn't sure why she asked. It was a moot question at this point.

"You did. In my defense, I never sleep in clothing."

She felt herself blush and her mouth go dry. "I'm sorry. I didn't mean to invade your privacy. I don't seem to have any control over it."

"May I hold you?"

The question caught her off guard and then she remembered. Nothing without her permission. He'd given his word. She nodded moving aside to let him join her on the stairs. It was crowded and close. He gathered her in a gentle hug and put his cheek on the top of her head. Comfort rather than seduction.

"Newly Awakened witches crossing the Veil have to rediscover their magic. It's more powerful on this side. You will get the hang of this. In the meantime, you are welcome in my bed whenever you want to be there. I'll buy pajamas if necessary."

The absurdity of the situation made her giggle. They had already kissed and slept together but they had yet to have a full conversation or dinner. "We have this dating thing so out of order. Can we start again please?"

"No," he chuckled using a finger to tilt her chin up. "I like the direction this is going." He kissed her softly. "The restaurant we have reservations at is about an hour from here and worth the drive. Alex distracted me and I've left Honey's lobster downstairs in the car. I'll go back to get it and join you inside with your permission."

"Be my guest," she replied with a shrug. "Do I need to change before we go?"

He gave her a brief squeeze. "Never for me. I like you

the way you are."

Sliding her key into the front door, Phoebe could feel herself smiling. As the door swung open, she saw a sudden flash of green. Before she was Awakened she'd always assumed that the green flash was a reflection coming from one of the many windows in the hall, but now she recognized it for exactly what it was. Her wards.

Believing had never been hard for her but seeing her magic in action, really seeing it, made her feel wonderful. Walking over the threshold she put her handbag by the couch and her keys in their designated bowl. Having a place for everything and everything in its place was the motto that held her world together but when she looked around her living room, it was chaos.

Although she'd arranged Honey's bed, toys, and bowls next to the kitchen door, the bed had been dragged under the window, toys and kibble were scattered like confetti around the house, and Honey was snoring on the couch.

Just as she opened her mouth to greet Honey, a bright orange ringing toy ball came rolling into the room, a moment later a black and white fluffy kitten came tearing out of her bedroom. The kitten caught sight of her and skidded to a stop right in the middle of her living room next to the ball. They stared at each other for a long minute. She felt more than saw January appear in the doorway behind her.

"Who is that?" He stepped through the glimmering doorway cautiously carrying a silver tray complete with a decorated lid like some lost butler from a television commercial. His voice seemed to wake Honey who glanced irritated over her shoulder, got up, turned a circle, and then plopped herself back down with her back to them.

"I have no idea. I only had one cat when I left this

morning."

The kitten sat down where it stood looking first at Honey and then back at them as if to say that it was supposed to be here.

"Hmm." January said as if this sort of thing happened all the time. "I'll put the lobster in the kitchen for them but not the butter. It's not good for kittens."

He moved off to the kitchen. The kitten's eyes followed him and the tray with longing, but it stayed in the middle of the floor beside the ball.

Phoebe crouched down to get closer to its level. "Hello sweetheart." She held her hand out for it. "How did you get in here?"

The kitten yawned and then said, "Came through front door with mailman. Yowled at this door until neighbor opened."

Phoebe screamed, lost her balance and scrambled back. The kitten turned in the direction Phoebe was looking, back arched, tail puffed, claws at the ready. It let out a deep menacing growl that should have been impossible for a cat its size. In an instant, January was at their side, crouched like the tiger she'd imagine, teeth exposed and ready to fight.

"What did you see?" he asked the kitten.

"Didn't see," the kitten said between growls. "Witch saw and screamed."

They looked first at one another and then at her. She was trying to remember how to make air come in and out of her lungs.

The kitten glanced at January sheepishly. "First witch. Forgot supposed to stay quiet." The kitten sat down crestfallen wrapping its enormous tail around its feet and drooping its head. "Too excited. Honey said this witch my witch. Ruined it."

Phoebe sat up alarmed. "Hey. Don't be sad. You were

wonderful. It was my fault. I'm a new witch. I have a lot to learn."

January stood smoothing his clothes out as if he'd not intended to rip something in half with his bare hands.

Phoebe tugged his jeans. "Help me out here. Tell her I'm new."

"Him, not her," the kitten said sadly.

January shrugged heading back for the kitchen. "It's her second day of being Awakened. Most witches don't get a familiar until after their 5th year, unless they create one themselves. You look a little young for a fully trained familiar."

Honey chose that moment to come down off the couch. She picked the kitten up by the scruff of the neck and deposited him straight into Phoebe's lap. She gave January a meaningful side-eyed stare that told him clearly not to interfere.

The kitten looked up at her hopefully. "Learn with you. Honey said so. Say name and we family."

January came back into the room, leaning against the doorway with his arms crossed. "He can't tell you his name. If you're his witch, you should already know it."

Yellow green eyes pleaded up at her. As she stroked the kitten's beautiful silky fur she felt the same type of breathy air travel up her arm and whisper in her ear that she had when she'd stroked Honey.

"Bramble," she said. "Your common name is Bramble."

"Yes!" Bramble put his paws on Phoebe's shoulder and rubbed his forehead across her cheek. "Honey right. You my witch." The sound of his ragged purrs and the soft rumbling purr from Honey made Phoebe feel like the smartest human in the world.

January came forward and crouched beside them. "Congratulations Phoebe and Bramble. You are now familiar and witch."

"Family," Bramble corrected happily.

"Family," January repeated stroking Bramble's head.

Before Phoebe could really take in what had just happened, Honey took a very happy Bramble by the scruff of the neck and headed towards the tray of Lobster.

By the time January laid the lobster out in the way Honey wanted it, Phoebe had straightened the cat toys and exchanged her jeans and tennis shoes for a black sundress and strappy sandals. A long silver pentacle hung from her throat and her beautiful red hair drifted in loose waves around her shoulders. January thanked the Goddess for bringing her into his world. Bramble had eaten his weight in lobster before heading to Phoebe's bed for a snooze. It took him a lot of convincing and bribing to persuade both Bramble and Honey that he could protect Phoebe on their date.

It was fully dark when she walked to the curb and he opened the car door for her. Putting her hand on the top of his car she stopped and looked back at him.

"I need a photo of you and to know where we are going so I can text my Dad."

Intrigued, January came closer to look at her phone. A photo of Phoebe, a man with round glasses and long brown hair, a dark-headed woman with the same green eyes Phoebe had, and a scruffy-looking younger man stared back at him.

"Your family is close?"

"Too close sometimes," she said looking down at her phone with obvious affection. "They live up towards Salem and we spend most holidays and birthdays together. My dad and I made a deal when I moved to Boston that I would keep him informed."

"Let's take one together, then. It will help me look normal."

"You don't have to worry about that. My brother, Joshua, is an artist. Every time I see him, he's experimenting with a new, and not always safe way, to create something beautiful. My mom makes and sells up-cycled furniture and my dad is a horticultural therapist. Being normal in this family is not a valued asset."

She came up beside him and put her arm around his waist. He followed suit loving the feeling of being matched. Looking up at the screen, he focused his gaze on her image and smiled without showing his teeth. The click of the electronic shutter always made him chuckle. He wondered if some of the younger people knew why it made that noise. He was glad that she had the sense to be safe and that she had a family that would help make her so.

"Can you send me the photo too? I'd like to have it."

She didn't look up from her screen but the light of her phone highlighted her pleased smile. "Sure." She handed him the phone. "Put your number in."

He added his number and sent himself a text so he would have hers. It wasn't something he did often. He loved technology but he'd never been a fan of phones. "We're headed to The Sailor's Catch. It's a vampire-exclusive restaurant. If you want to text Olivia or Melissa, you can tell them where we're going. I promised Bramble I would have you in bed by dawn."

"Why Melissa or Olivia?"

"I don't know if your parents are Enlightened but if they aren't they won't be able to see or get inside the venue. Melissa or Olivia can at least knock on the door."

Phoebe blew out an astonished breath shaking her head. "Vampire exclusive restaurant. Just when I thought my life can't get any weirder."

She got into the car and he closed the door.

8

VAMPIRE RESTAURANTS

The Sailor's Catch was close to Crane Beach. The way Phoebe's face lit up when she realized the restaurant overlooked the moonlit ocean made him almost forgive Alex for choosing it. The last time he'd been here was with Alex who probably chose it because it was a place that January could feed without consequences. That the visit would bring Phoebe to the attention of just about every vampire on the East Coast probably hadn't occurred to him.

Explaining the vampire politics of the situation would complicate the romantic mood he was trying to establish but would be essential for her guide. The grey area they were in now gave her time to become accustomed to him and him a chance to be himself without all the red tape. When she had a guide, he would need to have visits like this approved first.

Although his break-up with James likely happened before Phoebe was even born, in vampire terms it was still recent history. January brought Alex here only a couple of months ago in order to confirm January's pledge to guide him. Coming here with Phoebe would also make his application to become her companion official. His people understood this introduction meant that his interest in her was personal and progressing.

Rather than walking ahead of her as he would have done as her guide, he came to her side of the car and opened the door. Helping her from the seat, he retained her arm so that she would walk directly beside him. Because individuals truly capable of being a companion were so rare, courtship was valued and respected above all other things in the vampire world. To walk beside Phoebe was the first of five levels of declaration. This signaled to his people that Phoebe was protected.

It was rare for a vampire to bring their mortal companion across the threshold of death. Real love kept most of them from attempting it. Sure, if you were successful, your companion became a vampire and could live with you for the rest of your life. If you failed, however, the person you loved died and you were responsible for their death. Not many vampires survived that guilt. Most tried to choose a companion from the long-lived Enlightened such as the Fey but falling in love with mortals happened more often than anyone, including himself, wanted to admit.

That he was even thinking about the possibility of being in love with this mortal was unsettling. The doors opened and he walked through holding Phoebe firmly beside him. The murmurs of surprise were soft and instantaneous but most likely undetectable to her ears. Whether it was the sounds or the expensively decorated lobby, Phoebe chose that moment to step closer to him. The vampire at the door stepped forward. His waist-length black hair blended flawlessly into his semi-formal black and white kimono called a *haori*. *Daiki*. The attendant's name came to him suddenly.

The attendant stepped forward with a deep bow. "January. What an unexpected pleasure. Alex has made arrangements for you and your friend."

"Daiki," January returned the bow, "this is Phoebe's first time here. Can you impress her?"

Phoebe chuckled reaching forward to shake Daiki's hand. It was an honor in the House of Yūrei to be offered physical contact of any kind. He met January's eyes for permission to accept Phoebe's hand. Nodding, January waited for the flare of possessiveness to take him. Rather than shaking her hand, Daiki held her hand between both of his for a moment giving her a gentle squeeze.

"You honor me, Phoebe. Welcome to The Sailor's Catch. I will do my best to impress."

"Consider the job done. I've never been anywhere like this."

Her honesty must have caught Daiki off guard. The formality he normally showed January dropped and he gave her a genuine smile. He brought her hand to his lips and pressed a gentle kiss to her palm.

It was almost more than January's temperament would allow. He didn't think he'd made a move but Daiki instantly let go of Phoebe as if he'd suddenly remembered himself.

"You both set me a wonderful challenge. I will see what I can do to exceed your expectations."

He led them through the lobby. The tables were almost all set up outside because of the warm night and outstanding view. The restaurant was partially suspended above the sea on stilts. Each table was set up for maximum elegance and maximum privacy. For blood family gatherings the temporary barriers created by screens could be removed but the restaurant prided itself on keeping matters classy and quiet. Vampire feeding in private was often sexual. Here, a vampire companion could get a gourmet meal and then become one with no one but the sea to bear witness.

Mila, the vampire who owned the restaurant, came across the lobby from the kitchen to greet him but her eyes were solely on Phoebe.

"January. You've been gone so long we thought you might have returned to Europe for a spell."

"Sorry Mila. Alex is a bit shy when it comes to these sorts of places."

Mila snorted with laughter. "There is nothing on that boy that is shy. Introduce me to your friend."

"Phoebe, this is Mila founder of the House of Yūrei. She owns the place. Mila this is Phoebe Pierce. I'm currently seducing her into being my companion."

Phoebe made a sound somewhere between a gasp and choking.

"He's always been too honest," Mila said taking Phoebe's outstretched hand and raising it to her lips for a kiss. This time January didn't resist the urge to pull Phoebe back towards him. Unlike Daiki, Mila would think nothing of crossing January if she believed the prize was worth it. There was no doubt in his mind that she was worth it. Were the situation reversed, he would have pursued Phoebe.

Mila gave him a knowing smile and a deep polite bow. She waved Daiki away. "You are both welcome. Come with me and I will seat you myself. Phoebe, do you like red wine?"

"Yes."

"Good. So does January. As a treat, I will select one for you both."

The seating area featured a Japanese Chabudai table sat on a plush dark rug with a series of lounging pillows around it. Mila's personal preference was to hold her companion in front of her when she fed them and fed from them. This was reflected in all but the most formal dining areas here. January sat first facing the sea. Before Phoebe could choose a spot across from him, Mila immediately moved the pillows to create a backrest and lounging area for two. Phoebe settled beside him close enough for him to easily take her into his arms. Mila handed her a menu and then left.

"So why do vampires need exclusive restaurants?" she asked scanning the menu.

He read with interest over her shoulder enjoying the look of pleasure on her face as a cool ocean breeze tangled through her hair. "They don't. Companions do. Eating together is a type of bonding in most cultures. Vampires crave close bonds. Our feeding isn't appropriate for public spaces. This is a happy compromise."

Two bottles and glasses were delivered to the table by a dark-headed vampire. One bottle was jeweled and green and the other one was dark purple. The green one was for him, the purple one was wine for her. The waiter poured both with care before leaving them to drink. January sat beside her keenly aware that this might be the first and last time she allowed him to do so.

Bringing the warm glass to his lips he took two deep long swallows. She watched him holding her own glass halfway to her mouth.

"Do you miss eating human food?"

Her question helped him relax. That she asked about his feelings rather than what he was dining on was a good sign. "I miss sharing food experiences sometimes, but not the act of eating itself. The food I remember was more for survival than joy." He took another sip watching her carefully.

She sipped thoughtfully looking out toward the sea. "I think I would miss it. You know, certain flavors like pumpkin pie at Thanksgiving or chocolate fudge at Christmas, even the toast my mom burns every time I eat breakfast at her house, they provide the nostalgia backbone of my memories. I think it would be hard to give that up."

He took another long drink waiting for her to decide if this gap between their cultures was too far for her to cross. If she couldn't cross this boundary, there was almost no chance she would feed him directly. It was best to know now, before he was any more attached to the idea of her as his companion than he already was.

"It would be hard, but not impossible. There are many...sensations that could make up for the loss." He laced his sentence with innuendo and gulped the last of the blood from the glass before it grew cold. "Sometimes, to recall a flavor or experience a new flavor, vampires will use a scent on the glass while we drink."

She sniffed the wine she was drinking before taking another sip. "Does it work?"

He shrugged and sat his glass beside the bottle. "It makes the taste different but whether it is similar to what I'm supposed to be tasting, I wouldn't know. I have nothing to compare it to."

"How do you prefer to eat?"

He leaned forward picking up the purple bottle and topping up her glass even though it didn't really need it. "I prefer to feed right before I make love. With my lover in my lap, legs and arms wrapped around me. There is a soft place, just above the clavicle, where the scratch of my fangs is almost unnoticeable."

He heard Phoebe draw in an unsteady breath.

"Does your lover also drink?"

"In my fantasies, yes. In real life, I have yet to have the honor. Drinking my blood is how the conversion begins. It has to be done by someone willing to face death to spend a lifetime with me."

Phoebe's brows raised. "So tonight, you're going to

watch me eat?"

"No, I'm going to feed you, if you will allow it. You eat, and if you're willing, describe what you are eating so that I learn what you like and why. Then if you're comfortable, I will ask you to feed me. If you're not comfortable, the bottled blood will be enough."

Phoebe tried to tamp down the thrill in her stomach. The soft carpet under her backside, the pillows, the candlelight and moon light, and the sound of the ocean lapping under them. It had to be one of the most beautiful places she'd ever been. The thought of being fed by hand like some pampered pet amused her on a lot of levels but it was the thought of feeding him that really had her interest.

"Does Alex feed you?"

January wrinkled his nose. "No. If he were truly trying to be a vampire, he would. He's holding out for a werewolf worth his loyalty."

"Who feeds you now?" She wasn't sure why she wanted to know.

"I order from a blood bank called Sangre. It's like a vampire grocery store. It's expensive but the store makes sure the donors are safe and well compensated." January leaned way closer than was necessary to read the menu. "The crab is good."

There were no prices on the menu which suggested this was probably going to cost her more than her entire months' worth of groceries, but it would be worth it.

"How can you suggest food if you don't actually know what it tastes like?"

He gave her a wicked smile. "It's one of the few foods I do remember. Some of the foods I can't even imagine a taste for."

"Like what?"

"Avocado. It looks repulsive and smells like water on grass. Alex says it doesn't taste of anything but James used to eat them like they were one of the best foods on earth."

Avocado. Closing her eyes, she recalled the taste. The memory was vague around the edges even though it was a food she liked. What would a hundred years do to that memory?

"To me, avocado tastes like a very moist firm large mushroom with a subtle watery green flavor rather than an earth. I like it with a little bit of salt or as guacamole but only in moderation."

January's eyes lit up as if she'd given him a precious gift. "Now that I can imagine. I barely remember the texture of mushrooms, but I remember it. The taste of salt, I remember clearly. Occasionally I can still taste it on my skin."

An image of him tasting the salt on her skin made it difficult to concentrate for a moment. His smile as he continued to press his body close to her told her he knew exactly what he'd done.

The tapas-style menu was extensive and included several dishes she'd never heard of. Each of the dishes also had a date beside them. For example, a Genovese Onion Tart, 1570. January explained this was so that a companion could choose something their vampire recognized. She chose three dishes and then January chose three more including the tart.

"That's a lot of food for one person."

"You can take what you don't eat home if you want or I will take it to Alex. He loves leftovers."

The thought of Mr. Perfect eating leftover onion tart out of the fridge made her laugh. "Not a trait I would have assigned to him. How long have you been living together?"

"Come here, Phoebe." He opened his arms and made a gesture for her to come to him. "Sit in front of me. Lean back against me so you are comfortable. We will watch the water and talk while Mila prepares your food."

Torture. Her choice was to give up looking at him and sit in his arms to view the sea or not touch him and watch the moonlight illuminate his skin. He pushed his hair over his shoulder and her gaze traveled to the strong column of his throat. She moved herself into his arms feeling her desire rise as her back made contact with his chest.

Her head dropped back to the cradle of his shoulder and she felt a low growl of pleasure rumble through his body. His hands traveled slowly down the length of her arms, threading his fingers through hers, he bound her arms across her chest with his. Her head dropped to the side exposing her own throat. She felt him brush his lips against the delicate skin and wanted to feel the bite of his teeth.

"I would like to taste you, Phoebe. May I?"

"Yes, please."

Completely immobile, she felt the soft lap of his tongue and then his mouth suckling the juncture between her shoulder and throat. The bite was powerful and the sting made her struggle. Erotic yearning hit her suddenly. When she gasped January held her tighter, the power of his body holding her completely helpless while he fed. If he'd given her control, she would have turned and straddled him, taken him then and there to complete the joining, but he held her still. She heard him drink, felt the pressure of his mouth on her neck. Then he closed the wound with his tongue and gathered her close.

"I will never get enough of you," he whispered in her ear.

She pushed to turn in his arms and he let go. Looking up at his face in the moonlight Phoebe felt his eyes searching her expression for acceptance. She leaned forward and kissed him.

"That was incredible."

Mila appeared at that moment with a knowing smile. "Your food will be here in a moment."

Her acceptance of what he was humbled him. The taste of her desire made him want to join with her completely here under the moonlight. Only, he didn't want their first time together to be observed or rushed. He had only meant to take a taste but the intensity of her reaction meant that he'd fed well and for the first time in a long time he was completely comfortable. He'd forgotten the richness a true companion could bring to the experience. In recent years feeding had become a necessary act of survival.

Purchasing blood was now the norm rather than the exception. Pouring her a glass of wine, he settled her against him again opening his arms so that she could pick up and set down her glass without interference. Her hand rested on his thigh exploring the texture of his pants and he recognized something that he should have noticed before. She was reluctant to lose physical contact with him.

He drew her silky auburn hair through his fingers. "It is not normally like this for me. Vampires build a relationship and through that relationship, the desire to feed and to join grows."

Phoebe took a large drink of wine and then another. "Grows? If it gets better than that, I might die of pleasure."

He laughed. "Then I'm afraid we will die happy together. Tell me truthfully. Is this level of passion natural for you?"

"Yes and no. I uhh, do tend to initiate the physical side of things but it typically takes me a while to build up the interest. I don't usually move this fast." As if her statement made her aware of where she was sitting, she began to shuffle forward and moved to his side.

He placed both hands on her shoulders moving her back towards him. "Stay please. My question wasn't meant to embarrass you. It is my ego asking whether you feel the intensity between us as keenly as I do." He placed an apologetic kiss against the wound on her shoulder.

"I feel it too," she replied looking out over the water.

The food arrived at the table delivered by two of Mila's current lovers. They sat down finger bowls and towels alongside the trays of food. There were a great deal more than 6 choices. Each plate offered three portions in dishes almost as beautiful as the food itself. He picked up a calamari ring and offered to her.

She grinned up at him over her shoulder. "You're serious? You plan to feed me?"

"Handling the food is nice for me. It reminds me of being human. Sharing it with you gives me a chance to share the experience. You can tell me what you enjoy, explain the taste if you want. If you don't like it or if I am moving to slow, just say so and I will sit back and watch you enjoy." He offered her the calamari again and this time she leaned forward and took a bite.

Chewing slowly, she looked up at the stars. "The batter is salty rather than greasy and the calamari is tender rather than rubbery. It is difficult to taste under the batter but I like the combination of the soft and crunchy."

It was one of the best meals of his vampire life. After her first hesitant bites he began to play with her. Asking her to close her eyes when he chose a dish and then asking her to guess which one it was. She described what she was eating in a thoughtful way, answering his questions on flavors and textures, not rushing the experience.

By the time she'd sampled all the dishes on the table she was too full for desserts. He allowed her to move away from him to claim her own seat only because he enjoyed looking at her almost as much as he enjoyed holding her.

She arranged the pillows so that she could lounge across them.

He refilled his glass and took a drink to keep his hands occupied.

"What are you drinking?"

"My guess is a mixture of human and animal blood. Mila made the mixture in case you were not interested in feeding me."

"You're still hungry?"

It was an unmistakable invitation. The thrill of being desired almost made him change his mind but his desire to learn every way to make her gasp with pleasure was at war with his understanding that in order for them to have a real relationship, they needed time to learn one another.

"I don't need the blood. I am drinking it to eat with you and give us a little time to get to know one another. The next time we feed together, we will complete the joining."

She looked at him confused. "We can't complete it now?"

He moved fast snatching her from where she lay and sitting her firmly in his lap. He let her feel his hardness through her thin sun dress, see his desire to have her in his eyes, understand that he wasn't rejecting her. "Temptress. You would take me to your bed and I would be lost for life."

"A girl can hope." She put her arms around his neck. "Come to me when you're ready and we will see who is lost."

Phoebe excused herself to the bathroom. Getting up and walking away from him, she realized that her knees were actually weak and it had nothing to do with blood loss. Real sexual attraction, the kind that made your stomach flutter and your body ache, was rare. Her instinct was to reach out and grab it with both hands. That he intended not to take her to bed immediately was frustrating to say the least.

As she washed her hands she caught sight of the mark on her shoulder in the mirror. Rather than puncture marks like the movies, the place that January had taken blood looked more like a small hickey but it bore a shallow scratch, not much more than she might have received from a cat, and it was already showing signs of healing. She ran her fingers over it. The desire to try that again wasn't diminished by the distance or the understanding that he was literally taking her blood.

A stall behind her opened and a golden-haired woman in a long red dress came out. Everything about her was exquisite. Unlike the dreamy expression on her own face the woman was attempting to repair her mascara where she'd obviously been crying. Even with her makeup smeared she was an elegant woman.

"Are you okay?" Phoebe asked feeling the answer before she asked it.

The woman gave her a trembling smile. "I will be, I think." She raised her hands to touch the mark on Phoebe's neck but Phoebe stepped back.

The woman shook her head. "Sorry. That was rude."

"It's okay. This is still all very weird for me."

The woman tilted her head. "What is weird?"

"Vampires. Enlightened. Even standing in the bathroom talking to strangers is a bit outside of my comfort zone."

The woman laughed revealing long sharp teeth. "It's not something in my repertoire either. Excuse my dramatics. I didn't want to do this. I hope you understand, he left me no choice."

It was all the warning she had. The Vampire leaped forward to grab hold of her and Phoebe threw both her arms up to defend herself.

9

BROKEN PROMISES

With a flash of white light, Phoebe was standing behind the counter of The Craft Shop. Knees trembling and head spinning she looked around wildly for the vampire in red. Doubling over, she dragged in a couple deep breaths trying to keep herself from passing out again. She was getting pretty damn sick of fainting every time something weird happened. In fact, she was getting pretty damn sick of so many weird things happening at once.

Yes, she had always dreamed of living in a place where the supernatural was natural, but she'd failed to consider how hard it would be to re-learn how to function in such a place. For a moment all she really wanted was for her life to be blessedly boring again.

Familiar hands patted her gently on the back. "By the Goddess, Phoebe. That was incredible. You scared the crap out of me. Are you okay?"

"I'm going to throw up," Phoebe whispered.

Melissa helped her sit on the floor and then sat down cross-legged in front of her. Putting one hand in the middle of Phoebe's chest and the other on the ground, she began a soft chant. Almost immediately the sickness stilled and her head stopped spinning. She looked at Melissa who had her eyes closed and was whispering something that disappeared into the darkness before it could be heard. Candlelight twisted through Melissa's black hair and for once, she looked completely in control. The nausea and some of the fear that was knotted in Phoebe's stomach dissipated.

"What are you doing?"

"Grounding," she said finally opening her eyes. "You need to ground the extra energy after you teleport. Olivia says you can store it in an amulet for later if you need it but that it's best just to send it back where it came from. You're lucky I was here. I hurled the first time I teleported." Melissa tilted her head in a puppy-like fashion. "Why are you here? I thought you were supposed to be on a date with a vampire."

"I was. Someone attacked me…"

Melissa hissed. "That pointy-toothed bastard! He gave us his word."

"No. It wasn't him. A woman, a vampire, she attacked me in the bathroom at the restaurant."

"Why?"

"No idea. One minute she was crying in a stall and the next minute she said, "He left me no choice. And then, wham! She's leaping toward me."

"He? Do you think she meant January? Like a crazy ex-girlfriend or like January asked her to attack you?"

Phoebe blinked in horror. "Why would he do that?"

Melissa sat for a minute and frowned. "Forget I said that. I can tell a bad guy from a mile off and there's no way your vampire wants to hurt you. That he carried you through my wards like a knight in shining armor proves it. Speaking of, did he see you go or did you just disappear?"

Phoebe groaned. "I just vanished. And he has my purse so I can't call."

Melissa's lips pinched together. "He was supposed to protect you. I should let him just sit there and work out what happened."

"It's not his fault. Up until that point, I was actually having a really good time."

Melissa leaned forward to draw her finger over the small cut on Phoebe's neck. "I can tell."

Phoebe felt herself blush and she pulled away from Melissa's hand. "It was my choice."

"I didn't say it wasn't. Vampires are extremely charming when they want to be and terrifying when they don't. Your vampire has a reputation for being both."

Phoebe leaned back against the counter looking up at the till aware of two things. The first was that it was after dark, a long time after dark, a beautiful Lammas night and Melissa was still in the shop. The second was that Olivia had reset the wards for Lammas and Phoebe technically shouldn't have been able to teleport inside.

"Why are you still here? You're usually the first one out the door on a major Sabbat," she asked Melissa point blank.

"I came back to move the book while Olivia wasn't here."

"What book?"

"That Vampire witchcraft book you and Olivia keep looking for."

"I don't keep looking for it."

"Yes, you do. So does she. It's okay. The compulsion is pretty strong."

"Any idea what it wants?"

"To leave. Olivia said that I needed to hide it from her because she was starting to feel the effects. I put it in the last place she'd look for it." Her grin was infectious.

"You put it in the storeroom, didn't you?"

Melissa shrugged her shoulders but her smile got

bigger. "Now my turn. What are you doing here? I mean, you obviously teleported to save your ass. Why here?"

Phoebe looked around the darkened shop. "No idea. I have no control over it. I get freaked out or worried and wham, I show up somewhere else. I managed to send myself back to my bed once, but that's the only time I've shown up where I expected to."

Melissa stood up with a big stretch and reached down to help Phoebe to her feet. "Sounds about right considering how new you are to all of this. I can help you control it. I can only go really short distances. Like from my kitchen to my bedroom and I find it absolutely exhausting. Most witches can't do it at all." Pulling her handbag from across the counter, Melissa took out her phone.

"What was the name of that restaurant again?"

10

SHADOW CURSE

January was still watching the moon and waiting for Phoebe to return from the bathroom when Mila dragged a young female vampire to the table by the hair. He sat up immediately. "What's going on here?"

Mila hissed in the woman's ear. "You will tell him."

She turned her dark eyes on January and then back to Mila. "I am bound to silence. I can't."

Dread pooled in January's stomach. "Tell me what? Where is Phoebe?"

"This traitor in my house attacked your friend."

January jumped to his feet but Mila held up her hand. "Your witch is unharmed but only because she is fast and this one is stupid." Mila shook the young vampire viciously. "I received a call from a witch named Melissa. She said you would know who she is. Your Phoebe is at The Craft Shop and is safe."

Relief made his knees weak, but it was followed swiftly by rage. "I gave her my word she would be safe here, Mila. She was attacked in your home. Who is this woman?"

Mila flinched at the force of his words. "I apologize, my friend. My word has been broken and I will pay the price.

This is Marina. She is of my house. The shame of her action is mine to bear."

Marina looked frantically at January. "No! Please, my lady. No. It's not your fault. It was me alone. I did it. Please! She had nothing to do with it."

January ignored the young vampire meeting Mila's black gaze. "It is so. Mila of the House of Yūrei for this violation in hospitality and your lack of control of the vampires in your house, you are stripped of the right to offer sanctuary or guidance for one solar year. For every minute it takes your child to answer my next question, she will fast a week."

With clenched teeth Mila nodded and bowed in agreement. "Hai."

Mila threw the girl at January's feet. Reaching down, he grabbed her arm and pulled her to face him. He used every bit of his power to compel the truth from her. "You are loved and well fed here. Why did you attack Phoebe?"

Marina looked at him with panic rather than anger. "I..." She cried out suddenly as if she'd been struck.

"By my blood you will tell him," Mila ordered, her command reinforcing his compulsion.

The girl began to grasp at her own throat as if she were choking and January realized that she was cursed. Bound by a dark magic he hadn't seen in centuries. Mila's blood flowed through Marina's veins. The compulsion to obey the command was tearing her apart.

"Stop. There's something wrong."

January's warning was too late. Before Mila could call back the command Marina's throat split in half from just below her chin to the middle of her chest. January pushed her away and she fell to the ground. A formless darkness climbed out of her throat and then out of her body moving swiftly over the floor towards him. January put one hand on his necklace and picked up the green jeweled bottle from the table. A spell filled his mind even though he had not been able to cast a spell since he was a human.

"In the Lammas light of the moon, Darkness you are bound.

Confined in this bottle until it breaks on hallowed ground."

Like a genie sucked into a bottle, the dark thing was dragged back from the bloody ground and trapped in the bottle. The rush of power that flowed through January to bind the darkness left him breathless. He held the bottle up to the moon light in shock. For his entire life he'd been told that Vampires couldn't cast spells as witches did and yet he'd done so.

As his senses returned to him, he became aware of Mila standing in a pool of blood over the body of her lost companion. Unshed tears glimmered in her eyes. If it were anyone but Mila, he would have wrapped them in his arms to comfort them, but in the House of Yūrei, only Mila was permitted to initiate physical contact.

Moving to her side, January bowed his head quietly in respect. "I'm sorry," he whispered knowing that his words were no comfort. "We can't touch her until after the Recovery Unit has been here. This is dark and forbidden magic."

"What is this thing?" she motioned to the bottle with her chin.

"A shadow curse. It's a dark soul given the power to move from body to body. Once settled into a body, it feeds on its host until there is nothing left of them." January tilted the bottle carefully holding it up to the light noticing nothing but the remnants of the blood in the bottom.

The shadow was in there, but it was hiding. A shadow curse should have been impossible for anyone but the Seelie Queen and the Unseelie Queen to summon. Not because they required so much power but because the method to summon them required the blood of the Seelie Queen to open the book that contained the spell. A book only the Unseelie Queen knew how to find.

They signed a peace treaty together to forbid either of them from using the curse. What he held in his hands was either proof they were working together or evidence that someone close to both of them was willing to start a war to keep the Veil in place.

"I will find out who did this to her." Mila clenched her fists, the only indication of her true anger. "When I do, they will pay for every moment of her time they have taken from me. This I promise to you."

January nodded. "I will help you."

11

A SHAPE IN THE DARKNESS

James was sitting in his office at the Boston Recovery Center staring at a list of the recently Awakened in disbelief. The list was long enough to scroll through the names. There were more Unguided cases in Boston this last year than there were in the previous ten years combined. Most of those cases occurred within the last six months.

A rumor amongst the more fanatical Unseelie was that the Veil was being destroyed by the Seelie Court. That the same rumor existed in the Seelie Court about the Unseelie was typical. There was precious little information about how these new Unguided people had come through the Veil and absolutely nothing that appeared to connect the unsanctioned Awakenings to one another. In the Recovery Center, the Unguided recalled the first Enlightened person they encountered after they were Awakened but none of those encounters would have been labeled as extraordinary.

James focused on his task. He compared the names on the list he'd given Isla with the names of the newly Awakened who were listed as shut down, dead, or missing. In the first weeks of his reporting, there was a direct correlation. Had anyone but Isla known about the list, James would be in jail as a murder suspect.

In the last month, none of the names he'd given Isla were on the list of the missing or the dead. That meant one of two things, either the Unseelie Court was covering their tracks better or Isla was holding the information back. He thought back to her control over the children, her quiet deadly warning.

Would she risk her status and safety for strangers? Staring down at the blank piece of paper where he was supposed to write the names of the newest Unguided witches, his heart whispered an answer. No. Isla hadn't built the reputation she had by being stupid and only someone with a death wish would directly defy the Dark Queen. It would be someone close to her. Someone she trusted.

His phone rang and he picked it up without checking the number. "Hello?"

"James? It's January."

James closed his eyes letting the moment flow over him. Every time he changed phones, he gave January his phone number. Until now, he'd never called. "Are you okay?" He tried to make his inquiry sound professional.

He heard January sigh. "I was attacked by a shadow curse tonight. So was Phoebe."

Gripping the phone tight he felt like he couldn't breathe. A shadow curse was a soul, an evil soul, trapped between life and death. Its driving desire was to take over another body to have the opportunity to live again. It used the body until there was nothing left in it and then moved to the next body. They were banned by both the Seelie and the Unseelie courts in the 1600's. The souls were volatile often turning on the spell caster.

"Is she dead? Phoebe? Did the shadow take her?" James didn't want her to be. Phoebe was competition and he wanted her out of the way, but he didn't want her dead. The thought surprised him. He'd never wanted any of them dead.

"No. She teleported just as she was attacked but she was the target. How can I find out who sent it?"

"I'm not sure. I can ask around, but I can't guarantee anyone would admit to it. The Unseelie Queen herself signed the treaty that bans them. No one crosses her lightly."

"I know. I was there when she signed it. The Seelie court doesn't deal in that kind of Magic and the White Witch Council has any magic user capable of it under observation."

"A shadow curse is as likely to turn on its creator as it is to do their bidding. If we can find it, we might be able to bribe it."

"That's a good idea. I need a favor for a favor."

James shifted in his chair caught off guard for the third time in as many minutes. He wanted Phoebe's contract to trade her back for a favor. That favor was being offered without her. Now that the moment was here, he wasn't sure he had the nerve to ask for the favor he wanted. A second chance. It was within his grasp.

Looking at the names of the dead or lost witches on his screen, he knew that he didn't deserve one. In the hundred years since they'd parted, he'd learned nothing. He was still too selfish to deserve a chance with January.

"What do you need?"

"I need you to protect Phoebe. We aren't at the stage in our relationship where I can stay with her all the time and no one is a better bodyguard than you."

The request shredded the last of James's hopes for reconciliation. Even though he'd known on some level the request was coming, it still shocked him. "For how long?"

"Just until Yule. If I haven't been able to find the

shadow or the person who cast it against her by then either one or both of us will be dead."

If it hadn't been for his promise to the Unseelie Queen to agree to January's request, he might have hung the phone up right there. That she'd predicted the request, just as she predicted him driving to see Isla, made him understand that she was more involved in what was happening here than anyone might understand.

"Agreed." The sound felt torn from his heart.

"Be sure, James. We have history. I know you say we're just friends now, but I would understand if you told me to get lost. I wouldn't ask except that you are the only person experienced enough with the Unseelie to be able to recognize the shadow. The only one I would trust with my companion's life."

"Your companion? She's accepted your offer?"

"No. I haven't even made the offer formally, but I will. I just need her to give me a second chance. I failed her tonight. What do you want in return? A favor for a favor."

James felt tears moving down his cheeks but his heart was so numb he didn't recognize them as his own. "Can I have a blank check? I don't need anything right now and I don't know what I'll need in the future."

The silence on the phone was so long that James wondered if the line had dropped.

"You know I can't do that. Friends or not, no one in their right mind gives an Unseelie that kind of promise. We both know it would be used against you."

James cleared his throat and crumpled the paper he held in his hands. "You're right. Then give me somewhere to go that no one knows about but you. A house somewhere I can live comfortably on my own for five hundred years without anyone the wiser."

"Somewhere to hide from the Unseelie," January said thoughtfully. "A fair deal. I'll get it done. When its ready, we will meet in person, and I'll tell you and only you where it is. Is it a deal?

If there was such a place in the world, January would know where it was. When the job was done or Phoebe was dead, he would disappear and hope that five hundred years was long enough to grow another heart.

"It's a deal." James tossed the crumpled paper into the trash and began to shut the computer down. "I'll ask around and find your shadow."

"You don't have to. I trapped it in a bottle of blood." His phone indicated a delivery and James saw a jeweled green bottle in the driver's seat of the car.

"How?" A shadow could be trapped by mirrors but James had never heard of one in a bottle.

"I cast a spell. I haven't been able to do it since I was converted but I took Phoebe's blood and while it was fresh in my body, I could use her magic."

"Be careful. That shadow will be angry when it is released. You might be immortal but you're not invulnerable."

"You too, my friend. I am in your debt."

James hung up the phone without saying goodbye. There had to be a way out of this that wouldn't cost him his life. If he could find the source of the Awakenings, then he wouldn't need to report newly Awakened witches to the Unseelie court. There was a doctor in Larkshead, Selene Hernandez, who was already working on it. It wouldn't be hard to get a hold of her data.

A bargain was a bargain, but he couldn't bear to watch January fall in love and spend a lifetime with Phoebe. He would make another trade and find someone else to guard Phoebe from the shadow.

. . .

January walked to Phoebe's front door carrying her handbag. He'd stopped by his own house to stash the bottle in his safe and to warn Alex about the shadow. Their home wards were strong and not for the first time since meeting Phoebe, he wished he could also teleport. As it was, it was just after midnight when he arrived in front of her door. A light scratching from the other side let him know that either Bramble or Honey sensed him here. The door opened slowly and Phoebe peeked out. Still dressed for dinner, her smile was relieved and welcoming as she pushed open the door.

"Come in. I'm so sorry for disappearing. Are you okay?"

Coming inside, he held out her handbag as a kind of offering. "I'm sorry. I said you would be safe and I lied."

"You didn't lie," she said taking the bag and stashing it by the couch where both Honey and Bramble sat peering at him with exasperation. "Melissa said on the way home that The Sailor's Catch is one of the most exclusive vampire restaurants in the world. It's not the type of place you expect to be attacked in the bathroom. Tell me the truth. Are you really okay?"

The knot of tension in his throat eased. She wasn't angry or afraid, she was worried about him. He wrapped her in his arms and held her close. "I've never been more terrified in my life. I don't know what I would have done if something happened to you."

Her hands drifted up and down his back. "It's okay. I can't say that it's on my top ten things to do again, but I'm not hurt. Other than scaring the hell out of me, she didn't touch me."

January manoeuvred them towards the couch arranging Phoebe in his arms. "Did Marina say anything about why she attacked you?"

"She said, 'He left me no choice' and she was crying

about it. I know it sounds insane, but it felt like she didn't want to do it. I'm worried about her."

He hugged her close treasuring her generosity. "Marina was possessed by a shadow curse. They are almost unheard of these days. Once she allowed the shadow into her body, it could make her do things she didn't want to do."

Phoebe pushed back searching his face for a moment. "Something happened after I left."

"The shadow was still in her when Mila caught her. It tore her apart to keep itself safe."

Phoebe closed her eyes shaking her head. "How can you live in a place with so much violence."

Gathering her close he held her quietly. There was nothing to say. The Unenlightened and the Enlightened both lived on a knife edge of civility. There was only ever an illusion of control and safety.

"I'm sorry you were attacked, Cariad. Give me another chance and I will prove to you that my world, our world, has as much kindness as it does blood."

She pressed a soft kiss to the hollow of his throat that sent a shiver through his body. "It's not your fault but I need a couple of days to find my feet before I jump into this next life."

January nodded even though his mind rejected what she wanted. "I'll give you some space. Not too much." He kissed the top of her head holding her close for a second longer. "You've got my number. When you're ready, just give me a call."

He helped her up from the couch and they walked hand and hand to her door. Before he could open it, she caught his arm and pulled him toward her for a kiss. A slow sensual exploration that left him tight and breathless.

"Temptress." He whispered against her lips. "Do that again and I will forget I'm a gentleman and you'll spend the rest of the night under me."

She arched a brow brushing his hair back from his face. "Is that supposed to be a threat?"

He swept down to kiss her, moulding her body to his, allowing her to taste the strength and wildness he was capable of. Now it was her that was breathless.

"It's a promise."

He left before he could change his mind.

The light tickling sensation of her hair being stroked woke her from a restless sleep. Glancing up through her lashes she recognized the shape of January in the darkness. She was sprawled across his chest, his naked chest, with her leg thrown over him. His eyes were closed in the half-darkness but his fingers drifted through her hair. If this was his idea of giving her space, she'd hate to think what the alternative looked like. Before she could work up any indignation, she recognized that the blankets tucked around them were not hers.

Her sleep shirt had ridden up around her hips leaving nothing but her socks between then from the waist down.

"Good morning sleeping beauty."

The soft sound of his amused voice rumbled under her cheek. She pushed herself up on one arm to look down at him. He tried to give her an innocent look as his fingers drifted to the small of her back.

"Where are we?"

"In my bed. It's a little after 5 am. You arrived about 1 am."

She began to roll off of him but he caught her leg and pulled her back into their original position. "Stay. I'll drive you home in a couple of hours and you can pretend this didn't happen."

Phoebe snuggled into his chest too tired to think of what the logical thing to do in this situation was. "Until I come back tomorrow. Any clue why I keep coming back here?"

"You want me, and I want you. Your magic brings you here because you want to be here."

She smiled against his chest. "That's very presumptuous of you."

His hands moved from her hair, to the small of her back, and then to cup her backside and bring her in direct contact with his hardness. "Tell me that I wouldn't be welcome and I will move away."

It would take almost no movement at all to join with him. When she didn't answer he began to move away from her but Phoebe hooked her heel around his leg and stopped him. "I don't want you to go."

He settled them again but didn't allow her to put space between them. "Then I won't. But I'm also not going to make love to you until you walk through my door willingly." His hands traced the curve of her spine. "It might kill me, but I'll die an honorable man."

"It might kill us both." She laughed trying and failing to relax. "There's no way I'm going to be able to sleep."

He resumed stroking her hair. "I can help you."

"You just said you weren't going to help me until I asked."

"Not like that," he chided tugging a piece of her hair a little harder than was necessary. "I was a witch before I was a vampire. In my own time, I could use my voice to persuade people to do what I wanted them to do. Although my other magic is gone, I still have that gift."

"How does it work?" She let her fingers drift over his chest and arms, a light touch meant to soothe rather than stimulate.

"It's a compulsion. I give the command and your mind will follow it."

Looking up at him with a frown, she realized he wasn't joking. "That's a scary gift."

Cupping her face, he kissed her forehead. "You never have to be afraid of me, Cariad. I would die before I used any of my gifts to hurt you."

She returned his hug. "Okay. Let's try it quick because we either sleep or I walk out that door for a glass of water and back in for something better."

He stilled for a moment as if mentally counting to ten.

"You have a devilish streak, woman."

Phoebe wasn't joking. Her imagination was conjuring up some triple X versions of what she'd like to do with him tonight, none of which were sleep.

"Okay. Command me."

Tangling his hands through her hair he whispered, "Sleep deep. When I speak your name, wake refreshed."

12

FALLING IN LOVE

The pattern continued. January called it courtship and stepped into the role of Victorian gentleman so completely that she felt out of place and time. During the day she worked at The Craft Shop while Melissa and Olivia showed her and Bramble the magical ropes. At night, January arrived to take her and sometimes Bramble on dates. Real dates. Art galleries, aquariums, bookshops, pottery painting, a ballroom dancing class, anything that meant they had to do something together. If he didn't stop feeding her 'things he couldn't imagine a taste for' she would have to go up a size in clothing.

Although Phoebe would have considered herself knowledgeable about Boston, it was nothing compared to what January knew first hand. Sometimes they spent the entire date walking unremarkable streets of the city while he told her stories of bandits, gardens, scandals, families and triumphs. Everywhere they went, he pointed out the stars. He was so excited about the exhibitions in the Boston Museum of Science that they had to go three nights in a row to get through all of the information.

Some nights it was just like dating a human, some

nights his whispered commentary on the side of that made her hyper aware of how old he really was. Bramble attended school in the early evening but still complained about not getting to go with Phoebe on all her dates or to January's home when she unwittingly "appeared" there.

Sometimes she would wake back up in her bed, but more often than not, she had to face Alex over the coffee pot and have January drive her home. Pajamas became a must for her and as a courtesy January chose to wear silk harem style pants that left absolutely nothing to the imagination.

She was deeply considering leaving some of her own clothes at his house to avoid wearing any more of his clothes home. Grinning wickedly, he'd said when she walked through the door of his bedroom, she would be welcome to leave anything she wanted but not until then. He liked her in his clothes. He'd already purchased two beds, bowls, and toys for Bramble. Two beds because Alex insisted Bramble have options.

January was picking her up tonight for a Mabon ritual at the stone circle where they met. The night was warm for the end of September and the dry weather meant that the leaves were at their best. She'd packed an overnight bag for herself and she'd packed Bramble. If he wanted her to come through is door, she was ready. A woman could only handle so much temptation.

By the time he picked her up she was starving. The excitement of the day meant that she'd had coffee for breakfast and she'd missed her lunch. A normal evening human date involved food but as they left the city lights behind and entered the woods, she realized that dating a vampire might have drawbacks.

"Tell me what I've forgotten." January's eyes didn't leave the road as he shifted gears.

Phoebe opened her mouth and then closed it again. How did he know? "Do vampires read minds?"

He gave her a sexy little half smile. "I wish. You keep looking at me and looking back towards town. Your heartbeat is regular so you aren't frightened. That means I've forgotten something."

"Is there going to be dinner at this Enlightened Stone Circle Ritual? Because if there isn't, we need to stop somewhere so I can pick something up."

"We're heading to my house first for what we need. It's a festival, so there will be some treats available to purchase but were expected to bring food, drinks, and blankets for ourselves. I also have an offering for the coming harvest. Don't worry. Alex has trained me well. He's an absolute Diva if he's not fed regularly."

A hundred questions should be floating through her mind, but in the dark car she found herself simply enjoying the opportunity to watch him. Moonlight made his pale features and hair glow with an unearthly beauty. His concentration was absolute and he obeyed every road rule to the letter, including the speed limit.

"How long have you been driving?"

January looked over at her briefly with an arched eyebrow and a smile. "Do you actually want me to answer that question? I noticed you get spooked when I talk about my past."

Phoebe smiled back. "That long ago, huh?"

"Let's just say that I learned to drive before you needed a license to do it."

"Is it rude to ask how old you are?"

"No. I wondered when you'd ask. It's a natural question. As a courtesy, vampires make a distinction between the age we appear to be and the age we are. I was transformed in my late twenties. A vampire's conversion is normally done slowly by their companion over several years. Mine was done unintentionally and very quickly by my maker in 1263 at a place then called Gannoc but now called Deganwy, Wales."

"Unintentionally?"

"My maker, Enir the Norn, and her companion Nesta, were taking advantage of a Norman skirmish against the Prince of Wales, Llywelyn ap Gruffudd. Enir was teaching Nesta to feed on her own. Before the blood banks, it was a skill vital to survival. I came upon Nesta unexpectedly feeding off the dying. I thought she was a monster and I killed her. Enir was too far away to stop me. She caught me and meant to destroy me but something went wrong. I survived her attack and awoke fully converted. She went to my village, collected my belongings, and told my family I'd been killed in the skirmish."

"I'm sorry." It was all she could think to say. Two facts warred in her mind. January was 760 years old, and he'd killed a woman, a vampire.

"Don't be. I've had the opportunity to build several different types of life since then. I have the advantage of knowing I have the time to start again and again until I get it right. The transformation was a blessing in the end. My wife, Angharad, died unexpectedly of a fever earlier that year. Her death hit me hard. She and my brother, Madyn, were all I had in those days. I tried to find Madyn after my conversion but by the time I got back to my village he'd already gathered his family and left for Gwynedd."

The foreign words mixed into his English made his accent sound musical. "Do you miss her? Your wife?"

"When she first died, I wasn't sure I would survive without her. Even though death seemed to sit at the table with us every day, nothing felt normal after she went. I was angry at God and the world for taking her from me. It was only that grief understanding that helped me comprehend Enir's reaction. Her rage matched mine, only she had somewhere to lay her anger."

"Is she still angry with you?"

"I don't think she will ever forgive me completely, or herself. Eventually, we both recognized that what happened to Nesta and to me was an accident of timing that one could call fate."

Phoebe let silence fall between them again, her mind caught in his story.

January turned onto a heavily wooded road, and then onto a drive. The wood and wrought iron gate looked like two dragons intertwined with one another. It swung open as they drew near. In the moonlight she could make out a modest horse stable, a garage, a guest house, a swimming pool, and what looked to be a large stone Queen Anne styled home complete with an impressive central turret and fish-tale shingles in the gables. Like a miniature castle in the woods. It was breath taking.

"It's beautiful."

January smiled with genuine pleasure. "Thank you. It's one of my favorites. It took me two lifetimes to build and costs me a moderate income to run, but of all the homes I have, it's my favorite."

"Because it looks like a castle?"

"Yes. And because the White Stone Circle where we met is about a half mile down a path and into the woods."

"You own the circle?"

Taking off the seatbelt January leaned over to kiss her briefly before opening his door. "I built the circle."

January brought Phoebe into his home hoping she would relax a little once she had a look around. She put her handbag and a smaller overnight bag over her shoulder before she collected Bramble off the back seat. With Bramble in her arms, she looked like a lost orphan coming to stay. His body was hot and tight with wanting her. That she was finally consenting to stay the night with him willingly only made him want her more. If he'd not specifically promised to bring her to the Mabon Ritual, he would have just fed her and taken her to bed.

Her long green dress hugged her hips and brushed the tops of her feet. Telling her about Enir and Nesta was important for both of them. He couldn't hide his past, and it was unlikely that Enir would leave them alone once she knew that January was interested enough to formally request Phoebe as a companion. He could have easily packed food and blankets before he left to pick her up for their date but he wanted to see her here, walking the halls of his home, leaning against the kitchen counter while they decided what she wanted to eat without the rush of having to bring her back home.

She stepped through the door and looked up to the second floor. Although she'd been through the front hall a couple of times, she normally only had time to go to the kitchen, get some coffee and breakfast, and then leave. He could almost see her putting distance between them. Reaching forward, he took her hand and tugged her and Bramble into his arms.

"I brought you here to show off, not scare you off. What's wrong?"

"Nothing." She sat Bramble on the floor who yawned and then began exploring. "It's beautiful. I'm just feeling a little out of my league. You are 732 years older than me and your front hall is bigger than my apartment. What do you do for a living, anyway?"

January kissed her cheek and then her forehead. "If I tell you, you have to promise not to be intimidated."

She took a deep breath looking up at him seriously. "I promise."

"I'm an accountant."

He watched the information work its way through her expectations. Her adorable mouth dropped open and then she slapped her hand over it to stop herself from chuckling.

"You are not."

Her laughter washed over him and he kissed her cheek and then her neck again. "Listen, young lady, the IRS is no laughing matter."

Tears flowed from her eyes like laughter from her throat. She relaxed into his embrace still looking at him with disbelief.

"I thought you hunted demons or were some sort of supernatural cop."

"I have done both in my time, but they don't pay well. I like to be comfortable. Vampires have very complex tax needs and pay generously to have those needs met."

"You are a surprise on every level." She shook her head. "Okay, show off this house of yours."

He led her through the bedrooms and bathrooms enjoying the way each of the rooms caused her to hmm or tsk. Bramble followed sniffing, jumping onto tables, chairs, and beds, generally inspecting the place. Eventually, he lost interest and abandoned them to go find his bowls. The time period for each room was different. Persian baths, a Victorian library complete with a cabinet of curiosities and fireplace, one art deco bedroom, one early medieval bedroom, Alex's bedroom reflected January's time in 17th century Japan.

Some of the artifacts in each room were real and some were pure fancy. Vampires often had a time period that was their favorite and their home decoration reflected that preference. This was his favorite home, so he made sure to have each of his favorite time periods displayed here.

Coming to his own bedroom door he hesitated. He was a man who enjoyed pleasure in all of its many varieties. Some people embraced that side of themselves and some people couldn't. He stalled.

"The utilities are now in the garage because Alex hates the sound of the dryer worse than he hates hanging out in the garage folding his laundry. I figure that will last until mid-October when it starts really getting cold."

"He's a werewolf who doesn't like the cold?"

"Neither of us like it. Me because I spent the first 300 years of my early life trying to avoid freezing to death and him because the cold reminds him that he's not completed his transformation."

He pushed open his bedroom door slowly. The decision was hers. Even though she had a bag and Bramble, he would let her walk away if she wasn't ready yet. When he'd first decided on the Arabian Nights-themed bedroom, he'd been in a low mood. He needed something to stimulate his senses and give him hope so he designed a room meant for pleasuring a companion.

Lush reds and purples were embroidered with gold and silver, cut wooden screens cast patterned light around the room, stained glass windows, Turkish lamps, silks, brocade, and a ceiling painted to resemble an azure star-lit sky. His bed was the Centerpiece of the room, large, low, and round rather than square. It was draped with a heavy damask fabric and full of pillows of every shape and size. There were intricately carved candle holders, incense burners, and a narrow tantra sofa designed to accommodate just about every sexual position imaginable.

Phoebe had been in his room before but it was always dark and she was mostly half asleep. Watching her move around the room running her fingers over the fabrics and surfaces made him feel exposed, like The Beast watching Beauty move through his castle. He wanted her to love this house as much as he did.

She turned a circle in the middle of the room with her arms thrown wide looking up at the ceiling. "I love this place. When do I move in?"

She was joking, her grin said so, but he felt his heart leap with excitement. "Say the word and I'll send for the rest of your things now."

Crossing her arms over her chest she stalked toward him. "You would not. We barely know each other."

"We sleep together almost every night." He moved toward her because he had to. "In the 1800's, we would be engaged by now. Besides, what better way to learn from one another than to have exclusive access?"

"Exclusive?"

She was challenging him. Everything from the twinkle in her eye to the tilt of her chin said so. It was exactly the right way to get his attention. "I won't make rules for you but until you make it clear that you don't want a relationship with me, there won't be anyone else. I have my heart set on you."

"Says the man with a bedroom literally built for sex. You don't strike me as a guy who denies himself pleasure."

"You're right," he said gently pushing her hair behind her ear. "There was a time when I'd go to bed with just about anyone but that was a long time ago. I've got nothing to prove." He reached for her uncrossing her arms and wrapping them around himself. She stepped into his embrace, a creature of pure temptation. "Besides, how could I have another lover when a half-naked temptress appears in my bed at will."

Phoebe laughed. "That's a good point. Do you think I'll stay here through the night?"

"I think you will. This is where you want to be."

Her breath fluttered and so did her heartbeat. She was nervous but her expression was anything but intimidated. What he wanted was to take her to the bed right now and taste every bit of her but there was dinner to eat and a ritual to attend. Picking her up, he threw her over his shoulder and left the room before he changed his mind.

"Come along, Temptress. We have a Sabbat to celebrate and I promised Bramble a good meal before we head to the circle."

Setting her back on her feet in the kitchen, he thanked the Goddess for Alex. On his own, he didn't bother to stock the cupboards with much beyond the occasional drink and snack for visitors. Alex, on the other hand, loved to both cook and eat. As a result, the cabinets and the fridge were stuffed with a variety of quality foods. The delight on Phoebe's face, when she opened a dish and found falafel on a bed of couscous complete with Tahini sauce, made the time January spent cleaning up the mess Alex made in here almost worth it.

He watched fascinated as she opened dishes and rummaged through shelves. Making a sound of triumph, she dumped the whole concoction into a bread wrap.

"We can take that and some other things with us to the ritual, but if you eat it here, you can heat it up and have some of the wine I bought for the evening."

She opened another cabinet pulling down a large plate. "Is it as good as the stuff I had at The Sailor's Catch?"

"It's the same. When you said you enjoyed it, I purchased a case. Alex doesn't like it but that normally means most other people do."

It was all the convincing she needed. Phoebe put the wrap in the air fryer that Alex paid a fortune for and began to open cabinets looking for something else.

He caught her hand when she opened the fridge again. "Go sit down. Let me see if I can serve you the right things for this dish."

She looked intrigued.

"Please?"

Nodding, she left the room and seated herself at his dining room table. He brought her olives, cheese, a braided bread loaf he'd bought for the ritual. Adding two types of dipping vinegar, and a salad that had pomegranate and raisins in it, he arranged them as neatly as he could on a series of colored bowls and plates. Laying out lace napkins he'd purchased in Malta, he lit the long white candle Alex insisted on keeping on the table just in case. It was a feast fit for Mabon.

Bramble refused falafel but accepted shredded chicken in gravy, especially when he learned that Alex had made it, especially for him. He insisted on eating at the table, having a napkin, and his food heated so the gravy was runny. January indulged him while Phoebe tried not to laugh. Hoping that she made as many happy sounds when she made love as she did when she ate, he prepared his own meal.

The bottled blood was kept in a hidden compartment in the fridge door and then placed in a specifically designed bottle warmer. As the science of how they fed advanced, so did the ease and convenience of getting fed. Once they had skulked in the shadows hoping to find a human who could be trusted, and feeding as often as was safe was a thing of the past. They now had a blood donor's union, scented bottles to bring out certain tastes in blood, and bottles designed to be both functional and beautiful. He poured the blood into a tall dark blue warmed tankard. It was more than he generally ate in a week but he wanted to be in full control of his hunger when they made love tonight. He couldn't remember ever being this happy.

Alex came into the kitchen just as Phoebe's food finished cooking. He made a face as January placed the wrap onto a plate.

"What is that supposed to be?"

"Something Phoebe invented from leftovers." He cut the wrap open and Alex's eyes widened in appreciation.

"That woman is a genius. Phoebe!" He yelled toward the dining room destroying any romantic atmosphere that still remained. "Can I have half of your Falafel wrap?"

"Only if you bring me a knife when you come in. Watch Bramble, he's right by the door."

"You brought the cat? Did he like the chicken?" Alex fetched a plate out of the cabinet and then silverware before scooping up Phoebe's plate and heading to the dining room. In the quiet of the kitchen January tried to decide whether to be amused or irritated.

Alex came back into the kitchen heading for the library. "That looks awesome. I didn't know you could cook."

"You cooked. I warmed and put it on the table. Where are you going?"

"Bramble can't see over the table from the chair. I'm going to get him a cushion."

Bramble followed Alex into the kitchen sitting at January's feet looking just about as bemused as January felt.

"Family?" he asked softly looking down the hall and back at January with his ears twitching back and forth.

January leaned down and wiped the gravy from his whiskers. "Yeah. I guess we are." He lifted the familiar up and went back to the dining room.

Bramble had two servings of chicken before he discovered the bed Alex had laid down for him in the library right next to the fire.

"Fire ritual here?" he asked Phoebe looking up at her with a hopeful look.

"In the woods at a big white stone circle with lots of other witches and familiars," Alex replied kicking off his shoes and getting himself settled on the couch with the rest of Phoebe's wine.

"Bramble go?" He looked at them and then back at the bed with obvious longing.

Alex grinned. "He can stay with me. Rosalind is busy tonight and I could do with a film-watching buddy."

Phoebe picked Bramble up and gave him a kiss. "It's your choice, baby. Do you want to do magic in the stone circle with me and January or snooze and snack with Alex?"

Bramble looked at Alex worried. "Alex stay with Bramble?"

Alex held his arms out for the familiar. "I'm not going anywhere, and they aren't going far. If we get bored, we'll go find them."

"No scary movies," Phoebe said handing Bramble to Alex. "They give him nightmares."

It was all the convincing he needed.

13

MABON MAGIC

Although Phoebe insisted she couldn't possibly be hungry after that meal, January put snacks, water, more wine, some tissues, a small first-aid kit, two pairs of warm socks, a blanket, and their phones into a backpack. Going to the closet under the stairs, he pulled forward the rack that contained his ritual cloak. He threw it over his shoulders loving the familiar pull of the warm cloth. Over the years, he'd embroidered the hem of the cloak with silver runes and protective patterns, some so old that he'd almost forgotten their true meaning.

It would be too warm to wear all evening, but that's not why he brought it. Phoebe's dress was thin, and her shoulders were bare. When the night darkened, and the fire dimmed, she would be cold. Before the end of the evening, he would drape the cloak over both of them and begin his seduction properly. Closing the simple silver cloak pin and putting their pack over his shoulder, he offered Phoebe his hand.

"Shall we go?"

She was in a castle with a vampire in a green cloak about to head to a moonlit ritual at a stone circle reserved for supernatural people only. All that was missing from this fairy tale was a wicked witch. Her stomach was full of good food and even better wine. Her cat was snoozing by the fire with a werewolf she liked more every day, and she had nowhere to be tonight or tomorrow except for here. It was time to admit that life didn't get better than this.

She moved towards the car, but January stopped her in the middle of the driveway.

"There's no road to where we're going. It's a path through the woods."

Phoebe smoothed her dress self-consciously. "I'm wearing sandals."

January smiled at her but didn't pull her toward the path. "You could probably walk it barefoot if you wanted. The path is Wild Fey tended. If you have an invitation from me, you can't get lost or hurt on the path." With a gallant bow, January kissed her hand. "I'm inviting you into the circle, Phoebe Pierce. Whenever you want, the path to and from my home is open to you."

The words had no sooner left his mouth when she spotted a white stone-lined path running from the edge of his yard into the woods. There were no lights that she could see, yet the path itself glowed a subtle white gold, even between the trees where she knew the moonlight couldn't reach it. Magic pure and simple.

"You know, a lot of horror books I read start something like this. I'm the kind of person who has insurance on my insurance, and now I'm following a vampire into the woods by myself."

His cloak brushed against her arms catching her dress, tugging it softly as if to urge her under its fabric. She shivered even though she wasn't cold.

"You're a witch. We're in the woods moving towards a stone circle full of witches on a major sabbat. In your movies, which one of us would be the victim?"

"You make a good point." Phoebe laughed.

They walked a while in silence both aware that the forest around them moved and shuddered.

"Do you watch a lot of horror movies?" he asked watching the moonlight dance through her hair. He was more of a fantasy man himself.

"No. I have a wild imagination. I love Samhain, but I have to limit my intake of scary stories or I have nightmares. Do you?"

"I also like Samhain and I know some stories that could turn your hair white."

"Is that what happened to you?"

January twirled her around making her giggle. "Yep. Chaucer published some good stories but the ones he saved for the taverns after he was drunk could convert anyone to the Seelie side of things."

She stopped dead in her tracks. "You did not know Chaucer."

He shrugged leading her down the path. "I didn't but Shakespeare and I both wish we had."

As if on cue the path widened and Phoebe could hear the sound of music and laughter. They came into the glade she'd first seen January. Between the white stones of the circle, there were tall goblet-shaped fire pits that sat on black square fire mats to protect the grass. Where before, the Center of the pit had been clear, now it contained a large fire pit and a heavy stone table filled with plates that had everything from honey, apples, and grains to small poppets, paintings, and photos. There was a cheer as January came fully into the light.

"Merry Meet!" he shouted at the guests.

"Merry Meet!" was shouted back. The music seemed to come from everywhere. Lively. Like nothing she'd ever heard before. Around the outside of the circle were tiki torches and blankets filled with people laughing, eating, and drinking from what appeared to be bone plates and mead horns. People and yet not people.

Phoebe could see horns, fangs, claws, skin that looked as if it were made only of spider webs and a range of shapes and sizes that boggled her mind. In fact, the people shaped people were in the minority. No one pointed or sat by themselves. They blended completely rather than to sit in similar groups. The conversation buzzed and in the air was the pure happiness of being alive.

"Let's find a spot where we can see." January's excitement was obvious. He led her almost to the very spot where she'd first seen him crouched outside the circle. Putting his pack between his feet, he reached in and spread a blanket woven thick enough almost to be considered a rug. There was a howl in the woods and like a chorus, all of the people around the circle threw their heads back and howled at the moon. Phoebe felt a smile split her face.

January rolled his eyes. "Werewolves think they are so funny. Okay. What do you want to do first? Drink? Dance? Conjure?"

"Phoebe? Phoebe Pierce? Is that you?"

She turned to see a very very short woman dressed all in brown approach her with a smile as wide as her face. A face full of very sharp pointed teeth. The woman held her hands out towards Phoebe and gave a little skip as she came forward as if they were long-lost sisters.

Without thought, Phoebe knelt down in the grass holding out her hands. The woman grabbed both squeezing them hard enough to make her wince.

"Merry Meet Phoebe Pierce. I'm Flaxseed. Bramble said that you would be here. Let's have a look at you. Bless your heart. I'd almost given up hope."

"I'm sorry. I didn't know you were waiting for us," January replied kneeling beside her.

"Oh no. Not giving up on you. On Bramble." She reached forward to grab Phoebe's chin turning her head first one way and then another inspecting her. "Yes you're new, but you've got strong blood. Yes. That should help."

"Help what?" January asked putting a hand on Phoebe's thigh.

"Bramble. He's absolutely useless at magic. Can't think why. His sister, Brindle, is magnificent."

Phoebe drew her head back with a frown. "He's not useless, he's young."

Flaxseed clasped her clawed fingers over her heart. "Ahh, listen to her. Isn't she divine? She's already protecting him." She patted Phoebe's cheek. "I've trained familiars for the last 160 years, dear heart. Every one of them has been a joy, even your Bramble, but he's got zero magical talent on his own. Feed him a bit of your blood, it might help. Or his blood." She pointed at January. "It couldn't hurt." She laughed as if she'd told the best joke and slapped January on the arm. "Jokes aside, you'll need to sign for him officially as soon as possible. I brought the paperwork."

From beneath her gown, she produced a sheet of paper and a pen.

January took the paper from her hand scanning it. "Why the urgency? He's not old enough to be a full companion, and Honey also seemed very keen the place him with Phoebe.

Flaxseed snatched the paper back with a growl. "Who am I to stand in the way of true companionship? She wants Bramble, he wants her. She needs to sign the paperwork."

January stood pulling Phoebe up beside him. "You are Flaxseed. Wild Fey, headmistress of the Bast's School for

Familiars. You were also the one who set a minimum age for familiar bonding on the Eastern Coast."

She gave an irritated sigh. "You have a long memory, Norn's son."

"I know." His look was direct, and for the first time, Phoebe understood that accountant or not, January was not a man to trifle with. "Why Bramble, why Phoebe, why now?"

A breeze sprung up around the circle whipping the fire into a sudden frenzy. It rushed up Phoebe's legs and down her arms whispering. *Help Bramble. Help Bramble. Help Bramble*. Phoebe looked at them both for a moment and reached down to take the paper and pen. There was a simple pledge on the paper, that Bramble would love and protect Phoebe Pierce no matter what, and that Phoebe would do the same. She bent down, signed the paper against her thigh, and handed it back to Flaxseed.

The wind screamed through the circle almost snatching the paper from between them, and then it was gone as if it had never been. The fires returned to their dancing rhythm, and so did the festivities. January stared into the dark forest as if he were watching the wind leave.

Phoebe knelt again, looking Flaxseed directly in the eyes. "There. He's mine and I am his. I will love and protect him no matter what."

Flaxseed clasped the contract to her chest looking at Phoebe again carefully before she tucked it under her skirt. "It is witnessed."

"Now we talk. Why does Bramble need help?"

A grin split Flaxseed's face once again. "You knew and you still signed? For that, you get an answer for free." She leaned close. "A witch's familiar is not only family, they amplify magic, and assist its direction. Bramble is like a magic sponge. He soaks magic in but doesn't release it. It has to go somewhere. I'm not sure even he knows what is happening to it. He needs your help."

Phoebe watched amazed as the woman appeared to pluck a bottle and two glasses from the air. "A toast to the new bond. Hobgoblin mead. Made in Larkshead, Maine, by a cousin of mine. The very best."

January opened his mouth to warn Phoebe about enchanted drinks, Wild Fey, and open contracts but the look of pleasure on her face as the drink passed her lips stopped him. Whatever Flaxseed was up to, she was doing it for Bramble. It was in Bramble's best interest that Phoebe lived a long and healthy life. He made a mental note to find Brindle or Honey and get some real answers. Flaxseed drank her glass down in one gulp and then refilled both hers and Phoebe's.

"To the future, whatever it may hold."

Phoebe raised her glass. "To the future!"

It was enough to make a witch weep with happiness. The dancing started almost immediately after her first glass of mead. However, it was in no way organized, the music and the dancers flowed into and out of the stone circle, and between the fire pits and blanket picnics, like water around stones. January pulled her into the midst of the fires and dancers twirling her around and leading her in increasingly complicated dances until her attention was exclusively on their movements together. He looked at her like she was the most fascinating woman in the world and she felt it.

When she and January had run out of breath twirling around fires and howling with the wild Fey who apparently had started the rumor about werewolves howling at the moon, they would find their blanket, cuddle close, and watch the festivities. She sat between January's legs, leaning against his chest, his cloak creating a cozy tent for two. He explained the difference between common and wild Fey, why a Fey witch was especially prized, and why Hobgoblin whiskey should be approached with caution.

A drum roll caused all the witches in the circle to return to their blankets.

"The Mabon priestess," he whispered against the shell of her ear.

An older woman with dark eyes and long white hair came into the circle. A tree nymph, January explained, a shapeshifter. Her skin and eyes seemed to be every shade of brown and green growing earth imaginable.

"Happy Mabon my wonderful witches!" she cried whirling in a circle of multicolored skirts and capes. "Shall we get this ritual started?"

Her call was answered by a series of whistles and howls.

The crowd separated almost instantly. The crowd was a strong word for the group. Even though they made a lot of noise, Phoebe figured there were only twenty in number all together. Some made their way to the edge of the circle and others to the larger stones that lay in the four corners.

Phoebe dusted off her skirt and removed her sandals. "I'm headed East. I'm a Bonafede airhead. Where are you going?"

January smiled sadly. "I've died and come back. Broken the natural circle of things. I can't do magic anymore."

Phoebe cocked her head and reached out to grab his hand. "Death is a natural part of life. Come on. Stand with me. It will be fine."

He took hold of her hand and she pulled him to his feet and to the easternmost side of the circle. She threaded her fingers through his with a smile that caught the firelight. The priestess went to the center of the circle with the offering table. Removing a long mead horn, she moved to the western stone and raised the mead horn into the air.

"Let's raise our glass and our voices on this blessed Mabon night to the West and the spirits of water, sea, blood, and movement. Come, and be welcome in our circle."

All of the witches standing by the western stone raised their arms and glasses. "Hail and welcome to the spirits of the west." They all took a drink.

The priestess handed the horn to a young man and then moved to the northern most stone. "Let's raise our voices on this blessed Mabon night to the North, to the spirits of Earth, body, and growth. Come, and be welcome in our circle." She knelt, putting her hand on the ground in front of the stone.

All of the witches standing by the northern stone reached down to touch the ground. "Hail and welcome to the spirits of the north." The group in the north stood. The priestess touched the shoulder of a dark headed woman all in brown. The woman knelt down again this time with both hands on the ground.

The priestess crossed the circle and picked up a red candle from the table. She walked carefully to the southern most stone and held the candle in the air. "Let's raise our voices on this blessed Mabon night to the South, to the spirits of Fire, spirit and hearth. Come, and be welcome in our circle." She handed the candle to Flaxseed, who held it in front of her face, whispered something against the wick, and it burst into flame. There were cheers and Flaxseed held the candle proudly in front of her.

All of the witches standing by the south stone raised their arms and glasses. "Hail and welcome to the spirits of the south."

The priestess crossed towards the eastern most stone and January knew without a shadow of a doubt that she was coming for Phoebe. She stopped at the stone table to pick up a lit incense stick. As she moved towards them,

January felt the air begin to move. He could feel the energy being raised by the group. The priestess held the incense stick high in the air. "Let's raise our voices on this blessed Mabon night to the East, to the spirits of Air, of breath, wind, and communication. Come, and be welcome in our circle." She gestured towards Phoebe to come take the incense stick and Phoebe moved without hesitation. Alone January watched her turn toward the center of the circle. The smoke from the stick began to swirl. The priestess smiled and then held her hand out to January.

Let's raise our voices on the blessed Mabon night to our generous host, January *ap Ionawr*. January, welcome to the circle. Come. Let us call the corners together."

January felt humbled. In the last 25 years he'd assumed his presence would not be welcome in the circle but from around him came cheers and whistles of encouragement. He walked to the priestess and bowed low before taking her hand. One hand clasped in unison, and the other turned palm up to receive energy, he felt connected to the magic and the witches around him.

In his younger years, his people had practiced the craft in secret. Creating this sacred stone circle had been an act of rebellion for him. Now he was proud to provide a space to practice magic where all were welcome.

The Priestess began the chant. "Earth, Air, Fire, Water."

The chanting rose around him synchronizing, harmonizing, and then calling the energy to them. Excitement bubbled in his chest. He looked over at Phoebe whose smile was ear to ear. Then it happened. The wind picked up from the east catching leaves and throwing them into the air, whipping fire and smoke up all around them, but the witches didn't notice. They continued to chant, each caught in his and her own call. Flaxseed, the young man with the mead horn, the woman in brown with her hands on the ground, and then Phoebe seemed to radiate light, their eyes turning silver-white in the darkness. Only once had January witnessed such a thing and long ago in a grove now called Plas Coch in Anglesey. A place once sacred to the Druids before the Romans slaughtered them there. The elements were here. The priestess squeezed his hand her head dropping back.

She shouted above the chants to the moon, "Earth is our body, water is our blood, air is our breath, fire is our spirit…we welcome you into our circle and into our lives. We ask your blessing, and we give you ours. Wassail!"

The witches in the circle stopped chanting and shouted, "Wassail!"

The wind swirled around and then suddenly stopped. Like all air had been drawn from the circle. The fire dimmed, and the witches around him suddenly gasped for breath. Phoebe's hair whipped around her, her hands held palms up, the incense stick suspended in front of her, her green dress billowing out around her.

The priestess dropped his hand grasping her throat and walked toward Phoebe. Phoebe's silver-white eyes looked directly at him and then at the priestess. They could breathe, but the air was full of whispering voices, like a thousand secrets being told all at once. The priestess stumbled forward to stand in front of Phoebe. He couldn't hear what she said, but Phoebe let out a high-pitched howl just like a gale across a dark moorland. The sound of Phoebe's otherworldly shriek drowned out all but one voice, a warning on the wind. Earth, Air, Fire, and Water, spoke as one voice.

The Veil will fall. It is almost gone.
Wind is here, and fire is called,
water will come, and earth is shaken,
when the truth speaker speaks,
the world will Awaken.

Phoebe looked at him, her silver eyes now green. Like an explosion, a burst of air knocked the witches around her flat including the priestess. He remained untouched. Then there was no sound. No air movement. Phoebe stood with her hands crossed over her chest, her head bowed, her eyes closed, the incense stick lying at her feet with its smoke just drifting serenely around her. The priestess stood up from the ground dusting herself off and laughing.

"We thank the elements for joining our circle. We accept this blessing and this warning with a thankful heart."

Other witches began to stand dusting themselves off and helping their friends up from the ground. January ran towards Phoebe and put his hands on her arms. The smoke from the incense that surrounded her moved across her arms to his in a complex pattern he immediately recognized as a handfasting cloth. A bolt of energy and awareness went through him, and suddenly he knew without a shadow of a doubt that Phoebe was his mate. She could cross death and come back to him. She lifted her head with a dazzled smile.

"That was intense."

Her throat was raw. She'd called the elements a hundred times before. Felt the power of what she was doing like a soft buzz of energy but this was like grabbing hold of a lightning bolt. She'd always known that air was her element, but this confirmation made her feel intensely powerful. Air was speaking to her. All she had to was turn her attention to a conversation, and the sounds came directly to her. January gave her some water, and Flaxseed gave her some more mead to soothe her throat. She should have felt tired, but instead, she felt electrified.

With the ritual complete, some of the witches were

packing up their picnics, some were sitting quietly watching the moon, the stars, and fire. There was a playful giggle in the wind. It whipped around her making her suddenly aware that some of the couples were disappearing into the woods hand in hand. It didn't take a genius to figure out why. January was gently urging her to their blanket. He sat down pulling her to sit between his legs and wrapped his cloak around them both.

"How do you feel?" He rubbed his hands up and down her arms as if to warm her.

"I've never felt so alive or powerful in my life. It's incredible." She turned in his arms to kneel in front of him. "Can I show you?"

He smiled looking deep into her eyes, and something about his gaze was different. There was a determination there that she hadn't seen before. Cupping his face, she placed her lips to his dropping her personal wards to push the powerful energy running through her body towards him.

The kiss between them deepened, and the energy moved back to her in gentle waves of amplified power. In the midst of the magic, she could feel January's personal energy and desire washing through her. Without real thought, she moved forward needing to taste more of him. He dropped back onto his elbows and then onto his back, allowing her to straddle his hips and crouch over him. Her dress moved up her thighs, but January kept his hands to himself. The power moved over and through her opening every sense to the unmistakable sexual tension between them.

Covering his face and mouth with a series of teasing kisses, she reached down to place January's hands on her exposed skin. He spread her thighs wide so that she could feel his excitement between her legs. For a long moment, she couldn't tell where his desire ended and hers began. He broke off their kiss gasping, his pale blue eyes burning with desire.

"Phoebe?" he said breathlessly. "It's too much."

But it didn't feel like enough to her. Dropping her chest to his so that she pinned him to the ground she kissed his chin and then his neck whispering in his ear. "You want me. I want you."

He captured her shoulders, pushing her back so that they were eye to eye.

"I want you with every fiber in my soul, Cariad, but our first time will not be in public on the ground." He raised his head to kiss her soundly using his greater weight to roll her under him on the blanket. His cloak settled over them.

"Allow me to bring you release."

She writhed under him feeling possessed by a sexual power that she'd never known in the bedroom. "Yes."

He threaded his fingers through hers holding her hands above her head. She wasn't sure what she expected, but it wasn't the single low-pitched command that came from his mouth.

"Come for me. Only for me."

As the orgasm hit her, she arched her back unable to move beneath him. He joined their mouths and rocked forward so that he could drink the first gasp of her pleasure from her lips. The waves of desire moved through her until her breath returned to normal and she became aware that her legs were wrapped around January's clothed hips. He was simply looking down at her with an expression the promised the next time she found release it would be with him deep inside her.

She twisted her writs to ask to be let go and his reluctance to do so re-kindled her interest. He let go rolling over onto his back so that they both lay side by side looking up at the stars. His breathing came fast and hard as if he'd shared her release. They said nothing for a long while. Phoebe's awareness seeped slowly into her and with it, the understanding that her appetite had been whetted, not sated.

She pulled herself up from the ground looking around them. There was no judgement or sly gazes. It was as if no one knew what happened. For reasons she didn't want to examine much closer, that excited her more.

January sat up slowly, a slightly worried frown on his lips. "Are you okay?" He reached toward her but Phoebe held up a hand.

"That was better than any orgasm I've had in my life but unless you want to finish what you started, you need to give me some space."

His face was a picture of male self-assuredness. "What I started? You started it, woman. You kissed me."

Phoebe laughed scooting away from him playfully. "I was sharing the power with you."

He stood up pulling her up from the ground and settling her clothes around her. "And I was sharing it back."

"It came to you innocent, it came back to me like an aphrodisiac."

He gave her a sly grin. "You were doing a good job of fulfilling a long-time sexual fantasy of mine. When we don't have an audience, I plan to bring you back, strip you naked in the middle of that altar, and show you what vampire magic looks like." He handed her shoes to her and began packing their things.

She picked up the blanket shaking it out and folding it. "Who says I would come?"

He arched a devilish eyebrow throwing the pack over his shoulder and taking the blanket from her hands.

"Don't say it."

January gave her a short courtly bow. "I'm a gentleman, I wouldn't dare." He offered her his hand. "Come on. I told Bramble I would bring you home before dawn."

. . .

January's thoughts were tangled up in the many ways he was going to enjoy Phoebe when he got her back to the house. They walked quickly and in silence, the clothes on his body feeling too tight and rough. Opening the door for her, he tossed the pack, blanket, and cloak to the side. She turned to look over her shoulder at him, a knowing smile playing over her lips. He walked up to her putting his hands on her shoulders to bring her close.

"Cariad, I want to take you to bed and make love to you until neither of us remembers how to love anyone else. It will not ease the call between us, it will make it stronger. Will you come to my bed?"

She stepped into his embrace. "Yes, please."

He swung her up in his arms and carried her towards his bedroom. She put her arms around his neck and relaxed into his embrace. The millions of thoughts that had been running through his mind all focused on one thing. She said yes.

Phoebe hadn't been carried since she was a child. Within the space of a couple of heartbeats, they were at his door and then in his room. He kicked the door closed behind them with a resounding thud and headed for his bed. Laying her down gently in the middle of it, he gazed down at her with a look of pure pleasure on his face. He took off her sandals one at a time and pitched them towards the door. Reaching up under her long skirt, he trailed his fingers up the outside of her legs until he reached her panties and began to pull them down. Phoebe moved to help, but he stopped her.

"Lay down and place your hands behind your head. I

need you to be ready for me. If you touch me now, I'll rush us both."

How she could be any more ready for him, she wasn't sure, but she was happy to find out. Laying back, she put her hands behind her head and tried to be still. He started pulling her panties down again, agonizingly slowly, kissing every inch of skin that he exposed. This was foreplay that bordered on worship. There were places on her ankles, calves, and thighs that she had no idea could be erogenous until she felt his lips there.

By the time her panties joined her sandals on the floor, she was holding her hands behind her head to keep from reaching out to touch him. He kissed her from ankle to hip and then from hip to inner thigh, his hands straying under her dress but completely avoiding the place she wanted him to touch most.

Moving onto the bed to crouch over her, he pushed her dress up and kissed her stomach and then the bottom of her rib cage. Normally she was ticklish but he seemed to know the exact right amount of pressure to apply. The swirl of his tongue and the threat of his teeth became an erotic game. Using his hands to support the small of her back, she found the brush of his long hair against her skin almost as stimulating as his lips.

Just as she felt she really couldn't take anymore, he sat her up to pull her dress over her head, leaving him fully dressed and her only in her bra. His gaze moved appreciatively over her body. Normally, she would have felt exposed, but his frank appreciation made her feel powerful. Laying back on the bed, she put her hands over her head and arched her back.

"You are so beautiful."

The words were whispered against her skin as he continued to kiss her everywhere that wasn't covered. From the underside of her ribs across the middle of her chest, down the length of her clavicle, and then her arm. When he put her wrist to his mouth, she felt the first hard scrape of his teeth and gasped.

"That's right, Cariad," he crooned, his tongue darting across the place his teeth had been. "I can hear your heart beating. Your excitement makes me excited." He kissed the place his tongue had been. "I want to taste you. Will you offer me your throat?"

Phoebe nodded. She would have loved to say something sexy, but she was in a haze of sensation.

He gathered her into his arms, facing him. The fabric of his shirt tantalized her excited skin. Cradling her, he kissed the crook of her neck so gently.

"I didn't hear you."

Dropping her head to the side to fully offer him her throat. She said the only word that occurred to her. "Yes."

Just where her pulse thundered under her skin, she felt the lap of his tongue and then his teeth. The sting lasted seconds, and then there was only the pressure of his mouth and the sensation of his tongue moving over her skin.

Whether she was there for seconds or minutes, she wasn't sure. Her body was on fire, and she was desperate to have him. Her fingers tangled through his gorgeous hair, and when he drew back, she kissed him. There was a slight tang of her blood in his mouth. It felt natural, like something she'd been missing her whole life and hadn't known it. She deepened the kiss, determined to get what she wanted from him.

He broke away with a growl. "That's right, Cariad. This is natural between us."

Unclipping her bra, he tossed it away as he lay her back down. He moved off the bed for a moment to pull his shirt off and drop it carelessly to the floor. His jeans followed, and so did his underwear. Viewing him completely for the first time, she vowed to herself that when he allowed it, she would take the time to worship him as he had done her. Joining her on the bed, he knelt between her legs and spread her wide. The anticipation was killing her. The whimper of need that came from her lips made him growl.

"Wait for me."

It was all the warning she got before his tongue entered her. The orgasm rocked her body. If she'd thought the one at the stone circle was good, it was nothing compared to this one. He nipped her sharply on the thigh.

"See what you've done. Now we have to start again."

And he did. No sooner had the first waves of her orgasm finished when his tongue found her again. He took his time as if there was nothing else to do but to bring her pleasure. As her next orgasm built, she tried to control her pleasure, but his fingers joined his tongue.

"That's not fair," she moaned as he slid first one and then two fingers inside her.

He loomed over her, his fingers moving in her and around her most sensitive area a little faster. "Fair? This is not fair." He leaned forward and whispered a single command, the power in his voice stealing the small thread of control she could manage. "Come for me."

Her back arched as a second, more powerful orgasm moved through her.

"Please," she begged, not sure she could handle anymore.

"Ask for what you want," he growled.

"Please come with me. Come inside me."

"Yes."

He moved on top of her, pulling her legs around his hips and sliding inside her. It was tight, but she was ready for him. So ready. The rhythm he created was fast and hard, but Phoebe felt she couldn't get close enough. She wrapped arms and legs around him, her mouth seeking his skin. Almost without thought, she bit him sucking his skin into her mouth to mark him.

"Yes. That's right. I am yours."

They came together. Phoebe felt like her body was breaking apart with the intensity of it, and the only thing that was holding her together was the weight of January's body on hers.

January reluctantly woke from a deep sleep. The late morning sun streamed through his bedroom window illuminating the mess he'd made with their clothing the night before. They'd made love until the early morning hours but it still wasn't enough for him. It would never be enough for him. In two weeks' time, she would make her decision on a guide and hopefully, accept his application as companion. It would be an anxious wait for him because Olivia and Melissa would be spending the next two weeks trying to convince Phoebe to remain a witch. During their learning time together, guide law dictated that he couldn't contact her until she contacted him.

It was an old law that helped each guide have time to fully show their potential guided what it would be like to live and learn with them. Olivia and Melissa had respected his time and limited their contact to work time only. In order for her to have a fair choice, he would have to do the same. He had refrained from giving her his blood so that their separation would be uncomfortable rather than unbearable.

She was sleeping on her side in a tangle of red hair and blankets. Sometime during the night, she'd tucked his hand under her face as if she were afraid that he would disappear. The sound of the door creaking open stirred her from her sleep. Bramble put his head in and then squeezed through the opening. January wondered how he'd managed to open the door and then rolled his eyes. Alex.

Bramble slunk inside low to the floor as if he were afraid of being unwelcome. The feeling of his light footprints on the bottom of the bed and then his little head peaking over Phoebe's shoulder made him smile.

Phoebe opened one bleary eye and let go of his hand, rolling onto her back and pulling Bramble onto her chest. With both eyes closed, she scratched under his chin and smoothed his hair. His purr was loud enough to wake the dead, and he reached out a hand to give the little familiar a stroke.

"Good morning, Bramble."

Bramble looked over at him with a cat grin and half-closed eyes. "Morning, good. Two breakfasts. Alex warm. Bed good." He gave a big yawn. "Now, nap with you. Everybody happy."

"Two breakfasts?" Phoebe's soft question made Bramble purr louder.

"Two. Had one. Alex, make now."

The smell of bacon wafted into the room through the open door, subtle enough that Phoebe wouldn't smell it. One of the many things he liked about this room was it was far from the kitchen.

"I think Alex is making you breakfast." January snuggled closer, still petting Bramble.

Phoebe looked down at him, her embarrassment clear. "Is that a vampire thing?"

January laughed. "We don't eat breakfast. It's a werewolf thing. Alex doesn't like to eat alone, so he's taking advantage while you're here."

She relaxed a little. "Do we have plans today?"

"I am going to try and fill the dreary hours until you return with some work I've been avoiding."

"Until I return?"

January kissed her shoulder. "Melissa and Olivia have a week from today with you to see if they can convince you to allow them to guide you. During that time, I was restricted from contact. That way, you can make the decision without being influenced."

Phoebe's hand paused, her smile wicked. "Oh, I am definitely influenced."

January kissed her lightly and then Bramble. "Good. Let's get you guys fed while I am still weak enough to let you walk out the door."

14

MAGIC AND DIVINATION

Phoebe's days were filled with her regular work and her nights were filled with her study of magic. The smell of sandalwood drifted through Phoebe's apartment reminding her of January's bedside table. Just about every-thing reminded her of January right now. A week felt like two years. With only a couple of days to go, she was starting to wonder if their connection was as good as she remembered it was and if January was as tempted as she was to break the restriction.

Olivia said that the restrictions meant no texts to and no contact with January until the end of the week. She'd given Phoebe an obsidian amulet to help keep her from teleporting unintentionally. If only she could find some way to keep her mind tethered to her tasks as easily.

Although she was doing her best to create a new life for herself, she knew that if the restriction hadn't been there, she would have gone straight back to January the first day. His absence meant that she could finally visit her parents like she'd been promising to do since Lammas. If they noticed anything different about her, they didn't say. It was lovely to have a little normality back again. Over dinner, her mom asked her if January was the reason for her recent silence and she'd blushed to the roots of her hair.

"I guess I'm a little obsessed."

Her Dad had winked at her Mom. "I remember what that felt like. We can come to see you. Take you both out to dinner. We might even be able to persuade your brother to come." They'd all laughed at that. Josh didn't do impromptu family time unless he instigated it. With a promise to bring January to them before Thanksgiving, she'd given both her parents a hug and vowed not to be a stranger.

She and Melissa were sitting on the floor of her living room with her altar between them. They had practiced magic together almost since Phoebe first started working at The Craft Shop. On full moons, they left work together and went to Phoebe's because it was both cleaner and closer.

They picked up a bottle of red wine, a pizza with extra cheese and jalapeños, and they cast spells together. It was a short round table with a pentacle carved into it that Phoebe's brother had made her for her birthday when she turned twenty-one. It had always struck her as powerful and today, she knew why. The oak altar was absolutely soaked in years of blessings and magic.

Together, she and Melissa placed the symbol of the pentacle on the north side of the altar, a small dish of water and a couple of sea shells in the west, a red votive on the south, and a small bowl containing a sage stick and a feather beside it in the eastern corner. Another white candle had been lit in the center.

Lights dimmed and candles lit everywhere, Bramble batted the feather a couple of times making them both laugh before he retreated to the left of Phoebe quietly observing what was going on. Music drifted from the speakers, something soft and melodic that Melissa had chosen to get them in the mood. The lights were dimmed and Bramble was looking so proud of himself that Phoebe couldn't help giving him a little stroke now and then even though she was supposed to be concentrating on quieting her mind.

In spite of everything they had done to keep up their regular routine, this felt different. They'd had to add chicken bites to their pizza order for Bramble and Melissa brought out a bottle of enchanted mead.

"I was saving this for a special occasion," Melissa said pouring the sweet-smelling amber liquid into the crystal goblet perched on Phoebe's altar to represent water. "Now we have two things to celebrate. Phoebe's Awakening into the Enlightened world." She set the decanter aside and picked up the glass toasting Phoebe and taking a sip. She handed the glass to Phoebe. Bramble put his foot on her to get her attention.

"Magic. Careful," he said.

Melissa grinned. "The person who sold it to me said that it was blessed but I wasn't sure I believed it. What's in the magic, Bramble?"

Phoebe brought the cup down to Bramble's level. He made a big deal of looking at it and sniffing it then sighed. "Good magic. Wild Magic. Open mind and heart." The cat nodded his head decisively before lapping up a small portion of the mead. Phoebe pulled the cup back just as he sneezed. "Good magic."

Phoebe held the glass up. "To an open mind." She took a sip and felt a purple light slide down around her. She handed the glass back to Melissa.

"To wild magic." She took a drink and handed the cup back to Phoebe.

Phoebe toasted again. "To good magic." The next sip intensified the purple. "Can you see magic? I keep getting these flashes of color."

"I can't see it. For me, it's a feeling in my chest. When I hold this goblet in my hand, I feel the power moving down my arm. When I drink it, the feeling is like heat spreading through my body. Olivia hears power. She says good power sounds like birds and bells and bad stuff sounds like hissing or scraping. Most people focus on the sense they use the most, but I've read that you can use mindfulness to be able to read magic through any sense you want."

Pressing the glass back to Phoebe, she grinned. "I bought it from Flaxseed. The best mead in Maine, apparently. Drink slowly. It packs an awesome punch."

"Wassail," Phoebe said and took a deep drink. Honey-flavored fire slid down her throat and spread across her chest like a warm blanket. There was a tingling in the middle of her forehead like she literally had a third eye trying to open."

Bramble touched her again. "Mind open. Time for the future."

Melissa rubbed her hands together with excitement. "He's right. We should do some divination. What should it be? Tarot? Scrying?"

"Pendulum," Bramble rumbled with excitement.

"No way," Melissa said with a shudder. I'm never touching one of those again."

Bramble got up and walked over to Melissa rubbing his fluffy body against her with a purr. "You safe. Bramble here. Bramble protect."

Melissa grinned and scratched his chin. "No offense, little lovely, but Flaxseed said you-"

"That you were learning," Phoebe cut in quickly giving Melissa a stern look. "Melissa and I want to keep you safe too but we're also still learning. We'll try pendulums later."

Bramble sighed happily. "Good. Will learn. Now the magic."

Phoebe leaned forward picking up the fat sage stick

from its bowl on the altar. She held it in the fire of the middle white candle rolling it to re-light its charred ends until they were smoking. Passing it in a circle around herself, Bramble, and her side of the altar, she handed it to Melissa to complete the circle. They did this three times then Phoebe sat the smoking sage stick back on its bowl. The smoke was heavy in the air, and they both breathed deeply. Together they repeated, "We are safe inside the circle."

They began to chant. Earth, air, fire, water. The purple color around Phoebe extended around the circle encompassing both Melissa and Bramble. The candles flashed three times and both the smoke and the mead in the glass began to tremble. The little altar shuddered and the pentacle in the middle went from black to bright silver.

"What's happening?" she whispered but Melissa's eyes were closed.

"Don't panic. Take a deep breath and just think about the moon. You know it's there, you see it every day, but when someone hands you a stone from the surface, it's more real. Magic is the same. It's always been here. Now you can see it."

Phoebe tried to calm herself. "You're right but I feel like I'm strapped to the moon rocket. Everything I think I know is changing."

Melissa opened her eyes and looked at Phoebe from across the altar. "For me, it was like looking for a secret door and suddenly finding it. I was so excited that I walked through before I even thought about what was going to be on the other side."

"And now?"

"And now I don't know how I didn't see it in the first place. I applied to guide you at first because I was afraid one of the other guys might not have your best interests at heart, but the more I think about it, the more I like the idea of really getting to show you how wonderful this world is."

Taking another deep breath, she felt Melissa's protection slide into place and with it, an understanding that she could use this time to really see what Melissa could teach her.

"How many Enlightened are there? If they have such incredible power, why don't they use it?"

Melissa picked up a pack of tarot cards from under the altar and began to shuffle them. "Olivia said that the Enlightened are outnumbered about 1000 to 1. Even though we're powerful, the world has a way of keeping the balance. The five main groups are Nature Spirits, or the Enlightened directly connected to the elements of the world. Witches are part of that group. Companions and Familiars which are Enlightened created by a bond with other Enlightened, that's what Bramble is. They are rare and valuable."

Bramble nodded, laying down and tucking his feet under him. "Bramble and Brindle born. Not created. No witch for us. Alone." He looked at Phoebe with absolute love. "Until now."

"It's happening everywhere. People and animals are Awakening without a guide or without warning. It's a scary world when you know what's going on. You can't imagine what it's like when you don't."

"Cards ready," Bramble said and Melissa sat them down in front of her cutting them into three piles.

"You said there were five?" Phoebe prompted.

Melissa nodded. "Shapeshifters who are Enlightened who change forms like werewolves. There is the undead, which is the group your vampire belongs to, and finally, there are supernatural animals. They are Enlightened who don't have a human form and were not created by other Enlightened.

"So, Bramble and Brindle are Enlightened animals?" Phoebe reasoned leaning forward to restack the cards and cut them again.

"Maybe. Flaxseed said she's never seen anything like it. Familiars are very difficult to create. You wouldn't just abandon them. Enlightened creatures tend to be things like unicorns and kelpies."

"Kelpies are real?" Phoebe asked with horror.

"Yeah. And not as choosey about what they eat as stories lead you to believe."

"So, I'm in the Earth Spirit group and I can't become a vampire?" Phoebe asked feeling bereft even though the thought of becoming one hadn't fully taken shape into her mind until that moment.

Melissa shrugged taking a drink and choosing her words carefully. "Anything alive can become a spirit or become undead, but to do that you have to cross over into death and then return. Most Enlightened don't make it back."

Phoebe frowned. "Sounds complicated."

"Now you know why you get a guide. Every continent has its own types of Enlightened so it takes a while to be able to recognize them all. In the five divisions, there is another split. The Seelie and the Unseelie. This is a personal choice that each Enlightened being makes eventually. You are either working for the general betterment of life on Earth or you're working for yourself. Most of us fall somewhere between the extremes."

"Cards ready," Bramble said again. "Read."

"What question do you want to ask?" Melissa said holding the cards in her hands.

Phoebe closed her eyes and let her mind go blank. She felt the air move over her skin. The Wind was talking to her. "*Veil. Veil. Veil,*" it whispered.

"How did I come through the Veil?"

The dim lights flickered and all around the circle the candles sputtered and then went out. Only the candles in the circle remained lit."

Melissa swallowed hard and laid the first card down. The Queen of Pentacles. The Earth Mother. She lay the second card down. The Queen of Wands, the Mother of Air. Then the Queen of Swords, the Mother of Fire, and the Queen of Cups. The Water Mother.

"Three more cards," Bramble said moving forward. Melissa laid them out. The Tower was a shaking of the foundations of life and belief until only what was true and steady was left. Death, both real death and the death of an idea or way of life, and then the World, an ending to a cycle of life, a pause in life before the next big cycle."

They all looked at the cards for a long while.

"What mean?" Bramble demanded.

Melissa wrapped her arms around her middle. "It means we need to call Olivia."

15

ECHOES OF THE FUTURE

Olivia stared at the photo of the tarot cards on Melissa's phone. "You're both sure that you set the circle correctly? There was no outside influence?"

They were behind the counter at The Craft Shop all staring down at the phone with varying degrees of worry. Bramble had looked at it briefly and then moved to the other side of the counter to push his paws through a tray of tumbled stones. The soft ticking sound of the stones rubbing against one another and the bright October sunshine streaming through the windows chased away some of the fear Phoebe felt the night before.

"Yes," Melissa said leaning over Olivia's shoulder. "We set the circle, we called the elements, we had Bramble to warn us if any energy came in from the outside."

"It was Bramble's idea to do the reading," Phoebe added stroking Bramble's head. He purred a moment and then spotted the display of pendulums on the opposite wall. His tail swished with excitement.

"But the question was Phoebe's," Melissa added.

Olivia enlarged the picture and then turned it over as if

that would help it make more sense. "What did you ask again?"

Phoebe sighed trying to figure out what part of the story Olivia wasn't understanding. They'd been over it a dozen times. "I asked how I came through the Veil?"

"It just doesn't make sense." Olivia handed the phone back to Melissa.

"What doesn't make sense? The cards, the question, what?"

Olivia looked at the door and then took her phone out of her pocket. "I did my own ritual last night. I asked the same question you did. Look." She handed the phone to Phoebe.

The image was a little blurry around the corners but the cards on the black cloth were easily discernible. The Queen of Pentacles. The Queen of Wands. The Queen of Swords. The Queen of Cups. The Tower, Death, and the World.

"Holy shit," Melissa gasped touching one of her pentacles for protection.

Olivia took the phone back tapping the screen. "That would be weird enough but look at this." Flipping the phone back toward Phoebe and Melissa she began scrolling through the photos of a chat group called 'Life's a Witch.' Every photo had the same cards.

Phoebe shook her head. "That's impossible. How could all of us get the same message at the same time?"

Olivia slid her phone back in her pocket looking around the shop. "I don't think I care how; I want to know why. What does it mean?"

"The Mabon ritual!" Phoebe said taking her own phone out of her pocket. "When we called the elements, for a moment, we were all focusing on being open to a message or blessing, just like we were last night. We got one then, too." Phoebe scrolled through the notes on her phone. "I meant to look it up later but with Bramble in school and training with you guys, I forgot it.

The Veil will fall. It is almost gone.
  Wind is here, and fire is called,
  water will come, and earth is shaken,
  when the truth speaker speaks,
  the world will Awaken.

Olivia wrote the words on the back of a receipt. "It's an old prophecy. Almost a fairy tale in the Fey courts."

"It's the steps of a spell," Melissa said excitedly taking the receipt from Olivia and laying it beside her phone. "The tarot Queens represent the four elements. Pentacles are earth, wands are air, swords are fire, and cups are water. If the Veil falls, it will definitely shake the world back down to its foundations, The Tower. It will be a symbolic Death, there will be no more Veil so essentially a way of life will be over. And finally, The World, a pause where everything is balanced before the next cycle."

"So, the spell requires an elemental witch to call each of the elements." Olivia made notes on her receipt. "That makes sense. Wind is here, meaning that Phoebe is one of the elementals."

"Then we need to find the others. Earth, Fire, Water, and the Truth Speaker," Melissa said sliding the spell receipt into her pocket along with her phone.

"How will we know which witch is the right witch? I mean, you said most of them aren't Awakened. There must be millions of witches around the world." Phoebe asked.

Olivia opened her mouth to speak but the door chime rang and all three of them looked to see who was coming in. James stood just outside the threshold with a friendly smile.

"Come in," Olivia said before Phoebe or Melissa could stop her.

James's smile got wider as he stepped over the threshold and headed to the counter. "Merry Meet."

Melissa moved closer to Olivia's side. "Merry Meet. What can we help you with today?"

"The Mabon Council sent me to collect Phoebe for her interview today."

"The meeting's today?" Olivia crossed her arms over her chest. "I wasn't notified, and neither was Melissa. We've combined applications to guide her."

James shrugged but the movement struck Phoebe as off. Bramble let out a low growl and moved across the counter to stand in front of her.

He glanced at her familiar with irritation but when his eyes met Phoebe's again, they were so calm she wondered if she'd imagined it.

"You'll have to take it up with the council. I withdrew my application. I still want to guide you but the situation with January makes it awkward."

Phoebe tried to remember if she'd ever heard January mention James. "What situation?"

James put his hands in his pockets and again, Phoebe got the impression that his movements were unnatural. "I-I thought you knew. January and I were companions for a long time."

Melissa whistled. "Nice try, Demon. I almost believed you for a second but then I remembered my vampire train-ing. You might have been lovers, but you weren't compan-ions." She looked at Phoebe. "Vampires don't have a 'till death do we part' clause in their companionships. Once they are bonded as companions, one follows the other into the next life."

James clicked his wings in irritation. "I broke it off. A vampire won't force a companion to stay."

Olivia cut in. "Or take another while their previous companion lives. January has applied to take Phoebe as a companion, and you are certainly still alive. So, my next question is why do you want Phoebe to be angry at January right before she has to choose a guide?"

"I don't want her to choose January. The only reason I was interested in guiding Phoebe was because of him. He was my guide before he was my lover. I wanted to save her the heartache I went through." He looked at Phoebe with an expression that was so sincere that she almost felt her resolve shake. "He will break your heart."

"Maybe," Phoebe replied. She'd never been approached by a boyfriend's ex but she'd heard plenty of stories about why it happened. "I appreciate the warning but-"

"Has he told you about Enir or Anghared?"

"Enir is his maker. He killed her companion on a battle-field. Enir tried to take revenge and kill him. Instead, she converted him. Their relationship is strained but civil. You still love him, don't you?"

James nodded hesitantly like he was confused about why he was having the conversation with her. "I will always love him and he will always love me. What did he tell you about Anghared?"

"Nothing because it is none of my business." In her opinion asking about a partner's ex's in a normal relation-ship was the equivalent of shooting yourself in the foot. The conversation always ended in jealousy. She imagined that was doubly true about vampires. "He's lived hundreds of years and we've known each other a little over 8 weeks. We've barely had time to discuss what's happening in this lifetime."

"That's long enough to tell you he was married." James's face flickered from sincere to sly and calculating.

Now she knew he was trying to make her jealous. "I know he was married. He told me himself. He also said he had many lovers. It makes sense. Eight hundred years is a long time to be alone."

James sat back on his heels his wings sweeping behind him. "And that doesn't bother you? That he's been in love before? That he might love me now?"

"Why would it?" Phoebe asked coming around the counter. "If he's still in love with you, he hasn't mentioned it. As for being in love before, I would be more worried if he hadn't had other relationships. I have."

"Have you told him you loved him?"

"That's also none of your business." She picked up Bramble from the counter determined to make her exit. "Olivia or Melissa can show me where the council meeting is. You can leave."

His smile was cold and although she had only seen him once she had the oddest feeling that this man wasn't the same man she'd met before Lammas. Bramble tensed and her hand drifted to her pentacle.

James moved forward ominously. "I was told to bring you."

"I'm not going anywhere with you. You came here to hurt me or January, or both of us." Phoebe snapped her fingers twice and a red ward settled around her and Bramble. Olivia and Melissa did the same. "Please leave." She felt more than saw Olivia and Melissa move to stand beside her.

He dragged his claws over the outside of the ward, and it sparked with power but held. "You will come with me one way or the other, witch. It's now only a matter of time."

Now she was sure this wasn't James. The face contorted around the edges and the voice split and wavered like a radio signal struggling to tune in. He turned away and hissed knocking the tray of tumbled stones from the counter with his wings. They skittered and bounced across the floor in every direction. The door chimed as he left and Phoebe felt Olivia and Melissa put their arms around her.

"I don't know what that was, but it wasn't the same demon we saw before." Melissa gave her a little squeeze. "Something's wrong with that guy, and I don't just mean in the obsessive ex type of way."

"Demons are a law unto themselves," Olivia added looking around. "We'd better get this mess picked up and the shop closed so we're not late for the interview." She reached down and picked the tray up off the floor and returned it to the counter. As she did, the stones began to march like ants back to the tray. Olivia laughed in delight. "Nice spell, Phoebe. What's it called?"

"It's called, Everything in its place. Although I thought it was supposed to urge people to return things where they picked them up." Bramble squiggled to get down to inspect the moving stones.

Melissa laughed as Bramble tried to catch the stones only to have them skitter out of his reach. "You're going to have to teach me that spell."

"Will you guys show me where the Mabon Council is?"

Both women gave her another gentle hug.

"We'll take you. You're one of us. We won't let you face this decision alone."

The Mabon Council interview room was located at a place called the Boston Recovery Center. Set in the Blue Hills Reservation, the center looked like a secluded private hospital and in many ways it was.

"What are they recovering from?" Phoebe asked from the back of Olivia's sedan. Melissa leaned back over the front seat.

"They aren't recovering, they've been recovered. Most of them are humans who were forced through the Veil. It doesn't happen often but when it does, it's devastating."

Phoebe sat back in her seat looking at the building again. There was so much calm and disinterested energy coming from the place that she almost let what Melissa said pass without comment. Recognizing the energy as a ward to discourage interest, she was impressed. "Why would someone force another through the Veil?"

Olivia looked up at the rear-view mirror with a sad smile. "Most people won't see magic no matter what you do. When an Enlightened being does something in front of an Unenlightened person that can't be rationalized, it scares the Unenlightened person into a kind of death. Their minds can't handle it. They faint with their eyes open and go into a waking coma. We call it a shutdown. They're kept as comfortable as possible at the nearest recovery center until they pass."

Phoebe remembers the feelings of her mind coming apart trying to take in the new information. If it hadn't been for Melissa or January, she might have shut down herself. "What happens to the person who has pushed the Unenlightened person through the Veil?"

"Most of the time, they are destroyed," Melissa said gently.

Phoebe sat back in horror. "That's barbaric."

Olivia turned slowly down a short, unmarked road and through a sliding gate into a wide parking lot. At first glance, the parking lot appeared only to have a few cars in it but as they passed through the gates, Phoebe saw that this was an illusion. The lot was filled both with people and vehicles.

"It is an old law and there are lots of Enlightened who want to see the law reformed, but there are even more who believe direct retribution is the only way to keep the Unseelie in line. That's why the investigations are so strict. The Recovery Unit has to prove the unsanctioned Awakening happened with the Enlightened person understanding the full consequences of the action. There are ways to request an Awakening but the chances of survival are so slim, no one tries it anymore."

They parked the car and got out. The trees gave the hospital a look of seclusion even though the recovery center itself was just a stone's throw from the heart of Boston. Melissa looped her arm through Phoebe's trying to comfort her. "Not all of these rooms are full of people. Some of the rooms are for the newly Awakened, like yourself, who are finding it hard to adjust. Some are for the Enlightened who need special treatment. Most of it is just offices for Recovery Units who enforce the laws."

She followed Melissa and Olivia to a large set of sliding glass doors.

"The Recovery Units make sure everyone is safe. They keep the Enlightened from being exposed, the Unenlightened from being Awakened, and keep the peace between the Seelie and Unseelie courts."

The doors slid open and the women were met by a short elderly gentleman in a formal suit complete with a button-down vest, cravat, and trousers. His long ears and an even longer tail were perked in their direction.

"You must be Phoebe Elizabeth Pierce." He offered her his hand and she shook it. "You have an appointment with The Mabon Council." He looked at Melissa and Olivia. "Who are these people?"

"Oh, uh. Colleagues? They've applied to guide me."

"From the Clay coven," Olivia said proudly.

The gentleman stepped up to Olivia and then to Melissa and asked them to hold out their palm. He looked at each palm with interest and then reached into his pocket and ran what looked like a short metal rod down the center of their hands.

"Yes. Yes. All good. Some problems with the Unseelie lately, Miss Olivia," he said pulling the lobe of one of his long ears. "I knew it was you but we're having to double-check identities and be extra careful."

Olivia bent down and kissed the old man between the eyes. "I understand, Finn. What kind of problems?"

"All of the normal Unseelie nonsense but now we also have rumors of shadow possession, soul binding, and Unseelie shape-shifters sneaking into recovery stations and stealing information about the Unguided." His tail whipped behind him in agitation.

"What are they looking for?"

The old man leaned close. "If you ask me, I think they're hunting someone connected to the Unguided cases. Everything that's been stolen is information collected in the last 6 months. You should take great care with Miss Phoebe; her name was on the list."

"What list?" Phoebe felt her mouth go dry. Rationally she knew she hadn't done anything wrong but the rules of the Enlightened world were very new to her so she couldn't be sure.

Finn motioned for her to bend down. She knelt in front of him so that they could be eye to eye. "There's been a lot of unusual cases of Awakening and then shutdowns lately. We've got a doctor, an epidemiologist. Selene Hernandez. Best in the field, in my opinion. She's tracking the Unguided outbreak to find the source. You're currently registered as one of the first Unguided in our area."

Olivia gave Phoebe a hand to get up. The look of worry in her eyes was unmistakable. "Thanks, Finn. We'll be careful." She gestured for Phoebe and Melissa to follow her and then stopped. "Finn, a Demon called James came to collect

Phoebe for this meeting. If he hadn't come, we wouldn't have known it was happening. Why weren't we alerted?"

Finn rubbed the tip of his ears. "James? That can't be right. He just got back from New Mexico. Been gone all week as far as I understand. As for the notification, I don't know anything about it. I could check for you."

The thrashing of his tail got faster and there was a definite gleam in his eyes.

"That would be great. You'd better double-check where James was too. As far as we know, he showed up at The Craft Shop about an hour ago. He was trying to take Phoebe."

"You think he's a shadow?" Finn's bushy grey brows seemed to meet in the middle of his forehead. "That's why we're using the silver. Won't bother a shifter but it disturbs the shadow."

"If it was a shadow, it's one of the best I've ever seen," Olivia said looking at Phoebe and then back at Finn. "He would have fooled me, but Melissa and Phoebe were watching closer than I was."

Finn nodded. "Better mention it at the meeting. I'll see if I can verify where James went and why that notification wasn't delivered."

Olivia gave him a warm smile and a short bow. "Thank you for sharing. Come to my shop. Bring your wife. Choose an expensive gift for me."

The old man chuckled and rubbed his hands together. "You do know how to make an old Goblin feel young. Hurry on. You'll be late. Fifth door in the second corridor."

Phoebe waited for her to catch up with them before continuing to the next corridor. "You know each other well?"

Olivia tucked a long piece of white hair behind her ear. "I'm an Earth witch. We have a special connection to Gruagach, Brownies as they are known here. Finn helped me connect to my Earth magic when I was very new."

"He just called himself a Goblin."

Olivia looked back at him over her shoulder. "It's an inside joke. Normally the Gruagach want very little for their help. Sometimes they do it for free. Not Finn. His help is always expensive."

Melissa tugged Phoebe close to whisper so the Brownie couldn't hear her. "She can't offer him a lavish gift or payment because it's an insult to his kind, but if she offers it to his wife, he can accept it. She's a genius. That's why I chose to study with her."

"If we didn't know this meeting was happening, do you think January knows?" Phoebe looked back down the corridor.

"Better text him," Olivia said stopping in front of the fifth door. She straightened her dress and ran her hands through her hair. "My bet is that none of us were supposed to be here today, especially you."

THE MABON COUNCIL MEETING

Olivia led them to a large circular boardroom with a circular table that formed a perfect "O" in the center of the room. Chairs of various shapes, sizes, and colors were sat around the outside of the table and there was a place that appeared to be a flap where one could walk into the center of the "O" to speak.

Three people sat side by side in high-backed green chairs around a table that could easily seat twenty. Olivia took a seat on the outside in one of the empty chairs closest to the door and Phoebe and Melissa remained standing. A woman with cat-like features that included whiskers handed a stack of papers to a well-dressed young man wearing a full set of ceremonial ritual robes. She then handed a similar stack to a barrel-shaped woman in a white gown decorated with enough moonstone to glow.

"Welcome to the Enlightened world, Phoebe Pierce," said the cat-woman. "My name is Lana. I'm the Mother of the Mabon Council. To my left is Jerry, the Maiden of the council. To my right, Cherry Blossom, the Crone of the council."

"Thank you, Lana, Jerry, and Cherry Blossom." It was all Phoebe could think to say.

Lana shuffled the papers in her hand. "Welcome also to Melissa and Olivia, of the Clay Coven. We'll start in just a moment. January *ap Ionawr* hasn't arrived yet and his application has to be considered seriously. Have a seat, ladies."

"Where?" Phoebe asked looking around the room.

Lana smiled kindly gesturing at the seats around the table. "Anywhere you like. This isn't an interrogation. You're safe inside the circle and your voice matters here. Normally as a witch, this would be just a formality where we would ask how you'd Awakened yourself, appoint a guide, shake your hand, and then have lunch together but your case is complicated."

"Why is it complicated?"

Lana looked at Jerry and Cherry Blossom as if silently consulting them for an answer. "As far as we know, you are one of the first Unguided Awakenings we've had in Boston. That alone would make you noteworthy. That January *ap Ionawr* of the Vampire House of Norn has applied to be your companion within the first days of your Awakening also makes your case unusual. According to our records, this is his first application for a companion."

Phoebe was trying to listen and to choose a chair at the same time. Melissa had gone straight to Olivia's side but if she did the same, that would have put the three of them directly across from the three council members and that felt confrontational. Sitting halfway between the two groups seemed like the best option. It also put her in a perfect place to watch for January.

Lana watched her sit with an appreciative nod. "You choose your own path. A good sign from a strong witch. Where was I? Yes. Flaxseed has filed paperwork as a witness to say that you've also taken a familiar called

Bramble into your care." Lana stopped and scanned the room. "Where is your familiar?"

Phoebe attempted to pull the chair closer to the table. "At home. He's studying for an exam." She had intentionally dropped him off at home before the meeting in spite of his protest. Honey would take him to school later. She wasn't sure what was going to happen here and she wanted him somewhere safe.

"If he's a full-fledged familiar he shouldn't be taking exams." Lana flipped through her paperwork. "If he's still training, he'll have to be returned to the school."

Phoebe shook her head. "Absolutely not. I signed the contract and Flaxseed witnessed it. He's mine, I'm his, or however, it works. We stay together. Talk to Flaxseed. She's the one who insisted that I sign paperwork immediately."

Cherry Blossom tapped Lana on the shoulder with her stack of papers. "Loyalty is also a good sign from a strong witch. We will trust the judgment of Flaxseed in this matter. If she feels Bramble is best off with you before he's completed his exams, then so be it."

Jerry leaned forward looking fascinated. "If you're a new witch and you have a new familiar, why do you want to become a vampire?"

The door swung open and January strode inside with Alex at his heels. His silver-blue eyes scanned the room until they landed on her. The smile he gave her made her breathe catch in her throat. He didn't even look at the other chairs. He walked straight to where she was seated and pulled out the chair beside her.

"Apologies, Cariad. Thanks for the text." He gathered her hand from the table and kissed the top of it. "I've missed you." Turning to the council, he bowed his head with a stern look. "Why was I not informed this meeting was today?"

"Neither were we," Olivia added. "We learned about it from one of the Recovery Agents, James. You sent him to collect Phoebe."

Cherry Blossom looked at her colleagues. "James? He's just returned from New Mexico. We didn't send him. We sent the notification of this meeting by personal carrier."

"We received no notifications," January repeated. "Did your carrier come back? May I speak with them?"

Lana nodded. "Of course. We'll double-check where the messages went. That's very odd. Under the circumstances, I'm both surprised and pleased you were all able to make it."

Alex considered his seating options for a moment and then went to sit beside Jerry. Squinting at Alex, Jerry looked momentarily confused. "I remember you. You're the werewolf who wants to become a vampire."

Alex looked down at Jerry's paperwork with interest. "Something like that. I'm Alex Kimbos." He offered Jerry his hand.

"Jerry Santos."

Lana tilted her head. "And what do you have to do with Phoebe Pierce Mr. Kimbos?"

Alex looked over at her with an unapologetic grin. "I'm here for moral support."

"For Phoebe or for January?" Lana pressed, her twitching tail and expression somehow conveying both annoyance and amusement at the same time.

Alex shrugged. "Whoever needs it."

Cherry Blossom laughed, her whole body shaking. "The House of Norn picks some very interesting potential family members, January."

"If we can continue?" Lana said looking directly at Phoebe and then rolling her eyes as if they were sharing a private joke. Everyone nodded. "Let's start at the beginning. I'm going to summarize the documents that have been formally submitted, Ms. Pierce, and then you can fill us in on the relevant details we're missing or that are incorrect. Ultimately, we're here to help you make your first decisions as to where you would like to focus your learning in the first years of being Enlightened."

"Okay." Phoebe breathed a sigh of relief. That didn't sound so bad.

January moved closer to her whispering, "The simpler you make your answers the faster we get out of here and go somewhere nice."

Lana tilted her head toward them and continued as if she hadn't heard January although her ears tilted back and forth suggesting she had. "Melissa, your report says that when Phoebe came into work the day before Lammas, she wasn't showing signs of being Enlightened at the start of the day."

Melissa jumped as if she'd suddenly been called on by the teacher. "When she came in that morning, she was fine. She went into the stockroom to do the stock take and when she came back, she wasn't."

"What happened in the stockroom, Ms. Pierce?"

"You can just call me Phoebe."

January brought her hand into his lap and moved his chair closer to her. The feel of his shoulder next to hers did nothing to help her focus.

"I was taking stock and I dropped a spell book or it fell from where I put it. When I picked up the book, I read the spell out loud and-"

"Do you do that often?" Jerry asked with a good amount of judgment in his voice.

"I never do it." Phoebe shook her head. "I'm normally a very careful person. I don't know why I did it in the first place. I just felt compelled-"

Olivia jumped in. "There is a strong compulsion spell

on that book but only the person who ordered it should have been able to read it."

Cherry Blossom made some notes. "Who ordered it?"

Olivia reached into her sleeves pulling out a receipt. "A vampire named Nesta, but she never came to collect it."

The blood ran from January's face. Phoebe squeezed his hand. "I'm sure It's just a coincidence."

He squeezed back. "It's never a coincidence. It's always Enir."

The way he said Enir's name made Phoebe hope never to meet her. Cherry Blossom motioned for Phoebe to continue.

"I read the spell and…" How could she describe that first experience? She'd teleported a dozen times since then and hadn't felt anything like the white light connection she'd experienced the first time. "I think I disappeared and reappeared at the White Stone Circle near January's house."

Lana looked between them with a frown. "January's house? There's no report or record of you there."

January leaned forward. "I didn't file it because when Phoebe appeared, I assumed she was an Enlightened witch actively practicing magic."

His smooth confident delivery was accompanied by a brief squeeze of her hand.

"And you didn't think that a witch appearing in your private circle through the wards that I know myself that Flaxseed laid down was worth mentioning to the Mabon Council?"

Cherry Blossom's implication that January was hiding something was clear.

"I didn't think it was something you needed to be concerned about."

"Why is that Mr *ap Ionawr*?" Cherry Blossom now pushed her paperwork aside to fold her hands in front of her. Phoebe got the distinct feeling that this line of questioning wasn't by accident. "If I remember correctly, Flaxseed's ward requires a direct invitation from you in order for someone to find or enter the circle. An Unguided witch you've never seen in your life comes through that ward and you didn't feel that was significant?"

Phoebe's heart pounded in her chest, but January remained unruffled.

"I didn't know she was Unguided, and I think I did invite her." He looked at Phoebe rather than the council. "Not by name, because I didn't know it, but I invited her." He looked back at Cherry Blossom. "I was in the circle with an offering asking for a Lammas blessing. When she appeared, I presumed," he stopped carefully considering his next words. "That is, I believe that she is the blessing I'd asked for. My spell was the invitation that allowed her through the wards."

All three council members looked at each other before Jerry asked, "You believe that fate pulled an Unenlightened witch through the Veil and some of the most powerful wards on the East Coast as a blessing?"

"Bring me to my heart's desire," Phoebe said the last words of the spell she cast understanding why her connection with January had been so intense and instant. "It's a love spell. January, the spell I read from the book was a love spell. That's why our connection is so intense."

He smiled at her. "Is that so astonishing, Cariad? The spell I cast in the circle was also a love spell. I wished for you, and you wished for me at the exact same moment. Fate removed the obstacles between us so that we could find one another."

Lana cleared her throat. "As romantic as that sounds, Phoebe said she felt compelled to read the spell. What happened after you appeared in the circle?"

Phoebe looked back at the council members with her

mind still sifting through January's declaration. "I dropped the book when I appeared in the circle. At first, I was frightened by the book and then I convinced myself I was dreaming. I kissed January thinking it would wake me up and then I was back in the stockroom."

"You kissed an unknown vampire?" Jerry was looking at her like she was some sort of daredevil.

She sighed looking around the room. "It seemed logical at the time."

"If you hadn't dropped the book, I wouldn't have been able to find you again so quickly when you teleported out."

Cherry Blossom caught Olivia's eye. "Olivia, what is the name of this book and why do you have it?"

Olivia looked first at Melissa and then at Phoebe. "I don't know the name of the book off hand. I purchase a lot of stock from different places. This book was a special order that was never picked up."

"Witchcraft with Vampires and Other Enlightened Beings," Phoebe supplied feeling a bit shocked that the book had been ordered on purpose.

"A book for the Enlightened?" Lana turned her attention to Olivia. "Those are supposed to be warded for the protection of the Unenlightened."

"Warded," Melissa groaned. "Oh no! It's all my fault. I bought Phoebe a vacuum for Lammas. She was vacuuming the stockroom."

Lana tilted her head clearly confused. "You can't vacuum up a ward. It's an energy barrier. The only thing that breaks it is to doubt it."

Melissa groaned again. "I knew it was my fault. Phoebe said that vacuuming wouldn't hurt the ward, but Olivia said it did, and I believed Olivia. I'm so sorry, Phoebe."

Lana held up her hand. "This is going to need further investigation. Either the most complex series of coincidences I've ever heard of conspired so that Phoebe Pierce could be Awakened, or she was compelled to read a spell by a vampire who forced her through the Veil. A spell cast by January *ap Ionawr* who got what he wanted and immediately applied to take Phoebe as a companion."

January went deadly still. "That's a very serious accusation you're making."

"Or she was awake before she started cleaning." Alex's comments drew all eyes to him, and he leaned back in his chair. "Think about it. If Phoebe was vacuuming and believed it would have no effect on the wards, it wouldn't. If I understand it right, the wards were only damaged for Melissa. But Phoebe could see the warded spell book before she teleported. Something else must have Awakened her, she read the love spell at the same time January requested a love blessing. She teleported for the first time exactly where her life-mate was. The Stone Circle."

"I want the book brought here. We have experts who can easily determine what type of magic it has done recently." Lana turned to January. "Under normal circumstances, vampires can't cast magic but we know your case is different. If you have something to say, now is the time."

"I didn't force Phoebe through the Veil. Until she appeared, I didn't know she existed."

Cherry Blossom tsked. "We have other things to consider. Love spells have a mind of their own, we all know that. Now, January. the only report I have from you is from The Mabon Ritual. You say that Phoebe summoned, directly channeled, and held the spirit of Air at her first Enlightened ritual?"

"She did," January confirmed but Phoebe could see that something Lana said had disturbed him. "She's an Air elemental. Air talks to her."

"That's also unusual, Phoebe," Lana explained. "Most of us can offer an invitation to an element or spirit but in my lifetime, I've only seen two other witches in the last 20 years who can directly summon an element." She looked at Jerry. "True love aside, Elementals are powerful and rare. Why would you give up that level of magic and apply to join the Vampire House of Norn?"

Phoebe shook her head. "Why do you keep saying that. January applied to be my companion, I didn't apply to any vampire house. The only thing I've signed recently is the contract for Bramble."

"Bramble's contract." January said as if all the puzzle pieces were coming together. "Bramble and Brindle were created by Enir. The contract is between Enir and Phoebe, not Phoebe and Flaxseed. Bramble is the first exchange."

Jerry's mouth dropped open. "Didn't any of you advise her to read the contract before she signed it?"

"I did read the contract," Phoebe said indignantly. "It said I would love and care for Bramble and he would love and care for me. That's it. What do you mean first exchange?"

Alex raised his hand waving it around like a schoolboy. "Ooh, I know this one. There are three exchanges between an applicant and a vampire to officially enter a house. A promise, a gift of blood, and then a sacrifice."

Lana gave Alex a stern look and for once, the werewolf shut his mouth.

"Enir filed the application for Phoebe to join the House of Norn. The contract between yourself and Enir to care for the familiar counts as an exchange of promise." She looked at January. "Has she gifted you with blood?"

Phoebe felt her face blush scarlet.

"She has." January squeezed her hand again. "But the gift was only for me. We didn't know about the application."

Cherry Blossom shook her head. "The application is to your house, Norn's son. I don't know the politics of how your family shares information, but Phoebe has completed two of the three exchanges with your house."

January was quite a moment and then he laughed. "Then she's mine. She's an accepted applicant to the House of Norn and I am automatically her guide."

"But I didn't know I was doing it," Phoebe stood up pulling her hand away from him. "I didn't put in an application. I don't want to be a vampire, I just started learning to be a witch. I've never even seen Enir."

Lana tilted her head, first one way and then the other. "If you wish to accuse The House of Norn or January of manipulating you or your application, you can do so."

Phoebe looked around the table at all of the peering people waiting for her to make a decision. "What I want is some time alone to just think about what's happened before I decide anything else."

Jerry placed his hand on Lana's arm. "That's a reasonable request. January has had his time with her and so has the Clay Coven. James canceled his application. Giving her a week on her own to decide what she wants to do is fair."

Cherry Blossom tapped her lips appreciatively. "In light that there is also possible love magic involved, I agree. Some distance will help any remaining remnants of the spell wear off."

"No," January said standing up beside her. "I've already had a week without her. I don't want another."

Cherry Blossom continued. "We will re-convene on Samhain. During that time, the guides are forbidden to contact Phoebe unless she contacts you first. Phoebe, you will spend the first week of that time alone so that you can reflect and shake off any remaining effects of a love spell." She looked at both January and Olivia. "The Mabon Council will look into the circumstances surrounding Phoebe's Awakening to determine whether or not there was any force."

January clenched his fists. "She has to make a living and she works with Olivia and Melissa. I have obeyed the rules and waited for her to contact me. She didn't. She wouldn't have been able to resist if she were under a love spell."

Phoebe looked at him confused. "Olivia said I wasn't allowed to contact you."

Lana stood up. "She is not a child to have custody of. If you want contact with her, you will have to wait until she comes to you." She looked at Olivia. "That goes for you too. January didn't break the rules by contacting her but you did by not telling her that she had the right to contact him."

Olivia looked sheepish. "I was trying to help her gain some perspective."

"By doing the same thing the House of Norn has been doing, withholding information from someone you're supposed to be guiding." Jerry stood to gather the paperwork from Lana and Cherry Blossom. "If you ask me, none of you deserve to guide her."

"I'll give her some paid vacation time so she has the space she needs to make her own decision." She turned to Phoebe. "I'm sorry, Phoebe. I had no right to make that choice for you."

Cherry Blossom clapped. "Good. This is Good. Applicants can make their way home now. The Council will take Miss Phoebe to lunch and then make sure she has what she needs for her reflection time."

"May I have a moment with her?" January asked the council and then turned to Phoebe. "I didn't know about the application or the contract. I wasn't trying to manipulate you."

"But you didn't protest it either." She looked into his eyes hoping he would deny it but he didn't. "If Enir's plan had worked in your favor, would you have given me a choice?"

He drew himself up to his full height with his fists clenched to his side. "Phoebe..."

The council stood and she moved to follow them. January was suddenly in front of her, crowding her, looming over her, his gaze filled with hurt and indignation. He didn't touch her. The space between them was like a vortex drawing them together. They stared at each other and Phoebe could feel herself edging closer to him. Without saying a word, he stepped out of her way turning on his heel to walk out of the room.

A FAMILY AFFAIR

Lunch was a quiet affair and after it was over, all three Council Members gave her a hug. Jerry offered to take her where she needed to go and then sent an invitation to her phone to join a chat group created for the newly Awakened. Her head ached, and so did her heart. All she really wanted to do was run back to January and make sure he was okay but that's exactly what love spells did. They played with your emotions.

Their attraction might be natural but unless they gave it time, they would never know. The man had lived for 800 years without a formal companion, and yet he'd asked for her, Phoebe, a woman he'd only met once for a couple of minutes. It sounded ridiculous, but when she remembered the kiss and how right and natural it felt to be with him in this crazy world, nothing else but him made sense. When the week was over, she'd know if what they were feeling was real. If it wasn't... Well, thinking about that was too hard right now.

Before she returned home, she asked Jerry to take her to Bast's School for Familiars so she could pick up Bramble. Honey would have taken him to school by now. She wondered if he had done well on his test. Either way, she couldn't wait to cuddle him.

The school lived up to its name. It was a sprawling Victorian building surrounded by high red brick walls covered in English ivy. Through the black wrought iron gates, Phoebe could see an immaculate lawn and formal garden with a menagerie of animals scattered around. They all appeared to be in groups except one small and very sad-looking black and white fluff ball sitting by himself on the steps closest to the school door.

"Bramble," Phoebe called to him. He looked up instantly, and then his ears perked. She put her hand on the handle to open the gate as he came bounding forward. Before he could reach her, Flaxseed stepped onto the path between them, wrapping her long fingers around the gate to keep it closed.

"Phoebe. I was just about to call you. I've got some bad news. I'm afraid Bramble failed his exam this afternoon. He simply isn't powerful enough to be your familiar. I'm going to have to take him back."

Bramble hissed at Flaxseed coming out from behind her legs. "No fail. You cheat." He looked at Phoebe, pleading for her to believe him. "She cheat. So Bramble fail. Am powerful. No, stay here. Want to go home."

Phoebe knelt to Flaxseed's level, wrapping her hand around the other woman's fist. "I have a contract that says he's mine. You signed it. I have a witness. My familiar says he wants to come home." She put enough emphasis on the word familiar to make her point. "Let him through."

Flaxseed bared her pointed teeth. "Or what?"

Phoebe felt the air move over her skin and begin to rustle the leaves, then rattle the school windows, then roar around them. A gust whipped through the garden, causing all the animals inside except for Bramble to huddle close to the ground. Phoebe could feel the power around her through her. She had just about enough of other people deciding what she could and couldn't do.

"You will give him to me, or I'll huff and puff and blow your house down."

The wind continued knocking over plant pots and tearing the leaves off the surrounding trees with greedy fingers. Flaxseed laughed, yanking her hand from beneath Phoebe's and stepping out of Bramble's way. Bramble moved quickly through the bars of the gate and jumped straight into Phoebe's arms.

"Brindle, too," he said.

She barely had time to register his words when a slender, brindled colored tiny, short-haired kitten dashed across the lawn and through the gate to jump into Phoebe's arms to join her brother.

"Hello," Brindle said, touching her delicate pink nose to Phoebe's. "Go now. Not safe."

Phoebe stood up with both familiars, allowing the wind to die down. She glanced back over her shoulder to see Flaxseed opening the gate with a huge smile.

"Well done, Bramble and Brindle. You've done it. Top marks for both of you."

The other animals stood and came forward joyously to crowd around Flaxseed at the gate. Her hands lovingly skipped over them one at a time.

Bramble hissed at her again. "You cheat."

Flaxseed waddled toward them, waving off his comment. "Yes. Yes, I did. You didn't believe me, and your witch was willing to take you even though I said you failed. You believed each other, not me."

Phoebe looked at her incredulously. "Another test? Flaxseed, how can I trust you when you've lied to me twice."

Flaxseed clasped her hands in front of her, looking anything but contrite. "I have to be careful. A poor pairing

178

means heartache for all involved. Poor Honey is proof of that." She tsked. "Never mind. Honey's witch will find her."

The air moved over Phoebe's skin again, this time whispering, *Melissa. Melissa. Melissa.*

"Melissa," Phoebe said, suddenly sure of it. "Melissa of the Clay Coven is Honey's witch. She works at the Craft Shop."

Flaxseed clasped her hand to her chest, hopeful. "Is she? How do you know?"

Phoebe snuggled the kittens closer. "The wind told me."

"Is she kind?" Flaxseed asked softly. "Is she patient? Honey's been through so much on her own. It will take her some time to learn to work as a team again."

"Melissa already adores her. I trust her. It's more than I can say for you." Phoebe turned to walk away but then walked back. "What did you get out of it?"

Flaxseed didn't even pretend not to know what Phoebe was talking about. "It is not what she said she would do that convinced me." She moved forward and lightly touched Brindle's foot. "It's what she promised she wouldn't do if I helped. They were her familiars. She created them, and she said she would destroy them both if you didn't sign for him."

"Enir?"

Flaxseed nodded, and a black Labrador dog almost as big as she was moved through the gates to rub itself against her in comfort.

"Not created," Bramble said fiercely.

"Born," Brindle added with equal fervor.

Flaxseed gazed at them thoughtfully. "Then I am an old fool who has been tricked. Take care of them, Phoebe. If they are born, then they are the first I've seen in my lifetime."

· · ·

Flaxseed's words echoed in her mind long after they got back into the car. She would have preferred to go straight home, but Jerry insisted they stop at the pet store first for Brindle. He was fascinated by the familiars. Because Phoebe had forgotten the messenger bag she typically carried Bramble in when she shopped, Jerry had to hold the shopping basket while Phoebe carried Bramble and Brindle around.

They bought a new pet bed, more toys, a separate set of food and water bowls because Bramble made it clear sharing was not an option, a separate set of treats because Brindle didn't like fish and Bramble didn't like chicken, a shared carrier for riding in the car because neither Brindle nor Bramble liked to travel alone.

Jerry was no help. He held up beds, brushes, blankets, and treats, commenting on color and softness as if he'd been shopping for familiars all his life.

"I'm going to need a bigger house at this rate," Phoebe mumbled, heading out to the car with a fully loaded Jerry in tow. "Alright, we've got what we need. Let's go home."

"Collar," Bramble said.

"Collar," Brindle repeated solemnly.

Jerry looked at his watch. "Of course, you're absolutely right. We'll have to make it quick. I was supposed to be back an hour ago, but Cherry Blossom will understand."

Phoebe looked down at both familiars. "I didn't think you'd want to wear a collar."

Jerry opened the car door for Phoebe and then began arranging the cat carrier in the back seat, complete with a seatbelt. She put the familars down gently so they could inspect his work.

"They aren't normal collars. Think of them like the familiar equivalent of wedding rings. You all wear the same symbol so that other Enlightened know you're bonded."

Phoebe opened the pet carrier door, and Bramble and

Brindle went inside. "I take it we don't get those from a pet store."

Jerry shoved the last of the cat stuff into the trunk of his car. "No. They're commissioned. I know just the place."

Bramble and Brindle had a brief argument over which side of the carrier each was going to sit on, and then there was peace. The place they were heading to was the Harrison Avenue art district. It was full of beautiful small galleries and independent art studios. Jerry began a monologue about the challenges of living with his parents and working in the Recovery Center as the youngest Maiden on the council in the last century. He navigated the area like a pro, muttering a spell under his breath, which high-lighted the closest parking space. They parked without incident and filed out of the car.

Because Phoebe was trying to pay attention to Jerry and carry Bramble and Brindle in a dignified fashion, she didn't realize she knew where they were going until she was standing in the doorway of her brother's art studio. There was no sign on the door. In fact, if you didn't know better, you would think it was one of the many apartments. Phoebe had commented on the fact more than once, only to be told by her brother that his audience was the type that preferred not to be pointed out. She assumed at the time he meant mafia-type people.

Jerry knocked on the door. "We'll probably only be able to make an appointment. Mr Pierce keeps a very strict schedule."

"Joshua keeps a very strict schedule? The man who once showed up to Thanksgiving dinner 2 days late?"

Even as he opened the door, Phoebe couldn't believe it. In his signature khaki drawstring pants and multicolored geo print shirt, barefoot, with his brown hair almost recklessly disheveled, he came out the front door and put his arms around Jerry.

"Jerry. You're home early. How was the meeting today? Did you get that vampire witch thing sorted out?" He leaned forward to give Jerry a quick kiss, then spotted Phoebe. "Holy shit! Phoebe!" He moved protectively in front of Jerry. "What are you doing here?"

Phoebe shoved her way past him to go inside the studio. "Apparently, Mr Pierce, I'm making an appointment to buy collars for myself and my familiars."

"Not stiff," Bramble stated.

"Not green," Brindle added.

Joshua looked at her and then at Jerry and passed out.

At least she knew that fainting thing ran in the family. Phoebe put Bramble and Brindle down on the floor and helped Jerry drag her brother to a nearby couch. Normally, Phoebe spent the first 10 minutes in her brother's apartment trying to clear enough space to sit without touching anything she didn't have to, but today, the place was immaculate.

With the light shining through clean windows, she could see his easels were set up, and paint tubes, palettes, brushes, and jars were regulated to a long table in the back. There was another nearby counter filled with jeweler's tools. No take-out containers strewn through laundry or incense burning to cover the smell.

When her brother finally opened his eyes, he scrambled back from Phoebe as if she were a ghost. "Who are you?" he demanded.

"Who are you?" She stood up, waving her arms and walking around the place. "Your face is shaved. I don't think I've seen your face shaved since your high school graduation. And your apartment is cleaner than mine."

She sat down on the adjacent seat only to have both Bramble and Brindle jump on top of her and sit in her lap.

"Okay?" Bramble asked.

"We protect," Brindle added, growling at Josh.

Jerry sat down with her brother, patting his back tenderly. "I take it you know each other."

Josh rubbed his eyes as if doing so would change what was happening. "Jerry, this is my sister Phoebe. Phoebe, this is my life-mate, Jericho."

"Just Jerry," Jerry corrected, looking at Phoebe and then Josh with a good deal of embarrassment. "I thought you said your family was Unenlightened."

"They are. They were. Phoebe, how long have you been Awakened?"

Phoebe tried to decide which part of this situation was least believable. That Josh was Enlightened, that Josh had found a partner he was willing to fully commit to, that her artist brother was an exclusive dealer of collars for familiars, or that Josh's apartment was clean.

Jerry coaxed Josh onto the edge of the couch. "Put your head between your knees. I'll go get you some water."

Phoebe put Bramble and Brindle down on the floor and followed Jerry to the kitchen. "I thought you said you lived with your parents."

He went to a cupboard and pulled out a clean glass. Phoebe felt like she might need to go join her brother on the couch with her head between her knees.

"I do live with my parents. I spend a lot of time here, but I don't live here." He went to the tap and filled one glass, then thought about it and filled another, handing it to Phoebe. "Do you think Brindle or Bramble want a drink too?"

"Drink," Brindle confirmed, winding her way between Phoebe's feet to go to Jerry.

"Okay. I have dairy-free milk and some water. I think you're a little young for brandy, but you're your own boss."

She wound like a figure 8 between his feet. "Water. You make."

He blushed and bent down to pick her up, putting her on the counter. He reached above her to get a small shallow bowl. "I'm only doing this because you've been such a good girl today."

Josh came to the doorway of the kitchen carrying Bramble. Jerry put his hand over the bowl and closed his eyes. Phoebe felt the air around her vibrate and hum. Water seemed to concentrate around Jerry's hand and flow without a splash into the bowl. Josh looked at him with such an expression of unguarded love that it made her heart ache.

January. The image of him as she left the council room filled her mind. He'd been hurt by her choice. She'd been too overwhelmed at the time to comfort him. Brindle purred, turning a quick turn of excitement before bending down to drink the water.

"Delicious," she said. "Honey, say, water witch, my witch. Don't like water. Like you."

Jerry blinked, putting both hands over his heart. "Are you asking me to be yours?"

Brindle blinked her eyes slowly. "Say name."

Jerry looked at her a moment, his face a picture of confusion and then amusement. "Brindle." He said it with a laugh. "Your common name is actually Brindle."

"Yes!" She said and ran to Jerry. "Hide name in plain sight."

He scooped her up, cuddling her close with tears in his eyes. "Thank you for choosing me."

Bramble squirmed to be put down, and Josh sat him on the counter. He walked over to where Phoebe was standing and took a drink straight from her glass before looking up at her. "Okay?"

She rubbed his head. "I'm okay." Looking at Josh, Jerry, and Brindle, she couldn't do anything but smile. "We're okay."

Josh came forward and gave her a hard hug. "Please tell me you're not the vampire witch."

18

OLD VAMPIRES AND NEW TRICKS

Alex came into January's office buttoning a white formal shirt.

"So, what are you thinking, flowers? Chocolates? I don't think Amazon will deliver Falafel but I have a cousin who might take it over to her if we let him have a swim in the pool."

January looked at his screen without seeing much. "What are you talking about?"

He heaved his sleeves straight pulling silver cufflinks out of one of his pockets and putting one expertly through his sleeve buttonhole. "What are you going to buy Phoebe to begin apologizing for the shit storm that went down this afternoon?"

"I'm not going to buy her anything. I've got nothing to apologize for. She thinks this is all some love spell." January sighed rubbing his forehead. "She made her choice."

Alex crossed the room in two strides and slammed January's laptop closed, leaning over the desk to get right in his face. "You Enlightened are all the same. You think your way is the only way. What were Phoebe's plans before you decided to file paperwork so she could be your companion? Why should she have to turn her entire life upside down and become a vampire? What's in it for her? She loses her magic, then her job, then falafel, then her family. What are you giving up?"

January gritted his teeth. "You don't understand.

Alex strode away from the desk. "No, you don't understand. Do you want to be her life-mate? Start acting like one. Never above you, never below you, always beside you. That's what it means to be a life-mate. You support one another."

January sat back almost daring Alex to come forward again. "I have supported her."

"Bullshit." Alex ran his hands through his hair. His body wavered, on the edge of change. January pushed back from his desk to give himself room to fight if he needed to.

"Have you slept at Phoebe's house? Met her parents? Talked to even one of her friends?"

He hadn't, and they both knew it. "She hasn't asked me to."

"I know. She hasn't asked you because she isn't ready. You and Enir are signing her up for eternity, and Phoebe hasn't decided if she's going to be here for Yule."

January felt like he'd been punched in the gut. That she wasn't as committed as he was to a life together hadn't occurred to him. "She is my life-mate."

Alex rounded on him. "Then act like she has the right to choose the life she wants and you adapt to her plan. You sat there and let Enir and the Council take Phoebe's choices away and did nothing."

"I can't fight Enir. If she wants Phoebe in this house there is no way to stop her."

"You're just letting her win because deep down, she wants the same thing you want. Phoebe's a vampire. Enir doesn't give a shit about Phoebe, she's doing it for you."

Alex took a deep breath and then another, his form solidifying and all hints of his anger disappearing behind a calm facade. "Can't you see? They're both doing it for you."

"What am I supposed to do? You heard her. She doesn't want to be a vampire. I'm supposed to just watch her die one day at a time?"

"Yes," Alex growled. "If she's your life-mate, then you wait for her to be ready to join her life with yours."

Could it be that easy? Time was something he'd always had and taken for granted. Their bond had to be unquestionable on both sides before she faced the conversion. He shook himself mentally if she chose conversion.

Alex breathed a sigh of relief. "Join your life to hers, don't force her into your life. First, you apologize for being an asshole today. Second, you go to her family dinners and pretend to be a health fanatic on a liquid diet. She said her family was weird. Maybe they won't notice."

"What about Enir?"

"Enir went to a lot of effort to put Phoebe in your hands. She's not going to kill her. Ask her to give you some time." Alex huffed, tucking his shirt into his trousers. "Ask her after you apologize to Phoebe."

"I'm not allowed to contact her yet."

Alex grabbed his jacket from the back of the couch. "Good. That gives you time to think about what you're going to do to make it up to her.

Alone in her apartment with Bramble, Phoebe tried to remember how to live the life she'd had before she met January. This week she had methodically cleaned her home, opened the windows to let in some fresh air, watered her plants which looked like they'd done much better without her here than they had ever done with her, and took Bramble for a walk to buy some groceries.

At first, being without January, Melissa, or Olivia in the Enlightened world of Boston felt a little like taking the training wheels off her bike. She was trying so hard to act normal that she just came across as super weird. It didn't help that when he wasn't at school, Bramble insisted he go with her everywhere. Nothing said normal like sitting at your favorite fast food restaurant across from your cat.

Luckily, Bramble was like a sign to the other Enlightened that she was Enlightened too. On elevators, on the street, and at park benches, they talked to her about the Unguided and their feelings about the Veil. There were so many cultural rules about each of the Enlightened groups that Phoebe sometimes felt like she spent most of her time apologizing for being unintentionally rude. Someone should write a guidebook for the newly Awakened. She'd asked her brother if there were any books on the basics and he'd unhelpfully said that was what guides were for. As far as guides were concerned, there wasn't really much of a decision for her to make. For now, January wanted a relationship and so did she. Melissa and Olivia wanted to guide her as a witch, and right now, that's what she wanted too. She wouldn't choose between them; they were all just going to have to get along and work together.

Of course, she wasn't supposed to talk to January, Olivia, or Melissa until her period of consideration was over. She'd seen more of her brother in the last week than she had in the last year and her parents had disappeared on one of their no-phones-allowed camping trips. She sat down on the couch beside Bramble with a frozen pizza in the oven and stared at the door.

"Okay. Now, what do we do?"

"Magic?" He swished his tail excitedly and walked to her altar.

Phoebe stared at the array of objects there. They were Mabon pieces and the things she had arranged the last time she practiced with Melissa. "I'm supposed to be thinking, not casting."

"Casting help thinking," Bramble said, knocking the finished tealights off the altar.

Before January, Phoebe had done a little magic each day. A blessing, a little divination, a thank you to the elements and spirits that blessed her life. With Melissa and Olivia, she'd learned how to channel the magic from the energy around her rather than use up her own. She'd learned that although she could speak to the air with ease, the other elements were more difficult to connect with and she would have to practice reaching out to them in order for her magic to remain balanced. Opening a box she kept near the altar, she replaced the candles. Calling the circle as she'd done while Melissa was here, she closed her eyes and concentrated on quieting the noisy chatter of her mind.

"Pendulum," Bramble said with an excited flick of his tail.

Phoebe reached into the box and pulled out a small purple velvet bag. Opening it, she spilled the heavy Amethyst pendulum into her palm. She threaded its silver chain through her fingers and then turned her hand over to allow the stone to dangle. It trembled. Whether it was the stone's own energy or Phoebe's nervous grip, she wasn't sure. She placed her other hand palm up beneath it. Phoebe felt the quiet around her like a heavy blanket.

"Show me yes," she commanded the pendulum. At first, it only trembled, and then it began to swing in small circles.

"Thank you," she said, and the pendulum slowed its circles and hung between her fingers. "Show me no." It trembled again and then began to swing back and forth.

"Good," Bramble said, his eyes following the movements of the pendulum. "Energy good. Ask known question."

Phoebe nodded. Bramble was right. If she asked a question, she knew the answer to it, and the pendulum told her the wrong answer, then whatever was speaking to her would lead her astray. If it answered the question correctly, she could be reasonably sure the answers she got were the truth. "Is my middle name Elizabeth?"

The pendulum stopped swinging side to side and made an odd little wiggle on its chain before it began to swing in small circles.

Bramble moved close enough that she could feel the tickle of his whiskers against her elbow. "Ask question. Yes. No."

Spelling with a pendulum took time or required a spirit board, which sometimes meant two spirits trying to talk to you at the same time. You could only ask yes or no questions. The phrasing was essential. Before she could open her mouth, Bramble spoke.

"Phoebe, my witch?"

The pendulum swung in larger, stronger circles. Bramble did a little prance of delight. Phoebe grinned but kept her attention on the pendulum.

"Phoebe and January family." It wasn't a question. Bramble was telling her so. The pendulum continued to move in circles, confirming his assessment. He looked at her smugly. She didn't stop herself from laughing this time. She joined in. "Does the air speak to me?"

The candles flickered in a sudden draft of air. The pendulum kept swinging in strong circles. Phoebe knew what she should ask next. "Did January pull me through the Veil?"

The pendulum lost its circular rhythm and began to swing back and forth. She breathed a sigh of relief. "Did I bring myself through the Veil?" She expected the pendulum to change directions again and indicate yes, but it didn't. It kept swinging back and forth. There was no mistaking the answer. If she hadn't done it, and neither had January, who had? She went through the names she knew one by one. Melissa, no. Olivia, no. James, no. Enir, no. Flaxseed, no. The swinging became agitated, and Bramble hunkered down. She was running out of names. She thought about the book for a moment. "Was it an object?"

The pendulum continued to swing. If it wasn't an object or one of the Enlightened she knew, then it had to be a person she didn't know.

"Seelie?" Bramble asked, and the pendulum stopped swinging. It shivered violently in her hand and then hung perfectly still. They waited. Phoebe felt her hands tremble with the effort to keep still and not influence the movement of the pendulum. Finally, the trembling stopped, and the stone began to move. At first, the movements were so small that she could barely see them. Circles. Small at first, and then with conviction. Bramble looked up at her with his head tilted in question. "Seelie good?"

He was asking her for confirmation. If the Seelie were good, why would they force someone through the Veil? Something invisible tore the pendulum from her grasp. It flew out of her hand and skittered across the floor. Bramble hunkered down again and hissed. She felt it, too. Something dark lurking just on the outside of her wards.

Bramble growled. "Bramble fix." He marched towards the door with his tail up. Phoebe stood and followed him. At the door, he turned to look at her over his shoulder. "Open."

This is what they had been working on at The Craft Shop with Olivia. The ability to protect themselves. She opened the door quickly, and Bramble leaped into the hall with a fierce growl.

She stepped into the hall after him, throwing her ward forward like a shield. "You aren't welcome here." She felt rather than saw the energy scramble back and then disappear. In her apartment, the energy had felt dark, but here in the hall, it felt wild and scared. Now, there was nothing in the hall but the soft sound of traffic on the streets outside. "We did it!"

Bramble did another happy little prance. "Good team!"

She scooped him up from the floor, giving him a hug. "Great team." They walked back into the apartment. The smell of burned pizza was unmistakable, and so was the feeling deep in her chest that this place might have all of her stuff in it, but it was no longer home. She turned off the oven and dumped the charred disk into the trash. "Shall we go tell our family?"

Bramble picked up the pendulum and brought it to her to put back into the case. "Smudge. Then family. Then dinner."

Phoebe nodded. "Sounds good to me."

19

LOVERS AND TRUE COMPANIONS

January dreamed of Phoebe. If there was any doubt in his mind that the intensity of his feelings was being influenced by a love spell, they were gone. The moment the restriction was over, he intended to go and find her and apologize in person for being selfish. He'd chatted with a few of his clients across the world about how to "eat" at a family dinner and they'd firmly suggested he declare he was a vegan allergic to nuts, gluten, dairy, and eggs. That would make trying to figure out how to feed him awkward enough for most people to avoid it.

He'd called Enir to ask what she intended with Phoebe but as usual, his call went to voice mail. She would return it when she wanted to and not a second sooner. There was always plenty to do. One of his clients had decided to die and move countries 10 years earlier than planned. he was still guiding Alex through the politics of vampire houses while they looked for a werewolf territory that might be able to keep him safe, but all of the things that used to fill his life seemed to rattle around the space that Phoebe wasn't in.

Pushing himself away from his computer, he acknowledged that the bond for him was accelerating fast and she hadn't even taken his blood yet. He dreamed of making a different choice and finishing what she'd started at the circle. He dreamed of waking up beside her and inside her. He dreamed of seeing her in his kitchen drinking coffee or reading a paper. Did she even read the paper?

He dreamed of her so often that when she walked through his office door, he didn't really believe she was there.

"Phoebe?"

She smiled shyly with her hands in the back pockets of her jeans. "Am I interrupting? I tried to call to see if I could come over, but I couldn't get through. Alex said it was okay if I came in."

January looked for his phone on his desk and then remembered he'd left it in his bedroom so he stopped checking to see if she'd texted. He got up slowly and then rushed toward her wrapping her in his arms and burying his face in her hair. Feeling her body pressed against his, breathing her scent into his lungs, he relaxed for the first time since he'd left the Mabon Council chamber. Even without his apology, she'd come back to him.

She yelped and wrapped her arms around him hugging him hard. "I missed you too. I'm honestly starting to wonder if you're addictive."

He put his forehead against hers sighing with relief. "I hope so. I was just about to break the rules and come get you."

"Well technically, I broke them. I'm supposed to be reflecting one more day but Bramble and I couldn't stand it."

"You brought him with you?"

She shrugged. "Honey said to keep him close. I bought a bag so that I could carry him around like a crazy cat woman. He loves it. He's been to work, grocery shopping, everywhere I've been lately." She looked back towards the door. "In fact, this is the farthest he's been from me since my Mabon Council meeting. I haven't even been to the bathroom by myself lately."

January's blood ran cold. "Are you in danger? What did Honey say exactly?"

Phoebe shrugged. "I didn't talk to her directly. Bramble said he talked to her at school and told him to tell me not to leave him behind when I went out."

"At school?" January couldn't contain his grin. "There was no one around to verify her message, I take it?" He waited for the realization that she'd been duped by her own familiar to dawn on her.

She gasped. "That sneaky little—"

January leaned forward and kissed her. It was the best feeling he could remember in his life. "Shhh. He just wants to be close. I don't blame him. If I could convince you to carry me around also, I would have. This week has been hell." He hadn't meant to say that out loud but the way she smiled at him made the admission worth it.

"It's weird, isn't it? This…" she trailed off avoiding the word that would make her vulnerable to him.

"Need? I've not experienced it before, but it is common for my people. It is how we differentiate a lover from a true companion. The longer we're together, the stronger the call between us will get."

"I blamed the spell for a whole two days before I knew I was wrong. I'm sorry."

"It's me who needs to apologize. You're right. If the Mabon Council awarded you to me, I would have let them. I was only thinking of myself."

Phoebe opened her mouth to say something else when Alex strolled in wearing snoopy pajama pants and nothing else. He was cradling a very happy-looking Bramble to his chest.

"Phoebe. You found him. Good. He's been a love-sick zombie all week. Please take him to bed and put us all out of our misery. I can't stand the moping." He kissed the top of Bramble's head. "For reference, this guy is way too young to witness what you two are about to do. I'm taking him to my side of the house. What's left of the lasagne is in the fridge. We'll see you at breakfast."

Phoebe blushed scarlet as Alex strutted out of the room with her familiar.

"You're really going to have to work on his subtlety." She watched them go shaking her head.

Many happy hours later, they lay entangled and panting on his bed. He rolled off her more because he didn't want to crush her than because he wanted to. Pulling her across his chest, he smoothed her hair down her back enjoying the way the curls seemed to wrap around his fingers. The taste of her blood was in his mouth, he could feel the scratches of her passion on his back and the small throbbing of her bite on his shoulder. If he died right at this moment, he didn't think that there was a heaven that could create this level of happiness. He kissed the top of her head knowing he would do whatever was in his power to make sure that she would choose him.

"Let's get under the blankets before you get cold."

She snuggled closer. "I can't move. I think you killed me."

"*La petite, morte,*" he said hugging her close. "There is more if you want it."

She looked up at him devilishly through a tangle of red hair. "I could be persuaded."

They made love twice more before Phoebe told him she wouldn't survive another orgasm. Pleasantly tired, they drifted to sleep together. He dreamed of the stone circle.

Phoebe was sitting in the middle, her vibrant green eyes fixed on something he couldn't see. She hummed a song he couldn't quite make out, her body relaxed and peaceful.

There was a sound. A darkness, a shadow of something that was pure evil moved behind her on the outside of the circle. It stalked her. He tried to call to her, to warn her, but the words were stuck in his throat. The shadow slunk around the grass and then began to mold itself into a solid shape. His shape. She turned around and smiled up at him, her eyes full of love. The shadow smiled back. Its hand became a sword.

"Phoebe, watch out!"

The scream tore through his mind, but the sound that came out of his mouth was Enir's scream of rage. But the sound was different now. In the many lifetimes since she attacked him he had always associated that sound with anger but now he knew what it was. Pain. Soul shattering pain.

Opening his eyes in the early morning light he felt the trickle of tears slide down his cheeks. Phoebe was lying on her back beside him, her hand on his hip as if even the small space between them in bed was too much for her. For his part, the bond was now fully formed. All it would take to complete it now was to share his blood with her. He'd almost done it last night but that would have been selfish and unfair. A true companion had to choose to cross death.

Unlike the movies, the transformation required several slow exchanges of blood. The companion's body improved at first, and then as the organs reshaped, they sickened. In the early days, the final crossing was like a long fever that most companions never woke up from. These days, life signs and changes were monitored, but there were still more true deaths than crossings. He had applied to take Phoebe as a companion, but as he drifted to sleep again, he promised the old Gods of his childhood that he would choose death himself before he risked losing her. He would give her his blood to prolong her health and her life but their first true exchange would be their last.

It was early afternoon when he woke the second time. It was still too early for him to get up but if he didn't wake her soon, she would struggle to sleep tonight, and he was aware that she had to work tomorrow. Moving out of the bed as quietly as he could, he slipped on his discarded pants and went to the kitchen to make her some coffee. Alex was leaning against the frame of one of the kitchen's large picture windows in which Bramble was seated. He had added a Van Halen t-shirt to his snoopy sleep pants. They were both staring intently out the kitchen window towards the front gate.

"Good morning," he said, and both of them jumped. He laughed because sneaking up on Alex most days was nearly impossible. "What are you looking at?"

Bramble began licking his foot as if he hadn't been scared at all. Alex rubbed the back of his neck in irritation. "We're watching the gate."

January walked to the window glancing outside but saw nothing out of the ordinary. "Why?"

Alex looked at the familiar. "Do you want to tell him or do you want me to do it?"

Bramble straightened himself proudly. "Ward damaged. Phoebe can fix it."

January had paid a considerable amount of money to Flaxseed for laying down that ward. "How did it get damaged?"

"Bramble, no invited in. Only Phoebe. Did no want to stay out." He sniffed as if the whole affair was January's fault.

"So you took the whole thing down?" January was aghast. The little fuzzball twitched the end of his tail, tilting one ear back.

"Not all, just gate."

Alex walked toward the counter rolling his shoulders. "He tells me this just before we go to sleep last night. I can't go get Phoebe to fix it because you guys are…" He waved his hand towards January's door. "Anyway. I can't let someone sneak up on us so we sat up and watched the gate."

"Boring," Bramble said looking back towards the gate.

"Appreciated," January said stroking the familiar's head. "I invite you to my home whenever you want to come, Bramble. Will you ask Phoebe to repair it before you go?"

Bramble rubbed himself against January's hand. "Will ask. She fix. Fix better."

"Thank you. Alex, can you teach me how to make coffee?" January went to the cupboard and pulled out the coffee canister.

Alex took it out of his hand. "Coffee is an art, but I can show you the basics."

Bramble hopped down from the window with a big stretch and headed towards the bedroom. "I wake her. We go. Lots to do." He trotted down the hall with his tail in the air.

Alex waited till he was out of earshot. "That's a very nice hickey you have there. I thought you said that vampires don't bruise." Alex opened the top of the coffee pot and pulled out the carafe. He filled it with water and dumped the water carefully into the pot.

January's hand touched the bite mark on his shoulder trying not to smile. "It will be gone by this evening."

Alex pulled open a little basket on the side of the pot and placed a filter from a nearby drawer in it. "You don't have to sound disappointed about that. From the number of times you guys went at it last night, I have no doubt you can convince her to replace it." He poured the coffee into the filter rather than measured it.

January frowned at him. "How do you know how many times we…"

"Werewolf hearing. The soundproofing in this place is good, but she's not exactly quiet. I'm going to have to start sleeping with my earbuds in."

They looked at each other for a moment before Alex hit the power on the coffee pot. He was pretty sure the superior male smirk on Alex's face matched his own.

"It's good to see you smile, man. I was getting worried."

January nodded, moving to one of the cupboards to get two coffee mugs.

"Worried about what?"

Her voice made them both swing around. Face washed and hair somewhat tamed, she was carrying Bramble back into the kitchen. She was wearing yesterday's clothes, and for some reason, it irritated him. He wanted to see her in his clothes, in pajamas, in something that meant she wasn't going to go far from him today.

"Good afternoon, goddess. We were making your coffee in bed." Alex said taking the coffee cups from January's hands. "I hope you like it strong."

She nodded setting Bramble down on the floor and coming between them to claim a coffee cup. Her hip brushed against his. "Yes, please."

As the words came out of her mouth, she looked at him and winked. He felt his smirk turn into a full grin. "I was going to bring it to you."

"Another time." She reached forward and poured first Alex and then herself a cup. Inhaling it with her eyes closed, she sighed in happiness.

"Milk or cream?" Alex asked, going to the fridge. He had to do a little dance to avoid stepping on Bramble.

"Neither." She took a long drink. "You know I drink it black."

Alex shuddered. "That's too hardcore for me. Can you fix our gate ward before you disappear for more sexual shenanigans?"

She choked on her second sip of coffee, and January patted her gently between the shoulders. "Embarrass her on purpose again, and I will tie you to that gate like a guard dog."

Alex poured a generous amount of full cream into his coffee and then a little into a shallow dish for Bramble. "Sorry, Phoebe. I'm just jealous." His grin didn't look sorry.

Phoebe laughed. "What happened to the ward?"

"Bramble." Both January and Alex said it at the same time.

She looked down at the kitten with a face covered in cream. "What happened?"

Bramble came to her, looking like the picture of innocence and regret. "Only small break. Accident. Meant only me sized hole."

January pushed away from the counter to usher her to the kitchen table. "If you can't fix it, I'll have Flaxseed come back. She laid the first ward."

"What does it do?" she asked, sitting down.

"It keeps people who are not directly invited in by me from entering or seeing the place. Bramble didn't have an invite. You did. You found the gate for him, he opened it."

Bramble purred. "We good team." He jumped onto the table to sit beside Phoebe.

"I'm not sure I know how, but I'll see what I can do."

Alex clapped his hands. "Great. I'm going to bed. Will we see you tonight, Phoebe?"

She sat her coffee on the table. "Uh. No. It's the full moon. Normally, Melissa and I hang out and cast spells tonight." She looked over at January.

"Tomorrow night?" January asked.

"Not unless you're interested in having dinner with my parents first. We get together once or twice a month. I usually stay late."

Alex snickered. "January would love to meet your parents, but dinner is going to be out of the question unless they are both Enlightened."

January sighed. "I would love to meet them, but I can wait until you have time."

"That's news to me," Alex grumbled, draining his coffee cup and setting it in the sink.

January's temper got the better of him. "Alex, go to bed and go to sleep until I call you."

The compulsion caught Alex off guard, and he growled a low angry sound as he walked out of the room.

Phoebe frowned at him. "That wasn't very nice."

January sighed, running his fingers through his hair. "It wasn't on purpose. Normally my compulsion doesn't work on him. Either your blood amplifies my power, or he's more tired than I thought. Usually, he just flips me off and continues what he's doing." He came to the table, kissing her on the forehead. "I'm sorry. I'll go wake him and deal with the consequences."

Taking another long drink of coffee, he could see she was trying not to laugh. "How bad could it be?"

January sighed. "He's moody on the best days. A night of no sleep right before a full moon, he's going to be in full drama-llama mode."

This time, she did laugh. "Better get started. Bramble and I will see if we can fix your ward."

Bramble's head and tail drooped. "Can't help. Can't make magic. Can only take."

She reached down to give him a snuggle and a quick kiss. "Then go help January undo his spell. We're leaving in about fifteen minutes."

THE SUMMONS OF ENIR

January and Alex were seated in the stone circle. The small sliver of moon light was dotted with clouds and the cool October air rustled the leaves that were turning from beautiful shades of orange to dark shades of brown. The branches were not quite bare but there was no doubt in anyone's mind that winter was at their door.

On the ground cross legged facing each other, they sat with their eyes closed and their palms up on their thighs breathing deeply. Alex's face was covered in sweat and his form wavered in the darkness. January wasn't sure what to do to help him. He'd agreed to guide the young werewolf only because he couldn't stand fanatics or bullies and Marie Bernard, the so-called Alpha of the Boston Werewolf pack, was both.

She was building a werewolf army in order to protect Boston from the fall of the Veil. Convinced that humans would hunt and destroy the Enlightened once they knew of their existence, she'd begun to recruit local werewolves. That she did so whether they wanted to be recruited or not angered the locals but once recruited, none of the werewolves would challenge her.

Her obsession with Alex wasn't because he was powerful, it was because he was beautiful. Although Alex was a mature werewolf, he refused to take his wolf form because he didn't want to join the Boston pack. He wasn't interested in pack rank, Veil prophecies, or Marie. Rejecting Marie's request to guide him during his transformation, he'd told the Mabon Council clearly that he would take his wolf form when he felt the time was right.

Marie kept pushing, claiming to the Council that Alex was on the verge of an involuntary transformation and for the sake of Unenlightened, he should be handed over to the pack. Four months ago she and some of her pack had surrounded Alex outside a grocery store and attacked him to force him to change. He refused and barely survived. If January hadn't been in the area, she might have got what she wanted. The memory of Alex curled up on the ground refusing to transform or protect himself was still one of the bravest most defiant acts January had seen in his life.

He'd joined the fight claiming Alex as his own. A werewolf applicant to a vampire house, especially one as exclusive as his was almost unheard of. January had expected Enir to refuse on pure principle but in an unexpected turn of fancy, she'd not only accepted the application, she'd endorsed it. That endorsement meant that not only did Alex have the full protection of the house, but that should anything happen to January, Alex's contract would be passed to Enir herself. There was no legal or binding way for Marie to have Alex accept his choice.

January and Alex moved in together because it was expected that Alex would serve and learn the House of Norn rules from January himself. Both were naturally inclined to their own company, and the house was big enough for them to live alongside rather than with one another, but Alex was a werewolf, and werewolves valued family. January's intervention in the fight was a declaration to Alex and the Boston pack that they were family. He'd filled the fridge with food, filled the house with noise, and won January's respect with his determination to be an adequate applicant.

The attack on Alex sent the Boston pack into meltdown. They split into two groups, those who believed that Marie attacked Alex to protect the Unenlightened and those who believed the attack was unprovoked. Werewolves were extremely loyal, and the fighting between and within the groups was heartbreaking. The fighting plus unsanctioned Awakenings had spooked the Boston Enlightened into becoming more clannish. What they needed was a real Alpha, like Angela Hernandez in Larkshead, to bring back peace.

Marie's attack had brought on the very thing she'd accused him of. Alex was struggling to control his inner wolf. When the moon was full or Alex felt threatened, his inner wolf pushed to the surface. Their exchange this morning had undermined months of training. When January and Bramble had finally been able to wake Alex up, he'd been rightly upset about what happened. The trust between them was vulnerable because, in the past, Alex had easily ignored the compulsion in January's voice. Now that Phoebe's blood ran in his veins, January could literally command Alex to do anything.

Alex opened his eyes and fell back into the circle. "I'm useless at this. This morning it was everything I could do not to wolf out and eat you alive and now that I'm in the perfect place to do it, I can't. Maybe you should attack me."

January opened his eyes and relaxed his shoulders. "Absolutely not. I'm not going to teach you to wolf out as a defense mechanism. Every book I've read said that it should be a matter of relaxation, like taking your shoes off and putting them back on."

Alex laughed a genuine sound of amusement rather

than the sardonic sounds he'd been making most of the day. "What psycho-trash have you been reading?"

"Your Wolf and You by Dr. Beatrice Riggs," January said leaning back to look at the moon wondering for the hundredth time tonight what Phoebe was doing. "If you would read some of these papers, you might be able to develop your own strategy on transformation."

"My strategy for transformation is simple. Stay with you until I learn to control it, Marie is dead, or I decide to move out of this territory."

"Fine. You're hungry, I'm tired, and we're getting nowhere like this. I'm giving this one more month, and then we're heading to Larkshead."

"What's Larkshead have that Boston doesn't?"

January stood and offered Alex his hand. "Werewolves that don't want to kick your ass or make you join a cult."

"You do have a point, boss." He took January's hand and allowed himself to be hauled up from the ground. "On an unrelated note, first you're bruised and now you're tired. I'm guessing this is somehow related to Phoebe."

"My nature is to be nocturnal. Getting up in the daytime and sleeping at night is the equivalent of taking the midnight shift. I'll get used to it."

They headed away from the circle into the woods. A light breeze rustled the trees and scattered the moonlight on the ground. Alex walked beside him with his hands in his pockets.

"What's it like to finally find your life-mate?"

The question caught January off guard. Life-mate? A werewolf term but unusually appropriate for his feelings. Was it possible to live hundreds of years and have hundreds of friends and lovers and be waiting for just one soul?

"Before I was a vampire, I was married. If you'd asked me this question then, I would have sworn to you that it felt like a duty that had suddenly been turned into a pleasure."

"You were married? What happened? Did she not make it through the conversion?"

"She didn't make it to our second wedding anniversary."

Alex stopped dead in his tracks. "Why?"

"I was too busy warring alongside my brother to take care of her. Angharad caught a cold that settled into her chest. Something that she might take antibiotics or Aspirin for now, but we didn't know that then."

The crunch of the leaves under their feet seemed to echo and when they came to the fork in the path to take the short or the long way home, Alex chose the long way.

"I got a message on the battlefield that I needed to come home. I barely recognized her when I came through the door. The bright laughing woman that I loved was gone and in her place was a pale, thin, haunted creature. I put the broth in her mouth and cool water on her skin for a week and I really thought she might recover. I left one morning to find us some meat and when I returned, she'd gone."

Alex reached out to touch January's shoulder. "I'm sorry."

"Don't be. I had the opportunity to love her and I wasted it. I won't make the same mistake twice."

It wasn't long after the death of his wife that he'd come upon Nesta on the battlefield. He often wondered if he'd not been so deep in his grief that day, would he have given Nesta a fair chance. They walked in silence for a while the path turning slowly back to the house. January let his thoughts stay with the ghost of Angharad for a moment.

Alex cleared his throat. "Was she your life-mate or is Phoebe?"

January smiled in the darkness. "I've lived several lives.

In each one, I've been able to find love. Not always romantic love, but love just the same. I loved Angharad in my human life. I believed that love was true. Phoebe is different. It feels as if I was created only for her."

Alex sighed. "And you know that after a couple of months?"

"I think I knew it the first time my lips touched hers. I just hadn't admitted it to myself."

They came around the final bend in the path and January noticed the lights were on in their home.

Alex froze. "There's someone in our house." They both checked the breeze for scent. Alex's senses were far more developed.

"Is it Phoebe?"

"No. It's a vampire."

January's blood went cold. "Stay close to me. If I tell you to run, then run."

A woman January had hoped not to see for another hundred years stepped into the path directly behind them. "If you needed to run, you would both be dead by now. Honestly, my favorite mistake, I am constantly amazed you've lived this long."

January turned slowly bowing low. "My lady Enir. You honor me."

Alex swung around but not before Enir had caught him by the chin. He winced grabbing her hand but January knew from experience that it was pointless. She would let go when she wanted to. The last time he'd seen her was around 1968 in Atlanta where she'd summoned him to join her in the Miss America Protest. Before that, it was an 18th-century ball held in Sheffield.

In a white sweater and a pair of jeans with her long black hair braided down her back, it would be easy to mistake her for a teenage girl. Enir liked to be underestimated. She turned Alex's face one way and then another forcing him to his toes with her bruising touch.

"Ooh, he is pretty. He smells like a wet puppy, but I could overlook that. How is he in bed?" She sat him down unceremoniously and turned to January.

"I'm not sleeping with him, my lady."

She put her hands on her hips. "You haven't even tried him, have you?" She looked over her shoulder at Alex. "Don't worry, puppy. I'll put you through your paces before I go."

Alex shrugged rubbing his jaw. "Okay. You wanna go now or get settled in first?"

January tensed ready to defend Alex but Enir just laughed. "Ooh pretty and in need of a spanking. You know what I like, my little mistake."

January moved to Alex's side. "We didn't know you were coming or we would have prepared for you."

"Didn't know I was coming?" She flipped her hair over her shoulder with her hands on her hips. "Your application to bring this dog into our house was one thing, but to hear from the Mabon Council and not yourself that you want to take a life companion, that's practically a dare." Her smile belied the anger in her eyes. "Get on your knees and apologize for being rude."

The blood compulsion hit him hard. His body folded in on itself until he was on his knees in front of her.

"Stop!" Alex stepped between them to defend him. He got right in Enir's face. "Stop."

January's mind screamed in panic. Not for himself but for Alex. "I apologize for my rudeness, my Lady. And for that of my guide, Alex. He's young. They both are. Please."

She and Alex glared at each other for a moment. Anybody with sense would have backed down but that wasn't how Alex did things. He clenched his fists and growled a warning at her. As quickly as it came, her anger faded and she leaned forward to give Alex a quick kiss on the mouth. He jumped back in surprise and she came forward to offer January her hand.

"You've chosen well, my little mistake. He's got heart. Not the sense God gave a goose, but he has heart." He took her hand and she helped him to his feet. Alex came forward but she held out her hand. "At ease, puppy. I'm not here to hurt him, just wanted to see where your loyalty lay."

If anything, Alex looked angrier. "What are you talking about?"

Enir captured one of his fists and dragged him forward tucking his arm through hers and moving back toward the house. January followed at a respectful distance. "People who come into a vampire house either want to be vampires or want to be with a vampire. I gave you a choice, back down and live or defend January and possibly be killed. You chose January. I like that."

"It was a test?" Rather than being dragged, Alex fell into step beside her.

Enir smirked. "Almost. I am pissed off that I heard about both of these applications from a third party and the invitation into my bed stands."

Alex looked back at January over his shoulder with his brows raised but all January could think to do was shrug. He had no idea whether she was serious.

Moving up the front steps, January came around them to open the door for her. "How did you get through the wards?"

She smiled. "They are clever but you should know, my favorite mistake, that I never *meant* to harm you. When it happens, it's a surprise to us both."

They moved down the hallway and Alex led her to the

living room. "You ripped his throat out and left him for dead, didn't you?"

She shrugged taking a seat on the largest couch and pulling her legs up on the sofa. In the light of the living room January could see that she hadn't fed recently. "After what he did to Nesta, I felt we were even."

"I'm sorry, my lady. What happened was unforgivable." As January spoke he realized for the first time that he meant what he said.

She looked at him, her dark eyes sparkling. "I blamed you because it's easy."

Alex joined her on the couch. "You blame yourself?"

"Yes, puppy. Nesta was new, my responsibility. When she followed me through death, I promised to care for her." She took a deep breath and then another. With each exhalation, the sorrow she displayed disappeared. "I failed."

"You're hungry," Alex said moving forward to face her. "Do you want me to get you something? January has supplies in the fridge."

She wrinkled her nose. "No, thank you. After I've brought you to your third or fourth orgasm, you will feed me directly."

Alex sat back with a grin. "Ask nicely, and I'll think about it."

Her grin matched his. "Agree or I feed off you anyway and you get no orgasms."

He stood, did his best impression of a courtly bow, and offered his hand. "We'll do it your way."

She stood with a smile and followed Alex out of the room. January waited until he heard Alex's door shut before he breathed a sigh of relief.

The following day brought with it, the first of the truly cold weather. Enir was in the living room almost in the same place she'd been before. Her hair was loose and she was wearing Alex's t-shirt with her jeans. Werewolf blood was potent but there was no flush of feeding in her face. If anything, she looked worse than she had the night before. Staring sightlessly at the book in her lap, she sat like a statue hardly breathing.

"Good morning, my favorite. Are you well?"

January came fully into the room. "I was going to ask you the same question." He sat down beside her taking the book from her hands. "You didn't feed?"

"Hmm," she said. "I didn't want to weaken him. He's got heart, but he's holding on by a thread."

"If you don't want the bottled blood, I will feed you. I've fed well."

"Liar," she said leaning against him. "You have always been such a gentleman, my favorite mistake. Do you forgive me for how rotten I treated you at the start of our journey together?"

He put an arm around her and gave her a little squeeze. "No, but I think I understand now why you did it."

She looked up at him, her smile not quite reaching her eyes. "Because of your Phoebe."

"Yes."

The words hung between them for a moment. "When I first converted Nesta, she almost didn't make it. She promised me that if she didn't make it through this time, she would find me in the next life. I've been waiting for her, you know."

January kissed the top of her head. "I didn't know."

"I think she's angry with me for loving you. I didn't want to. I wanted you to feel as miserable as I did. I made you feel miserable. Now I have neither of you."

January stilled trying to make sense of what she was saying. "You've never loved me."

"No, my favorite, I have always loved you, not as a

companion, but as my son. You are the most beautiful thing that I have made in my many lifetimes. That is my sin and for it, I lose you both." She heaved a big breath and moved away from him. "When you begin to bring her over, I will feed you first. My blood is stronger than yours. It will help her."

January's heart beat fast. "She doesn't know if she wants to be a vampire. I will try to persuade her, but I won't force her. If she decides to remain mortal, I will follow her to the next life."

Enir hissed, jumping away from him. "I forbid it." Where before she had acted like a sickly girl, now she showed her full strength. Grabbing January's jaw like she had Alex's, she met his eyes squarely. "January *ap Ionawr*, on Samhain, before the sun is fully set, you will convert Phoebe Pierce into a vampire. If she dies, then her blood is on my hands. This is my gift to you." She tore her wrist open with her teeth and forced it into his mouth. He resisted her, but she was too strong. She leaned forward to whisper, "Before the conversion is complete or Phoebe is dead, you will have no memory of this conversation."

She pushed him away lapping the blood from her wrist and closing the wound. "Go clean yourself up and then sleep until your Alex comes to wake you."

By the time Alex came to check on him, Enir was gone.

21

THE WITCH'S BALL

Phoebe adored Samhain. On top of a step ladder suspending fall leaves and lace ghosts from the ceiling of The Craft Shop, she and Melissa sang along to a mix of Billy Pickett's 'Monster Mash' and 'Samhain Night' by Dahm the Bard. The last harvest festival, the first days of winter, the day the Veil thinned and ancestors crossed from death to speak to you. Phoebe loved any excuse to swap stories of being scared of the dark.

Even better? Samhain in the Enlightened world was celebrated all month with October 30th, October 31st, and November 1st being three straight days of feasting and celebration. The Craft Shop always went all out for Halloween, and this year was no exception—pumpkins, skeletons, ghosts, wreaths, anything that might cause a shiver or a smile. A mini cauldron of Halloween candy was set on the till counter for customers, but Phoebe was pretty sure that she and Melissa ate more than they gave out.

January surprised her with an invitation to a Witch's Ball on the 30th, they were hosting a Samhain ritual together on the 31st at the White Stone Circle, and

215

November 1st? That was the day Phoebe was going to fulfill that ritual fantasy January had shared with her. She couldn't wait.

"The Veil as we know it, does it really thin?" she asked Melissa straightening the lacy fall of the ghost shroud decoration.

"Yep. From Samhain to Yule the Veil is thin enough for almost anyone to cross. It's also the time when the Veil between the living and the dead is thin. It's one of the reasons the Enlightened in Ireland started the trend to wear masks on Halloween night. That way if an Enlightened being is observed, there's less chance of shutting down." Melissa ran her fingers through the hanging crystal pendulums sending them swaying in every direction. Bramble watched them swing with a proud gleam in his eye.

"Why do you think the Veil is thinner this time of year?"

"Honestly, I think it is because everyone believes the same thing at the same time. The Veil is basically like a ward between the Enlightened and the Unenlightened. During Halloween, the Enlightened believe they can be seen, and the Unenlightened believe they can see."

Remembering the prophecy at the Mabon ritual, Phoebe looked down at Melissa. "Do you think it will ever fall? That we could all live in the same world peacefully?"

"I do." Melissa grinned handing Phoebe another ghost. "If for no other reason than believing might make it happen."

James stood leaning against the silver railing at The North Bank Bridge Park holding a cup of coffee that had long since gone cold. The setting sun painted the space between the overhead bridge and the bay with beautiful shades of pink and purple. He snapped a few photos of it thinking he might paint it someday. Hundreds of photos were scattered across hard drives, memory sticks, and data clouds that he wanted to paint but never seemed to find the time.

Someday always seemed to be hiding behind the next job or at the end of some elaborate plan. When the Unseelie Queen found out that he was no longer giving her the information she wanted, all his schemes would come to an end. It didn't matter. He made his choice and snapped the photo anyway. He just wanted to disappear into a new life where he could start again.

The text from January asking for a meeting here was both a relief and a disappointment. For the first time in his life, James had failed to keep his word. Although he had traded a favor with the familiar Honey to protect Phoebe, Enir had found a way to get to her.

Enir craved power over January and while James had been chasing shadows, she'd found a way to get it. Even with a guide, it would be within Enir's rights to take Phoebe's blood that she was choosing not to seemed to James like a cruel game. He was suddenly glad that he'd decided not to follow Isla's instructions to shut Phoebe down. She belonged to The House of Norn now, and Enir didn't give up anything without a hefty price.

Although he'd told Isla that he would shut down the unsanctioned witches, on his long drive back from New Mexico he had found a small spark of honor that he hadn't even realized he still had. To end so many lives because of ancient divination that four Unguided witches and a truth speaker would cause the failure of the Veil was selfishness at its purest core. He wasn't a man known for altruism and he'd killed one or two people in his long life, but he remembered all of them. In the quiet moments, he remembered them and regretted his choice. For once, the reason he wanted to be good wasn't to impress January, it was to be true to himself.

His road to redemption was being thwarted. The questions from the Recovery Unit about his trip to New Mexico had been left half answered. Helping the Unseelie agents enter local Recovery Units to steal information about newly Awakened witches was getting more and more difficult. Convincing the Seelie that leaking the information was the fastest way to discover who wanted it was equally hard.

On the cusp of good and evil, no one trusted you. To compound it all, one of the agents, James wasn't sure on which side, had gone rogue and was masquerading as himself. The rogue agent tried to kidnap Phoebe but James couldn't figure out why. First, a shadow curse tried to kill her and now someone wanted to kidnap her. What was so important about this particular witch?

It didn't matter. Now no one, Unseelie or not, trusted him enough to tell him who had cast the shadow curse. Phoebe was now in even more danger. He failed to uphold his side of the bargain with January. There would be no sanctuary for him to paint, to start again, to forget about the hundreds of ways he could have saved himself so much misery if he'd chosen to be less selfish.

The scene at the magic shop came to his mind again and again. January standing over the top of the woman with his teeth bared at anyone who dared to touch her. That January was limiting his social contact almost exclusively to Phoebe had also been relayed to him. Maybe it was the blood, or the long lifetimes spent cultivating relationships, but Vampire's bonded quickly when they found a true companion. In their time together January had never spoken of spending lifetimes together. It was only now, looking out across the bay at the colors he would never paint, that James understood that January had always known that he would leave.

Seeing January's familiar silhouette on the horizon, James felt his resolve solidify. He would tell the truth and face the consequences. As January neared him, James felt a shiver of premonition. One moment he was leaning against the rail watching the last of the daylight glint off the water and the next he sat in the white sands of a desert with a broken wing. In pain, so much pain. He just wanted to lay down and die but someone wouldn't let him. Someone kept him tethered. Someone…loved him? The realization shook him. He'd chosen the light path and that path would lead him back to love.

He felt a hand on his bringing his awareness back to the present. January stood beside him smiling. Not the distant friendly smile he'd seen for the last 100 years but the smile one lover gives to another.

His heart skipped a beat. "January?"

January tilted his head and moved closer to James as if to kiss him but as he did so, James knew the person he was looking at wasn't January. He moved wrong, smiled wrong, smelt wrong.

"Who are you?"

The imposter's smile faltered and then turned into a leer. "I'm here to help you finish the job you can't. We must protect the Veil."

The imposter wrapped its arms around James and smashed their lips together. James struggled against him but the strength of the other being was incredible. A darkness forced its way into his mouth and down his throat. He choked and gagged to try and dislodge it, but it just kept coming.

A shadow was taking over his form. He closed his mind off from it quickly so that it couldn't read his innermost thoughts. Isla must have done what she had to. She'd relayed James's question to the Unseelie Queen. In return, the Queen sent both punishment and reinforcements. To fight was to die, so he let the shadow into his body and into most of his mind. He let it believe it had won. He could almost feel its triumph.

Retreating into the furthest part of his own conscious-ness, he waited. The shadow would take his body but without his permission, it would not be able to stay there long. When the time was right, he would dislodge it. The last thought he had that was purely his own was that once he relaxed, the shadow had stopped the pain. For the first time in his life, James felt nothing.

January allowed the valet assigned to him for the Witch's Ball to buzz around him. The young gentleman brushed hair and tucked fabric reminding January of the first time his personal fortune had been generous enough to afford a valet. He missed the man, Gabriel, but not the many pieces of clothing required to be fashionable and warm at that time.

As a rule, Enir did not provide the vampires in her household with a fortune to start them off. Beyond their basic education, she made members and applicants to her household earn their own way. As an exchange, she took none of their earned income even though she was entitled to half of it. Of the vampire houses, Enir's was one of the smallest with only three members and 2 applicants, Alex and now Phoebe.

He wondered how Phoebe felt being brushed, dressed, and pampered in preparation for the ball tonight. The choice of clothing was designated by the vampire house hosting the ball. This year, as luck would have it, The House of Norn was hosting. It was January's turn to choose the theme, and he'd decided on a 19th-century

Venetian ball mostly because Phoebe had a considerable number of romance novels on her bookshelves at home set in that century.

Enir insisted the location be a large hotel in Ipswitch called The Palace. It was as close to an authentic stately home as could be acquired near Boston. She was a woman who loved theatrics and had also insisted on acrobats, live music, and The House of Norn making a grand entrance altogether before the formal dancing began.

It was only because he'd matched Alex's costume to hers that he'd been allowed to make their grand entrance with Phoebe on his arm rather than her. Zaid, the third official member of their house had stated emphatically that he'd lived through the 19th century once and had no intention of re-enacting any part of it. Enir's response was to claim her fifty-percent of his earned income for the last three years to pay for her party.

In light of Alex's advice, he'd carved pumpkins with Phoebe, Jerry, and Josh. Brought Melissa and Olivia to the White Stone Circle and invited them to eat dinner with them. Bramble now had a bed, bowls, toys, and dominion at January's own house but he'd made a point of not only sleeping at Phoebe's house but doing so often enough that he was now comfortable. Phoebe's parents were the only regular people in her life he hadn't met. Phoebe explained they were an acquired taste best saved for closer to Christmas but Jerry hinted that in the Pierce family, no relationship was official until it passed the inspection of Ellie and Adam Pierce.

In preparation for the ball's finale, the Viennese waltz and the Slow waltz were being taught tonight on the dance floor. He placed his hand in his pocket fingering the small velvet box there. Although he did not have Ellie or Adam's approval, tonight he would give Phoebe the last gift her application required to be officially accepted into The House of Norn, a sacrifice.

In the box lay a silver oak leaf pendant, that matched to the acorn he wore. With it, he would make a vow to place her welfare above his own for as long as he lived and offer her his blood. If she accepted the exchange, then they would be bound as companions.

He looked around the room appreciating the crisp white linen and tasteful floral decoration and wished for the hundredth time that he could make this offer and this exchange at home. Unfortunately, Enir made it plain that when she woke tomorrow, if his blood did not run in Phoebe's veins, hers would.

If he was careful and her body accepted the blood, it would slow her aging and make her just a little bit healthier. If her body wasn't compatible, she would spend the night and the next couple of weeks very ill. He put his hand on his necklace and closed his eyes praying to the old Gods of his childhood that she would be safe and by this time on Samhain, she would permanently be his.

It was the kind of party Phoebe had always dreamed of attending. A young man called Rel had done everything but brush her teeth in order to prepare her for this ball and she was pretty sure he'd have done that too if she'd let him. Her hair was twisted into a half knot and curled within an inch of its life. Twisting through the curls were long ribbons of black, white, silver, and gold. Her gold and cream off-the-shoulder ball gown was embroidered with oak leaves, acorns, and twisting trees.

Rel had two pairs of shoes that would have made Cinderella die of envy. Beside her Olivia shined in opals and lace and Melissa's jet-black beaded and bustled taffeta made her look as much like a vampire as January ever had.

The other women around them were equally splendid but none so much as the dark-headed Enir.

January's maker was not the cold-controlled woman Phoebe had expected. She dressed with and spoke to all of the women there as if they were all young debutantes preparing for their first ball, and many of them including Phoebe were.

Her gown was black velvet with a bodice covered in silver, gold, and white floral hand-embroidered flowers that dripped across her hips and down only one-half of her dress. The asymmetry of the dress and a pair of tall black stilettos helped to transform her slender teenage form into that of a formidable-looking woman.

Wearing a small fortune in what appeared to be diamonds, she approached Phoebe holding out both of her hands much the way Flaxseed had the first time they'd met. Phoebe offered her hands and was pulled swiftly into Enir's embrace.

"Phoebe. At last. January has told me absolutely nothing about you."

She kissed first one and then the other of Phoebe's wrists. Phoebe waited for the sexual attraction to kick in as it did when January did the same thing but instead, she felt only mildly amused.

"Enir. You look beautiful."

She smiled. Her sweet features made disconcerting by the length and sharpness of her fangs. "I'd better. The way your companion complained about the price of my dress. Honestly, men from the Middle Ages are all the same. Always the steward of the estate and never the King."

Rel came up beside them with a large green jewelry case and opened it. Inside was another small fortune in amber jewelry. Enir picked up the necklace holding it between them for a second.

"You are the sun to my January's moon."

She clipped the heavy piece around Phoebe's neck, their cheeks brushing against each other before Enir carefully arranged the cascade of amber across Phoebe's throat.

"He is sacrificing a lot for you to be a part of this household."

Enir picked up two amber bangles putting them like cuffs around each of Phoebe's wrists.

"If he offers you his heart and you break it, I will make your death so terrible your screams will be remembered for centuries."

She picked up a set of earrings putting first one and then the other through Phoebe's ears, her touch so soft and sensual that Phoebe almost couldn't believe she'd heard Enir's words correctly. Enir put her hands on both of Phoebe's shoulders.

"Do we understand each other?"

Phoebe's mouth went dry. Where before the girlish delight in Enir's eyes had made her feel like they could potentially be friends, now the promise in her gaze made Phoebe understand exactly why people were afraid of vampires.

"I understand."

Enir's smile was soft and flirty. "Good. Now, go feed your companion and tell Alex I'm hungry. We make our entrance in half an hour."

January was in their shared bedroom leaning against the window frame looking out into the darkness. He was the very image of a vampire prince. His costume had a long black jacket and waist coat covered in golden moons. It also included knee breeches and white stockings which should have struck her as odd but he wore them like he belonged in them. In a way, he did.

"Are you wishing on a star?" she asked feeling suddenly shy.

He turned his eyes moving over her with obvious appreciation. "What could I possibly wish for that isn't already right here?"

Coming to her side, he picked up her hand and kissed the top bowing elegantly and low. "You look like a dream."

"So do you." Her heart felt happy.

Standing, he led her to the window and then reached into his pocket and withdrew a small black box. "I have something for you." He opened it and turned it around so that she could see it. Inside was a pendant, a small filagree oak leaf dipped in silver so that every vein in the leaf could be traced.

Phoebe ran her hand over it amazed. "It's beautiful."

He pulled his own necklace out of the cravat revealing the silver acorn that was so much a part of what he wore. "They are a match." Closing the box, he placed it in her hand closing her fingers around it and then wrapping his hands around hers.

"For my people, companions are a pair of things intended to complement or match each other. I want to be your companion, Phoebe."

The enormity of what he asked staggered her. The necklace was an engagement ring. "Are you sure?" It was a ridiculous question but deep in her mind she always believed that January's attention was temporary.

He kissed her again and then drew her into his arms. "I love you. You are the first thought that comes to my mind when I wake up and when you aren't in my arms at night, I ache for you. My life is yours, my blood is yours, my heart is yours. When you are ready to offer the same to me, put the pendant on. Be sure because once you say yes, I will never let you go."

He moved back intending to step away but Phoebe

caught his arm. He looked unsure, as if he were afraid of her rejection and she realized with a start that he was. With trembling hands, she opened the box and drew out the necklace. "Will you help me put it on?"

January searched her face for reassurance and when he found it there, the smile he gave her was unforgettable. Stepping forward, he unclasped the amber necklace Enir had given her and lay it aside. Phoebe handed him the oak leaf pendant and now it was his hands that trembled. He opened the clasp and placed it around her neck taking care to arrange the pendant. Then, he scooped her up and swung her around.

"You won't regret this, Cariad. I promise you."

Phoebe opened her mouth to tell him how she felt but a knock at the door interrupted them.

"Enter." January commanded not bothering to move away from her.

Rel entered the room carrying a small intricately deco-rated red bottle and a single small stemmed crystal glass. He looked at January and then Phoebe and spotted her necklace. He grinned. Stepping forward he handed the bottle and glass to January. "Congratulations to the both of you." Something about the exchange struck Phoebe as significant but she couldn't say why.

January poured a small amount of what looked like thick red wine into the glass and looked at it for a long moment. Then he raised the glass to her. "To our new adventure." He took a shallow sip of the liquid and handed her the glass.

"To our new adventure," she said and raised the glass back at him. Then she put it to her lips and took a drink. The smell hit her first, a dark rich smell of ancient forests and clean water, a smell she knew immediately was January's. Then the taste, pungent and dry like wine should be but with a slight metallic taste that she knew instantly was blood. His blood. A gift, a promise, and an exchange of blood. The final act to seal Phoebe into his house.

She closed her eyes and took two more long drinks then pulled the glass away from her lips slowly and looked at it. The smile faded from her face as the blood slid down her throat life fire. The room began to spin and the glass dropped from her hand. Her whole body was on fire and then she couldn't see.

"January!" she gasped but there was no more air, only the fire and her blood trying to escape her body.

He rushed forward to catch her as her knees folded. "Phoebe!"

Then there was nothing but darkness.

He kicked the crystal glass out of their way and carried her to the bed cursing his stupidity. Cursing Enir. Cursing the selfish part of his soul that told him this would be alright. She laid still, her panting breaths causing the necklace he'd given her to slide to the side.

"Her body is fighting, she's rejecting the blood," Rel said with panic. "How much did you give her?"

"Blood?" January replied choked with grief. "What blood?"

"You prepared it earlier. In the red flask," Rel said softly. "For the exchange."

The memory came back to him and he saw himself as if he were outside his own body, calling for Rel to bring him the bottle, making a cut in his palm and putting the blood in the bottle. Pouring it for Phoebe. Then teeth on his throat. Enir's instructions whispered in his ear. A blood compulsion.

No sooner had he laid her on the mattress when the doors opened. Alex came bursting through with his long black jacket swirling behind him like the wings of a raven. He pushed Rel out of the way.

"What's happened?" He came to the bedside sitting down and picking up one of Phoebe's hands.

Rel stood formally dusting himself off, his hands folded over his waist. "She accepted the offer of blood."

Alex looked at January's face. "She agreed to take your blood?"

"She agreed to become my companion," January's tongue felt thick in his mouth.

Alex gritted his teeth. "Did she agree to take your blood?"

January tried to make Alex understand. "It's part of the final exchange but I didn't mean-."

"Asshole," Alex growled picking Phoebe up from the bed. "Rosalind! I need you."

"Give her back to me."

Alex rounded on him cradling Phoebe to his chest. "You said you would wait for her. Rosalind!"

A flash of light appeared beside him. Rosalind looked ready for a fight and then she looked around the room confused. When she saw Alex holding Phoebe her confusion turned to sadness.

"It wasn't supposed to happen like this," he explained feeling like Jekyll excusing Hyde.

Rosalind's chin went up. She stepped to Alex's side, placed a hand on him, and then they were all gone.

Phoebe awoke in her apartment dressed in her favorite fleece pyjamas with Bramble on her chest. She was clean, comfortable, and better rested than she'd felt in ages. Opening her eyes, she saw Bramble looking down at her intently.

"Hello baby," she croaked, picking up a heavy hand to

stroke his face. Her throat and voice felt different, rough and unused. He purred, a sound that rumbled through her chest and down her limbs.

"Sick," he blinked slowly his long white eyelashes and whiskers trembling with emotion. "Bramble take. Phoebe well?"

"I'm okay." She sat up moving him to her side. In fact, she was better than okay. Other than a bad taste in her mouth, she'd never felt so well in her life. The weight of a necklace swung forward and she reached up to catch it. The oak leaf January had given her. "What happened?"

Alex came into her bedroom wearing nothing but the bottom part of a pair of her pyjamas. He was also drying his hair with one of her towels. Phoebe blinked twice but the image didn't go away. He smiled a smile that would have stopped traffic and came to sit on the edge of her bed.

"You're awake. Thank the Gods. How are you feeling?"

Phoebe shook her head. "What are you doing here in my pyjamas?" She looked around her sun lit apartment. "What am I doing here in pyjamas? We're supposed to be attending a ball." She put her hand on the oak leaf. "Where's January."

He leaned forward and pulled up her upper lip to check her gums. She grabbed his hand and he winced. "Easy. You didn't take quite enough for the full transformation but I'd say you're still a little over halfway there."

She let go carefully remembering the drink from the crystal glass.

"Rosalind and I brought you home. She said Bramble helped stop the conversion."

Bramble rubbed his body against hers. "Bramble help. Bramble take."

Alex sat the towel on the bed and leaned forward to pick the cat up and kiss him on the head. "You're the hero of the day."

"I didn't take enough what?"

"Blood. January's blood was in the wine. A lot of blood. More than was necessary for the exchange. It triggered the change. Your body started to fight it. I honestly didn't know if you were going to make it. Then this little genius puts his paws on you and draws the magic out." He tickled his fingers through Bramble's fur and was rewarded with a loud purr.

"January wanted to force me to be a vampire?" Phoebe said, but even saying it didn't sound right. "He said he loved me."

Alex snorted setting Bramble back on the bed and scooping up his towel. "Not as much as he loves himself, apparently. He swears up and down he didn't know about the blood but I talked to Rel and he said they made the drink together for you."

She reached forward and placed a hand on Alex's bared arm. "I knew about the blood. As soon as I put the glass to my lips, I knew."

Alex stood up astonished. "And you drank it anyway? I thought you said you didn't want to be a vampire?"

"I didn't. I don't. Actually, I don't know what I want. He handed it to me and it was romantic and I thought, well you're his companion now, you'd better get used to the blood." She pulled her knees to her chest wrapping her arms around them. "Now your turn. Where are your clothes and where is January."

"I'm sleeping on your couch because I wanted to make sure you were okay and after what January did, I can't look at him without wanting to rip him apart. I'm wearing your pyjamas because they are a hell of a lot more comfortable than 18th century breeches. I'm borrowing a t-shirt too. January's been here a couple of times but I told him to get lost."

"And he listened?"

"No. He said he needed to straighten up something with Enir and he'd come back and explain."

"Okay." She scooted to the edge of her bed, flipped the covers off, and swung her legs out to the floor. That she was wearing only the top half of the same pyjamas Alex was wearing registered just as Alex wolf whistled. She brought the covers back over herself mortified.

"I see what January sees in you." He waggled his brows for good effect but underneath his swagger she could see genuine worry.

"Well thanks, I think. Go get some coffee or something while I find some clothes."

"Where do you think you're going?"

"To work. My rent doesn't pay itself. Then I'm going to call January, find an industrial sized bag of Halloween candy, and celebrate my favorite holiday the normal way.

"Me go?" Bramble asked, his eyebrows raised with hope.

"Absolutely. A witch's place is with her familiar on Halloween. Go pick out some toys to take." He jumped off the side of the bed with such enthusiasm she couldn't help but smile.

"Come on bud, let's see if she's got any food in this place." Alex moved toward the door, then stopped with his hand on the jam to look back at her. "Be careful today."

"I will."

SAMHAIN CURSE

January didn't tell anyone he was leaving the ball after Phoebe was taken. Being separated from her while she was ill was unacceptable. He'd gone straight to Phoebe's house but when Rosalind opened the door, she said that Phoebe was still unconscious and that he was no longer welcome. Just like that, the wards Phoebe had taken down to let him in snapped back into place.

He'd sat in her hallway and waited for news. In the early hours of the morning, Alex came outside to tell him to go home. Phoebe was resting and would not need to be taken to the Recovery Unit. He'd gone only because there was nothing else he could think to do. At his home, he fed vigorously just in case Alex was wrong and Phoebe Awakened a vampire.

He went over everything that happened last night but no matter how many times he went through it, he couldn't make sense of what he remembered. He'd planned the evening to the letter. He would offer Phoebe his heart and the necklace if she said yes, they would dance the night away like the couples in her books, and then they would go back to their room and make passionate love.

He would tell her the truth about Enir's threat and ask her to take a small amount of his blood directly from his body. It would be erotic. They would enjoy it. Enir would be happy. It would buy some time to figure out how to either convince Phoebe to be a vampire or convince Enir she was better off a witch. What the hell had happened?

The joy of asking Phoebe to be his and her saying yes, her smile, the look of the oak leaf on her chest, those memories were fresh and bright. For moments he'd really believed that they would be happy. Calling Rel for the bottle to make a toast to their lives together, making the blood wine after he dressed for the ball, and handing her the glass, he remembered doing these things but he couldn't figure out why he'd done them.

When she'd collapsed, he thought he would go mad. Rel wanted to know how much blood she'd taken but he couldn't recall. He'd mixed the drink and handed it to her but he couldn't remember how much blood he'd put into the wine.

He'd promised not to hurt her and he'd essentially poisoned her directly after she'd agreed to spend her life with him. Why? Giving her the blood before the ball should have been out of the question. That vampire blood could cause sickness was common knowledge. Everyone knew that. Everyone but Phoebe, and she'd learned it in the worst way.

Alex walked into the kitchen carrying his costume and wearing very short pajama pants with tiny black cats all over them and a large orange t-shirt decorated with a black glittery Jack-o-lantern. January got up to see how Phoebe was doing and caught the soft smell of her emanating from the handsome werewolf's skin. He crossed the distance to block Alex's path in two strides.

Alex had the sense to put the costume down and his hands up in front of him. January actually hoped he would transform into a werewolf and fight. The anger inside him had to go somewhere. He bared his teeth to provoke the change but Alex just took a step back.

"What is your problem? First, you attack Phoebe and now me?"

"You're wearing her clothes."

Alex looked down. "Of course I am. Halloween or not, I'm not putting those breeches back on ever."

January growled. "Where is she?"

"Safe. Going to work. She said she was going to call you."

The slow clap of applause from the doorway surprised them both. Enir was leaning on the door frame still wearing her ball gown and silver crown from yesterday, her long, black, hair twisted into an elaborate style like some fairy tale princess.

The pleasant smile on her face belied the coldness in her eyes. She walked slowly between Alex and January running a long brown and black feather across the palms of her hands. January felt suddenly sick. The feather was an angel's feather. It was the only way that Enir could have walked through his wards again without triggering them.

She moved around Alex like a merchant inspecting a horse. "Nice outfit." She tickled Alex's chin with the feather. Once she was behind him, she grabbed his arm and yanked him down to his knees in front of her. His teeth clenched as he fought to change but this time, his wolf form was nowhere to be found.

Enir stared directly at January. "Alex, you have an application to join my house. I'm here to accept your offer today unless someone makes me a better offer. Because what I really want is the witch that disappeared from my party last night."

January stepped forward with his fists clenched. "No."

Her hand trailed up Alex's arm, across his neck, and

234

into his hair. She grabbed a hand and pulled his head back to expose his throat. "No?" She leaned down to whisper in Alex's ear. "Did you hear that, puppy? That's exactly what your little angel said. No. No, she wasn't going to tell me where Phoebe Pierce was. No, she wasn't going to tell me where to find you or the house."

"Rosalind?" Alex's voice broke around the name.

"Don't tell her anything. That feather could have come from anywhere. Enir's been here before so she knows where to find us. She wants something from you."

Enir wrinkled her nose. "Don't we all? That werewolf bitch Marie wants to make you into one of her soldiers, and January wants to ride in like a white knight to save you from yourself. Me? I want to make you the reason he regrets not accepting the position I offered him as my companion."

Enir had always had a sharp tongue but she was never cruel. She had also never wanted him as a companion. January watched her more closely. He'd known her for 800 years. She smelled right, she moved right, but there was an absence in her eyes that was wrong. He felt the compulsion to obey her in his blood but it was weak. Like an echo of Enir's real power.

She bent closer to Alex not breaking her gaze with January. "He wants two companions and I have none? Is that fair? After all, he killed my companion. That means I get to kill one of his."

She bent forward to bite Alex but January moved fast. Grabbing her by the hair he wrenched her away from Alex. She let go with a hiss dropping the feather and grabbing both of his wrists.

"You're not Enir and that's not Rosalind's feather. Who are you?"

She laughed wrenching her head to the side and tearing her own hair out. She brought January's arm to her mouth and sunk her fangs into him. He threw her away from himself but it was too late. The bite was like darkness running through his veins.

He fell to his knees clasping his hand to his chest. The ghoul crouched on all fours and then shambled towards him. Alex moved to stop her. January used every bit of the compulsion left in his body. "Stop."

Both the ghoul and Alex froze in their tracks.

He looked Alex dead in the eye. "Get out of here. Take Phoebe. Run! Hide from me."

Alex shook his head but January was firm. "Go now!"

He heard the door slam. Before the darkness could completely consume him, he launched himself at his attacker. She shrieked in rage but he pinned her to the ground sinking his teeth into her extended jugular. He sucked her blood into his body in great drinks hoping to kill her before the darkness took over. Her form wavered and where he had been holding Enir, now he held James. But it wasn't James either. Lifting his mouth from her throat, he let her blood soak unchecked down her shoulder and flow into the black remains of her gown.

"Who are you? What do you want?"

As the blood soaked into the fabric James's familiar face was slowly replaced by a slender Fey creature he didn't recognize. Unseelie. A shapeshifter. The taste of her tainted blood was all January could taste. He felt the edges of his vision blur. The Fey's eyes met his with the unmistakable mark of fanaticism.

"By my blood and the blood of your maker, I command you. You will take Phoebe Pierce's life tonight."

"No!" January scrambled away from her recognizing the power of his own compulsion in her voice. Even though her body lay lifeless on the carpet, her command filled the air. "By my blood and the blood of your maker, I command you. Kill Phoebe Pierce. You will protect the Veil."

The command closed around his heart. His body struggled against it and his mind screamed at him to stop but like a puppet trapped in his own body, he watched himself get up. Picking up the Unseelie's body he went outside and into the woods. The body wanted to be taken to the stone circle but no matter how many times he stepped into the woods, his feet could not find the path. He could feel the rising sun of Samhain tip over midday.

Without ceremony, he dropped the body where he stood and returned to his house but the wards were active now. The feather that had allowed the evil inside him to enter had been dropped on the kitchen floor during the scuffle. There was too much darkness in him now. He would not be able to cross the threshold of his house until the wards were destroyed.

He tsked at his own carelessness. The full daylight would weaken the darkness inside him, maybe enough for the vampire to find help. In the driveway was a car. The two-seater purple convertible that had been Enir's pride and joy. Without ceremony, he opened the door of the car and climbed into the small trunk. Angry and uncomfortable, he closed his eyes and slept.

The shop was closing. The Samhain spirit was in the air and in spite of Melissa and Olivia's objections, Phoebe sent them home early to enjoy the evening. She'd learned enough magic to keep herself safe until January came to pick her up. If January came to pick her up. The text she'd sent him was still unopened.

The store had been bustling all day with Enlightened of all sorts rushing in to purchase last-minute ingredients for their rituals. Bramble took turns being adored by shoppers and watching the door to make sure everything was safe. She was rearranging some sage sticks when she heard the door chime. The cold wind rushing into the warm shop set the pendulums swinging and brought a rustling warning from the breeze. *Danger.*

Bramble hissed from the counter.

She turned on her heels ready to defend herself but it was January who was standing at the door. He was there watching her, dressed all in black, his hair rumpled and unbrushed as if he'd just woken. Even so, his beauty took her breath away. Smiling she came forward.

"Come inside, you're letting all the heat out."

He moved forward slowly, almost reluctantly. Something about the way he was moving brought her to a stop. The wind whispered over her skin again. *Danger. Danger. Danger.*

He closed the door behind him, clicked the lock into place, and then turned the sign over from open to closed. She gestured for Bramble to hide. Turning slowly back toward her, he smiled and opened his arms. Normally she'd have run straight to him but everything in her body tensed. Something was very wrong. His eyes were flat, black, and cold, like an alligator in the water just waiting for something to swim close.

"January?" She called his name and his body jerked as if he'd been struck.

"Run." The word was torn from his throat.

It was all the warning she got. He lept forward closing the distance between them. She dropped low to the ground and rolled away. The blood, his blood, amplified her strength and dexterity. She got to her feet and headed for the basement. The door was thicker there and it locked. If she got there, it would give her enough time to call for help.

Even as she thought it, she knew she wouldn't make it

without help. Turning quickly, she made a B-line for the herbs. There was a crashing sound behind her but she didn't turn to look. Grabbing the containers of salt and vervain, she swung them in a circular pattern splashing the mixture around her.

"I am part of the light. I am safe within the circle."

She had to believe it. Closing her eyes and sitting in the middle of her makeshift circle she imagined a series of bell jars closing around her, one after another, larger and larger until she had enough room to get to the door.

January hissed in rage but the sound was both inside and outside his body. What had he said about demon possession? They had to have permission or they couldn't really take hold. Why the hell would he give permission for this? She opened her eyes slowly and saw him just outside her circle. He didn't pace or curse. He just stood there.

"January?" she said softly.

"Invite me in," he commanded.

His power tore through her and she watched in horror as she reached down to disturb her circle. Before she could disturb it, she felt Bramble's energy around her undoing the magic. Crying out, she yanked her hand away. January walked around the edge of the circle.

"January?" she said it again, not to whatever held his body, but to his spirit. "Can you hear me?"

He moved directly to the edge of the circle, his face twisted in pain. He began to push against the ward. She closed her eyes. She had to. She knew that he was strong and if he made any progress at all, she would doubt her wards. Only she could damage them. He screamed again but this time in pain.

She opened her eyes and watched the ward begin to singe his flesh. "Stop. You can't get through. You have to stop."

"Open the ward or destroy him. Those are your choices."

The voice. She recognized that voice. Enir.

"Okay. You win. I'll open it." Dropping to her knees she scooped up a handful of the Vervain and salt. January yanked her up to his chest using one arm to lock her to his body and the other to pull her head to the side.

"We have to keep you safe." Their voices were entwined. Enir and January. "We must protect the Veil." That voice sounded unfamiliar and hollow. Phoebe felt January's teeth scrape her neck as they had done so many erotic times before and although her logical self knew she should fight, some part of her recognized that she wanted this. She wanted him. Wrapping her arms around him, she cradled his head gently stroking his hair.

"It's okay. If you have to do it, it's okay."

"No!" January pushed her away from himself falling to the ground as if he were being ripped apart. "I won't."

He writhed in pain. His image flickered from the man she loved to that of a slender young Fey woman, to Enir, but none of the bodies were right. They blurred into the darkness around the edges. The darkness seeped out of January's body like a searching fog. It was looking for her.

She threw the handful of salt and vervain into the sky.

"By earth, by air, by fire, by water. Protect the life of your magical daughter. Conceal me from those who mean me harm From this day to my last, this is my charm."

At first, she thought nothing happened but then the darkness stalled in the air. Everything in the shop shook and vibrated. January lay on the ground as if dead. The dark shadow swung first in one direction and then another but it couldn't find her. It also flowed over and around January as if he too were invisible to it.

It knocked over bottles of herbs and stacks of stones and books trying to find the body it had lost.

Phoebe stayed still and quiet, hardly breathing. Finally, it made a hissing scraping sound and flowed out under the door into the night. The light returned to normal in the shop and Phoebe scrambled to January's side.

"Please be okay." She reached for him but her hand passed through him.

He sat up suddenly and looked towards her. "Phoebe?" he rasped.

She breathed a sigh of relief. "What was that?"

He stood and walked right past her. "Phoebe?"

She walked directly in front of him waving her hands. "I'm right here." She waved her hands in front of his face and then reached out to touch him. He moved away from her looking frantically around the shop.

"Cariad?"

Phoebe stepped back her heart in her throat. This couldn't be right. The darkness was gone. He should be able to see her. He pulled his phone from his pocket and dialed. Her phone rang from her bag. Following the sound behind the counter, he pulled it out.

"No. Please, no." He looked around setting the phone on the counter. "Bramble? Are you here?"

Wherever Bramble was, he didn't answer. January looked at his phone again and then dialed another number. Phoebe walked slowly around him like a ghost. He searched the shop almost as if he knew she was there.

"Alex? It's January. I came to pick Phoebe up from work but she's not here. It looks like someone or something trashed the shop. Call the Recovery Center and talk to James. Then go home and wait for her. I'll check her apartment and see if I can find Bramble. Call me when you get this message."

He hung up the phone with a curse. "Hold on, Cariad. I'm coming."

He opened the shop door and walked into the Samhain moonlight.

Phoebe stood in the midst of the wreckage, lost. The man she'd fallen in love with. The man she would have crossed death to stay beside meant to harm her. It didn't make any sense. She turned the lock on the door after he left knelt down and restored the ward. Behind her, all the smashed and spilled items in the shop made their way back to their bottles and shelves.

A sudden knocking made her jump back. Alex had his face pressed to the glass staring right at her. "Phoebe? Open the door! We have to go before he gets here."

She motioned for Bramble to stay hidden and opened the door. Alex walked straight in past the ward still wearing her pajamas and t-shirt but now carrying a rucksack. He looked at the destruction in the store as it slowly put itself back together again.

"Oh shit. I'm too late. Are you a vampire now?" He took a step back. "Or are you something else?"

Phoebe motioned for Bramble to come to her. He scrambled from underneath a stack of prayer flags and she picked him up from the floor. The kitten purred and purred. "What? No, I'm not a vampire. January-"

Alex pulled the door shut behind him looking over his shoulder. "That's not January. I mean it is January, but it isn't. I don't know what the hell that is but we have to get out of here before it comes back."

Bramble rubbed his fluffy head against her. "Don't cry. Now safe. Bramble here."

She rubbed her face against his. "Thank you for saving me. You were magnificent." Phoebe watched Alex open the rucksack and begin to put candles and other supplies in it.

"We can go to Olivia's. We'll be safe there."

Alex shook his head. "Whatever that is, it is looking for you. If it doesn't find you here or at our house, then it will go to your apartment. I got to your house first. I think I have enough of your things for you to survive until we find a store. We need to get the hell out of here."

Phoebe let the warning wash over her, one hand going automatically to her necklace. "January couldn't see me. Even after the shadow left him, he couldn't see me." She could feel the tears coming and she took a deep breath. Bramble rubbed against her again. "Bramble, see you. I protect."

"Why?" Alex asked placing tarot cards and a handful of pendulums in the bag.

"Spell," Bramble said. "Good spell."

"I asked to be concealed from those who meant me harm."

Alex stopped what he was doing and looked at her. "Listen. I know that looks bad but there's a reason. Something we're not seeing. He was being eaten alive by a ghoul thing, but he told me to take you and hide from him."

"Hide where?"

Alex came forward to set the sack on the counter. "January said if anything happened to him, I should go to Larkshead."

"Maine? Where we know absolutely no one? Why?"

"It's a werewolf Sanctuary. I'm a werewolf."

"We're not."

"But technically we're in the same house now. We count as a pack."

Bramble looked towards the door and then up towards Phoebe. "We go. Take green book."

Alex looked over his shoulder into the darkness. "Whatever you're getting, get it fast. We don't know if that thing is coming back."

Phoebe looked down at Bramble. "Melissa put it some-where. She said to leave it until we knew what it wanted."

"You need. Bramble know. Brindle said. I find." He wiggled out of her arms and jumped down. He began sniffing the floor like a bloodhound. "This way." He trotted towards the storeroom door.

Alex shrugged. "We need all the help we can get. Grab it quick. Get some stuff for warding. I'll let Larkshead know we're coming."

Phoebe walked through the storeroom picking up a large shopping bag and the things she might need to protect them. Salt, obsidian and rose quartz, sage, vervain, yarrow, black chord. She picked up a large green candle and turned it over reading the bottom. Enlightenment. The candle she'd lit when she first came through the Veil. The witch that made these candles was setting up a shop in Lark-shead. A witch setting up a candle shop in a werewolf sanctuary had to be Enlightened. It wasn't much but it gave her hope.

Bramble stopped to look at what she was doing. "Good magic. Witch made. We take." He jumped up onto a high shelf. "Book here."

She placed it and a couple of the other candles into the bag. She dragged the step stool to the shelf Bramble was on. Sure enough, the green book was there. *Magic for Vampires and Other Enlightened Beings*. As soon as she put her hands on it, the need to go back to the circle and wait for January was overwhelming. Bramble flattened his ears and put one paw on the book. Like a switch, the compul-sion was gone, erased as if it had never been there.

Phoebe's mouth dropped open. "How did you do that?"

"Brindle make magic, Bramble take magic." He looked smug. "Magic does not work on Bramble."

244

He'd been saying take and she assumed he was absorbing the magic into his body but that was wrong. Bramble reconfigured the spells to be neutral. That's how he'd destroyed January's ward.

Phoebe laughed. "You are a little genius."

Alex shouted from the top of the stairs, "Phoebe, Bramble! Let's go!"

LARKSHEAD OR DIE

January sat alone on his bed and read Alex's text for the second time trying to decide what to do next. The message simply said:

I've taken Phoebe and Bramble to Larkshead. You are shadow-possessed. Your shadow-self attacked Phoebe at the shop. We can't answer the phone until you're better. You know why. Find Olivia and/or Mira to get help. We will come home when it's safe. Sorry.

Teeth clenched he thought back for the tenth time to being in The Craft Shop alone. At first, all he could clearly remember was going to the door and then being inside amongst the wreckage desperately looking for Phoebe. He'd called and texted both Phoebe and Alex multiple times but until he saw Alex's text, he couldn't imagine why they didn't answer. Now he knew.

A shadow possession was different from another soul possessing you. It amplified the darkest most dangerous and selfish part of the self. It shielded the memory so that the person carrying the shadow curse stayed afraid and confused. If he couldn't find a way to banish it, the shadow curse would consume him. He picked up a piece of hematite. The stone absorbed shadows and dark energy from the mind and body. It wasn't a cure for a shadow curse, but it was a start.

He palmed the smooth cool black-grey stone and closed his eyes allowing it to draw the darkness from him. Like photos under murky water, he saw Phoebe from the doorway of The Craft Shop, the shadow not able to cross the doorway without a direct invitation. She invited him inside. Locking the door behind him, for a moment, his mind was in three places, the real him who wished as he locked the door that she would come join him willingly, a voice, Enir's, that urged him to begin her conversion, and finally the shadow who urged him to kill her.

It was like a horrible dream. Moving toward her, wrenching her to him, forcing her head to the side to have her blood. Then blood filled his mouth drenching his senses in delicious life. The soft feeling of her arms around his neck, pulling him close, accepting him fully. Her love had dislodged the shadow because, in that moment, his biggest desire was to keep her safe, to love her, to destroy anything that threatened her.

With the shadow gone, only Enir's compulsion remained but that compulsion was satisfied. She had consumed his blood and now he had taken hers again, the conversion had begun. His feelings were his own again and he knew, on some level, that he was pleased. Then she disappeared right in front of his eyes. Perhaps she'd tele-ported to protect herself as she'd done in the restaurant. He'd lost her.

The urge to smash his phone, tear apart the bedroom they shared, tear apart the life he'd built for himself here roared through him and the anger had nothing to do with a shadow. She'd been attacked three times while under his protection, twice by himself. He couldn't go near her until he knew why. He dialed Mila clutching the hematite in his hands.

Trees flew past them in a blur of headlights. Her fingers drifted through Bramble's fur as he snoozed in her lap. For the first hour of the journey, he had looked at everything with rapt attention excited to see the world. Now he slept the half sleep of cats occasionally licking Phoebe's hand or giving her a half rumble of a purr. Alex said nothing, just drove January's car at a speed that seemed impossible for anyone to do without having an accident. Her suitcase was in the trunk. Not the one she used to visit her parents but the one she used to leave the country.

Alex stopped at an outdoor center and bought some winter clothes for both of them, hiking boots, lanterns, blankets, and a first aid kit, the things you'd use to go on a long camping trip. They got to the till and the woman checking them out gave Alex a flirty smile.

"Happy Halloween. You have some great gear here. Where are you guys headed?"

"We rented a cabin. Not sure how basic it's going to be."

The cashier looked over their items carefully. "I'd get an axe, a utility knife, two fire lighters, and a small gas stove if I were you. Nothing worse than cold food in a cold cabin."

Alex handed her January's credit card. "Great let's add them in and whatever else you think we need. My wife and I are new at this, aren't we sweetie."

The cashier took the card and set it on top of the till. "That's so sweet. Listen though, don't take it too seriously. If you're miserable, save your receipt and go get a nice hotel room. You can return anything you don't use on your way back."

Alex placed a pair of outdoor pants and a fleece shirt on the counter. "We'll keep that in mind."

. . .

They loaded the car. Phoebe wasn't sure whether she should be offended on January's behalf. "Won't he be able to find us if we use his card?"

Alex pulled the label off two pairs of sunglasses and handed her one. "The real January will. I don't think the thing that is in January will remember to check his accounts."

"Are we really heading to a cabin?"

He sighed dramatically. "It's supposed to be a luxury cabin, but who knows what qualifies as a luxury in Maine." He shut the trunk and they got back into the car.

She sent a text to Olivia, Melissa, and Josh explaining what happened but not where she was going. In a text to her parents, she explained that she was going to visit a couple of potential store locations for the new business. Words of love and support poured back to her, and between them were messages and calls from January.

Are you safe, Cariad? Please. Just let me know you're ok.

She and Alex had agreed that they would send one text back to January. To send more might give the thing inside January an opportunity to manipulate them. Alex sent his text immediately but Phoebe didn't know what to say. In a car fleeing to a werewolf sanctuary, being chased by a shadow that wanted her dead, she didn't feel safe. On top of that, her mind seemed to delight in supplying more and more horrible reasons why January would mean her harm.

He fought the darkness inside him, almost tore himself apart to keep her safe from it, and yet she knew that if he hadn't pushed her away in those last moments, she would have let him finish the conversion. The wards in the shop would have kept her completely safe in the circle, but when the darkness began to push him through the ward, she'd opened the circle because she couldn't bear to see him in pain.

What's more, she didn't teleport. When she'd been attacked at the restaurant, she'd teleported to safety yet when January held her by the throat planning to drink the life from her body, she'd stayed. She'd unwittingly traded her human life for a life of magic and now she really was considering trading that magic for a man she'd only known a couple of months. Why?

"I love him."

Alex leaned forward looking back in the rear-view mirror. "Phoebe, tell me some of that awesome witch power of yours includes the ability to shield."

"Why?"

"Because we are about to have trouble."

Phoebe looked over her shoulder expecting something a little grander than the flash of red and blue lights in the background.

Alex was driving just under the speed of light. On the outskirts of Maine just over the Massachusetts line, that was a capital offense. The superior grin she was sporting as they began to pull over faded when she noticed the markings on the car.

"What the hell is a Boston police car doing this far out?"

Bramble opened his eyes scenting the air. "Woof."

Alex pulled over as far as he could and shut the engine off. His hands were clenched on the wheel. "Listen to me, Phoebe. He's going to try to take me back to Boston. I'm going to get out of the car when he asks. If he transforms, lock the doors, get in the driver's seat, and get out of here. Don't stop until you get to Larkshead."

Bramble got up and stretched walking over to Alex's lap and sitting down. "I protect."

Alex smiled down at the fierce little fluff ball. "Protect Phoebe."

The cop that got out of the car was a hulking man silhouetted by the flashing lights. If anyone looked like they should be able to turn into a werewolf it was him. He marched up to the car with absolute authority but also, a slight limp. Alex rolled down the window and waited.

The cop leaned down looking into the car. His eye was black and his lip was busted. He put his hand on the door to steady himself as he bent down. Bramble stood up on his back legs and placed his paws on the cop's hand. Phoebe leaned forward to grab him but stopped. The cop and the cat stared at each other for a long minute and then Bramble rubbed his head against the man's hand and began to purr. The cop's eyes filled with tears. With a gentleness that bordered on reverence, he stroked Bramble's head. Bramble gave him another rub and then got down and scrambled across the console into Phoebe's lap.

The cop sniffed, dashing the tears from his eyes. "Alex Kimbos. You are a hard man to follow. What's in this car? Rocket fuel?"

Although to Phoebe the words and the expression on the cop's face were friendly, Alex's hands tensed on the wheel. "Saul Baxter, you're a long way from Boston."

"I am." He said the words with wonder looking around as if noticing for the first time how far out of Boston he was. "I'm a long way from Boston. Where are you headed?"

"Larkshead."

Saul looked around again breathing a deep sigh of relief. "Not far enough away, in my opinion. I think I'll go to that New Mexico Sanctuary. Truth or Consequences. Always liked the name."

Alex let go of the wheel, his shoulders relaxed. "What happened to your face?"

Saul frowned tensing up and Bramble purred again. The expression vanished, replaced by a sad haunted smile.

"Marie. She's out of control. The pack is so big, there's

always someone picking a fight with someone else. All I do anymore is fight. I'm tired of fighting."

He looked at Alex and then at Bramble like the words surprised him. Then he smiled at Bramble with a look so tender that it made Phoebe's heart hurt.

"Didn't figure you for a cat person. I always wanted a cat."

Phoebe realized that he hadn't looked at her or spoken to her. His eyes scanned the car again and again, but even though she was leaning forward looking directly at him with Bramble in her lap, he only saw Bramble.

Alex touched his hand gently. "Get one in New Mexico. It will be good for you. I hear Truth or Consequences have a points system for pack rank, you lose rank if you fight. You and whoever you have a beef with have to live together in a one-room ranch house with wine and cheese provided and talk it out."

Saul stood up grinning. "Hope it's beer, not wine. I'm tired of wine. Don't have the stomach for it anymore." He looked around again his smile dimming for a second. "We better get going. Get off the I-95 as soon as you can. She's still looking for you. Good luck."

"You too, Saul."

They waited until the cop turned his lights off and pulled away.

"What did you do to him?" Alex's expression was half amazement, half fear.

"Good woof. Bad blood. Bramble take."

Bad blood. The words moved through Phoebe's mind even as the metallic taste of blood appeared in her mouth. "Is there such a thing as a blood compulsion?"

Alex tapped the satellite navigation system instructing it to avoid the I-95. "For vampires but not for werewolves. We're immune to most magic."

"Most, but not all. And that cop, Saul, was under a spell

until Bramble touched him."

They got back on the road. "Maybe he means Unseelie blood. My mom and Dad are Wild Fey. They told me drinking Unseelie's blood fed the evil inside you."

"Your parents aren't werewolves?"

Alex laughed but the sound was humorless. "I'm a genetic throwback. I've got no natural family pack. It's why Marie thought she could get away with forcing me into her pack. If I had a real family pack, she wouldn't dare."

"Family," Bramble said looking first at Phoebe and then at Alex.

"A familiar, a witch, a vampire, and a werewolf." He smiled. "I'll drink to that."

The red bottle flashed in her mind, the look of the liquid in the glass, the taste of wine laced with blood. "Wine!" Phoebe gasped in surprise.

"Sounds good. Red wine. None of that fruity crap," Alex said glancing in the rear-view mirror.

"No. Saul said he was tired of wine. January gave me wine laced with his blood before the ball. January said the vampire that attacked me at the restaurant was under a blood curse but we were drinking wine there too."

"You think the blood curse is being spread through blood or wine?"

Phoebe looked out the window and shrugged. "I'm not sure. Both. Maybe something in the blood activates the wine? What would be the benefit of drinking Unseelie blood?"

"Nothing. A pack that's constantly fighting is nothing but work for an alpha. You spend all your time rebuilding the bonds that are broken because of the fight."

"If it doesn't benefit Marie, why is she doing it?" She wished she knew more about the Enlightened or that she could see into the future better.

"I don't know but we should alert the Mabon Council."

HOW TO CATCH A DEMON

January stood with Melissa and Olivia watching the security tapes again. His heart cried out in denial as he watched the image of himself chase Phoebe through the shop, force her to open her wards, and then ruthlessly grab her to drink her blood. Melissa hit pause on an image of him on the ground. He expected for Melissa or Olivia to call the Recovery agents right away but instead, they rewound the image and watched again.

"What exactly are you looking for?"

Olivia took the remote from Melissa to move the recording forward frame by frame. "A shadow. Phoebe sent an email and said that you were possessed by a shadow that left your body and couldn't find you again."

Melissa shivered. "I didn't think you could be possessed unless you invited the spirit or the evil inside."

"Not anymore. It used to happen all the time. Shadow possession caused the war that eventually led to the creation of the Seelie and Unseelie Courts. There, right there." Olivia pointed to January's body on the ground but in the frozen image, there were two bodies—one a solid form and one a misty shadow.

"If he was already in me, why couldn't he come back?"

Olivia tapped her lips thoughtfully. "You'd taken Phoebe's blood before you pushed her away. Phoebe's spell hides her from those who mean her harm. Essentially, the magic in her blood shielded you so the shadow couldn't use you to hurt her."

They pushed play again and he watched Phoebe stand in front of him waving her hands but he walked past her. He remembered coming to the door to collect Phoebe for Samhain and to explain to her what happened at the ball. In his memories, he'd opened the door to find Phoebe missing and the shop ransacked. In the video, she tried to make contact with him but he didn't see her. When he left the shop, she stood by the door alone.

"What about here? The shadow is gone. Why can't I see her."

Melissa cleared her throat gently. "That's a good question but I think it's one only you can answer."

Olivia rewound the video to watch it again. "Why didn't you snap her neck?"

They both looked at her in horror.

"Sorry. That came out wrong. What I mean is, you're a vampire. You're easily ten times as strong and as fast as she is. You picked her up, but you bit her rather than snap her neck. Are you sure the shadow told you to kill her?"

January shuddered. "Yes. The shadow said kill her."

"Is that all it said?"

"No. It said something about protecting the Veil."

"That's what you said too! You must keep Phoebe safe and then you must protect the Veil." Melissa wound the video back.

"Yes! You bit her instead of killing her outright. I think you were trying to convert her at first but when the Shadow tried to push you to kill her, something interrupted the action." Olivia paused the video again. He was

255

drinking Phoebe's blood. The shadow was around him but then there was a bulge in his throat. He'd seen that before. At The Sailor's Catch."

"I'm fighting a blood compulsion."

"From who?" Melissa asked trying to see the screen around Olivia.

"There's only one person strong enough to compel me, that's Enir, my maker."

"And Enir wants Phoebe as a vampire, why?"

"She knows I want Phoebe to be a vampire, but I won't turn her without her consent. I told Enir I would follow Phoebe when she died rather than force her."

Melissa snapped her fingers. "Enir doesn't want to lose you. She gives you a command to convert Phoebe. The compulsion has a deadline. Samhain probably. Could be Yule. Vampire companions stand their best chance of surviving if their partner does the blood exchange. January won't do it. Enir compels him so January can't be blamed by the Mabon Council if she dies because Enir ordered it."

January gnashed his teeth. "And Enir can't be blamed because Phoebe is an applicant to The House of Norn." He looked again at the video. "And now I can't see Phoebe."

"Because becoming a vampire harms her in some way," Melissa finished gently.

He'd known it somewhere deep inside that the conversion shouldn't be done but understanding that it would hurt her broke his heart. It was too late to stop it. The blood Enir had forced him to give her would have started the change. That blood, his blood, would now overcome Phoebe's blood because he'd bit her again.

Olivia turned the recording off and put the remote on top of the screen. "We need to talk to James. The real James, not whatever it was that came into the shop the other day."

Melissa shuddered. "Why?"

"He's Unseelie. He might not know who is casting the shadow curse, but he might know how to protect us from it until we can figure out a way to banish it."

"Us?" January asked softly.

Olivia put her hand on his shoulder. It was the first time in their acquaintance together that she'd done so. "We all want Phoebe to be safe and happy. You make her safe and happy. We can help you figure this out."

"How?"

Olivia motioned for them to follow her. "You call that demon, James. We'll make something, an amulet or spell that compels him to tell the whole truth, not the demon version of it."

James was definitely up to something, but he'd given his word he would protect Phoebe. "What if he doesn't know anything?"

"We'll cross that bridge once we figure out how to make it."

Two weeks in a luxury cabin in the middle of 40 acres of woodland would normally have been a dream come true for Phoebe. A full propane tank filled the house with warmth and so did the fire in the little fireplace they took turns tending. There was wood in the woodshed so all they had to do was use their handy dandy axe to chop it into kindling. There was also a washing machine, and a dishwasher, the bath was big enough for a soak, the woods surrounding them led to the ocean, and if one was willing to walk a little further, they could walk right to the heart of Larkshead.

The famous Larkshead Christmas Village seemed to spring up overnight. Phoebe hadn't seen any signs of Emily Rollins or her store, but the Candle-Lit website had been updated yesterday with the announcement of the new permanent location. She decided to wait for Emily to be fully settled in her new location before she visited. What Phoebe didn't see was a single shop that didn't sell items for witchcraft. There was no need for a shop like The Craft Shop here because the whole town was run by witches, werewolves, and goblins.

Phoebe and Bramble practiced magic together every afternoon. Following both the book and the chat room Jerry had given her, she learned to bring her wards closer and push them out. Talk to the wind without channeling it, bless items for fortune and protection, heal vampire wounds, and feed a companion without getting woozy.

It was perfect, all except for a very irritable werewolf who paced the house glued to his phone and the fact that every thought she had seemed to be connected to January. It wasn't just that she missed him, it was like he'd been taken from her. She, in turn, felt angry and depressed that she couldn't just call him or put her hiking shoes on and enjoy where she was.

He continued to text her, sending her messages about his day, sharing photos, telling her about the hunt for Enir, and telling her he loved her.

Her parents were pleased that she was getting some time off and were more than a little presumptuous about Alex. So presumptuous in fact that she sent them a couple of photos of herself and January just to shut them up. She should have known better. When the questions poured in from both sides, she did what any good sister would, she also told them about Jerry.

Jerry and Josh were as in love with Brindle as they were with each other. Their social media was filled with photos of her snoozing, playing, eating, and going to work with Jerry. Bramble didn't like to be photographed. He tolerated three photos a week, one of which was allowed to be a selfie with Phoebe. Because she and January were friends online, she was careful about which photos she posted. Avoiding landmarks was pretty easy in the middle of the forest and sharing just a little bit with him made her feel less alone.

Alex opened and closed the refrigerator for the 5th time before Phoebe gave in and asked. "What are you looking for?"

"I don't know. Answers? A way out. Falafel."

She grinned. "If you find any of those things, especially falafel. Let me know."

He walked over to the oversized couch and threw himself down. "Let's go to Larkshead tonight and get some. I bet that fancy place, The Mermaid's Song has it."

"How are we going to pay for it? We've been shopping all over the countryside to make sure our paper trail doesn't lead to our front door."

Alex threw his arm over his face in exasperation. "Maybe it should."

She looked over at him to see if he was kidding. He wasn't.

"If you have a plan, I'm all ears."

"The alpha here. She's fair. She let us come here without any questions. I went to see her to say thanks. She assigned me a guide. A werewolf guide. I'm supposed to meet her tomorrow night."

Phoebe laughed throwing one of the sofa pillows at him. It hit him square in the stomach. "So, falafel is a bribe so you can go out tomorrow without me and play wolf?"

He winged the pillow back at her so fast she didn't have time to do anything but shriek as it hit her in the chest. "You're learning to witch. I'm going to learn to wolf. Then, when January gets here, we are going to cure him of whatever that thing is and get back to our regular lives, whatever that looks like."

"Deal," she laughed, hugging the pillow to her chest.

"I also think we should call him. Bramble can help us. You aren't eating, he's not sleeping. You guys are not doing well apart."

"I am eating. How do you know he's not sleeping?"

Alex looked at his phone and shrugged.

"You're texting him! You said one text."

"I'm not. I just asked Rosalind to keep an eye on him. He's spending a lot of time with Melissa and Olivia, out all hours of the day and night, trying to find Enir so you can come home."

Phoebe tilted her head. "You mean so we can come home."

Alex shrugged. "I don't think I'm going back. The only reason I was there in the first place was to find out how to be myself so I could go back home to my family. Marie won't let anyone teach me. I tried things with January, but..."

"He's a vampire. He can't wolf."

"That about covers it."

Bramble bounced into the room with his tail all fluffed up. "Storm coming."

Alex stood up. "I'll go get some wood, then drive down to The Last Stop and get some food. Call January. Tell him we're okay."

Phoebe barely heard the door click closed behind him before she hit dial.

January was waiting in the lobby of The Sailor's Catch for Mila to gather her things before they left for the hunt. James refused his calls and ran from him when their paths crossed close to The Craft Shop. Finn, from The Boston Recovery Center, told Olivia he'd been acting strange since he returned from New Mexico. Taking sudden trips and not reporting in. James was not only the agent assigned to monitor the Unguided witches in the area but also the agent in charge of letting Phoebe, Olivia, Melissa, and himself know about the Mabon Council meeting. By all accounts, James was looking for a way to get his hands on Phoebe.

The phone rang twice, and he put it to his ear, expecting Olivia or Melissa to tell him something about the charm they were creating. January traded a great many favors for information about shadow possession. Sent a request to Isla, the neutral servant of the Unseelie Queen, but without success. He was tired. He really needed to find his life mate, take her to bed, and sleep for a week.

"Hello?"

"January."

Her voice poured over him like water soaking the parched edges of a desert. He closed his eyes and let her voice wash over him. "Cariad?"

"I'm here." A deep shaky breath rumbled over the line as if she, too, were trying not to cry.

"I'm sorry, Cariad. I'm so sorry. I promised to take care of you-" he moved to the deck where they had shared their first meal together.

"Shhh. It's okay. You couldn't help it."

"You didn't answer me." It hurt that he'd begged her to speak to him, and she hadn't.

"Alex said you told us to hide from you. We weren't sure if it was safe."

He breathed deeply, the relief almost choking him. She wasn't angry or afraid of him. They were safe. They'd followed his instructions. "You did the right thing. I'm still not sure you're safe with me."

"The shadow is still there?"

She sounded worried.

"No. It left after I attacked you."

"Then why wouldn't I be safe?"

"Enir. She's put a compulsion on me to turn you into a vampire. Only she can lift it, and I can't find her." There was a long pause, so long that he wondered if she was still there.

"She can lift it, or we can let it happen."

He felt the breath knocked out of his lungs. "You don't have to."

"I know I don't. I want to. I want you. I'm in one of the most beautiful places in the world, and all I can do is look out the windows and wish you were here. Bramble and I are miserable without you. We can work on a spell to remove the compulsion."

"I want that. I want that more than I can tell you. There's only one problem."

"What?"

"Turn your camera on." He waited, hoping against hope that what he felt was wrong. Surely, if he wanted her to be a vampire and she wanted it too, then her spell would lift. She turned the camera on, and he was looking almost straight up Bramble's nose, but there was no sign of Phoebe.

"I still can't see you."

He heard her sniffle. Bramble rubbed against an invisible figure with a rough purr.

"Your spell shields you from people who mean you harm. That means that what I want from you is in my best interest and not yours."

She heaved a big sigh and then another. "Okay."

But she didn't sound okay. January wanted to crush Enir into tiny pieces to create this mess.

"Listen to me, Cariad. I am hunting for us; I am fighting for us. When this is all over, I am not going to be parted from you ever again. Family dinners, windswept rituals, bowling, whatever it takes to be close to you. You think Bramble's got it bad?"

She sniffed again, but this time, she laughed as well. "Bowling?"

He cradled the phone, wishing he could leave right now and go get her. "I hate bowling, but for you, even the borrowed shoes would be worth it."

This time, a real laugh.

"I love you too."

Her words wrapped around him, stealing his breath. Bramble beamed up at her, and he wished more than anything that he was there too. He could see the expression on her face. He felt like he'd waited a lifetime to hear her say those words. "I love you. Stay safe for me. You and Bramble cook up a spell to untangle this mess."

Mila came out onto the deck dressed in black *shinobi shozoku* with a small pack over her shoulder. She smiled at the screen and inclined her head.

"It's nice to see you again, Phoebe. I'm sorry to interrupt, but January and I have to go." She put a hand on January's arm. "James is at The Craft Shop."

"Be safe," she said softly. "The quicker we fix this, the quicker we can fix us."

January put the phone in his pocket and began to head for the car, but Mila stopped him. "You're not the only one to retain a gift when you were converted. Allow me." She placed a hand on his arm, and suddenly, he was filled with light. It burned him everywhere, inside and out. He felt himself vanish into the light, and suddenly, he was connected to everything: past, present, and future.

He understood exactly how it would need to happen. Five witches, one of them Phoebe. They called Earth, Air, Fire, Water, and spirit—the truth speaker. But there was more. It wasn't just these witches. It was witches across the world, all in their own circles, all calling for the same thing at the same time. They all lit green jar candles at the same time. Someone, a woman with short black hair, screamed and howled.

Then he was standing at the door of The Craft Shop with Mila at his side. He fell to his knees, and she sank down beside him. "Don't throw up."

She placed her hand in the middle of his chest and then on the ground, calming the energy that raced along his skin. He drew in a deep breath, then another. Finally, the shop came into focus, and he could stand. Mila pushed the door, but it was locked. She knocked, and Melissa's face peeked out. She looked surprised and relieved to see him.

"Come in. We have him downstairs."

They followed her into the shop and then down into the storeroom. James stood in the middle of a large black sigil drawn on the floor, surrounded by candles of every shape and size. Olivia was to the left, her eyes closed, softly chanting. James caught sight of January and looked relieved.

"Thank the Goddess, you're here."

January came to the edge of the circle. "I'm not going to let you out of there."

"I don't want out. I'm not in control of myself. She's making me hunt the Unguided witches. She wants Phoebe and a witch called Emily Rollins and something called the Truth Speaker." James sank down slowly to the floor, making every effort to keep all of his limbs and wings inside the circle.

"Who wants the Truth Speaker? Who is using shadow curses? Mila asked, stepping forward.

"Unseelie." The word was torn from his mouth. "Queen."

"Why?"

James thought about it quietly, and January could see for the first time how tired he was. "The Veil is a curse on humans. Punishment because they persecuted the Enlightened. She still wants revenge. She wants them to be divided, afraid, and vulnerable."

Mila took off her pack and put it on the floor between her feet. "She will kill you for what you've just said."

"She's already killed me," James said, and to January, he sounded relieved. "She's the one that sent the shadow curse."

"Then you won't mind if I try to help." Mila pulled out the large green bottle that January had trapped the other shadow in and tossed it to James. The bottle shook in his hand, and then a shadow seeped out of it like a dark genie. It was too weak to take a form, but it flowed in and around James, looking for a way inside. James screamed in pain.

"What are you doing?" January shouted.

"Two shadows can't live in the same person at the same time. They will kill one another in order to stay in charge of your friend's body. When they are both outside of him, we need to pull him from the circle without disturbing the sigil.

The outside shadow began to force its way up James's nose. He gagged but held himself rigidly still. His skin bulged, and the lights in the room flickered. Melissa turned her back on the ward so that she wouldn't damage it with her doubt. Olivia also continued her closed-eyed chant.

Then everything was quiet. Like a large force had closed off their ears so that they could hear nothing. James threw back his head, and from his mouth emerged two shadows. They writhed like smoke around one another, floating high over his head.

Mila moved like lightning, coming to the edge of the circle to pull him out, and he scrambled forward to meet her, but rather than fighting, the shadows blinked, one hovering around him like smoke and the other stronger one plunged into him again. His eyes flashed black and then gold.

"Don't break the circle!" Olivia cried, but it was too late. James, who was not James, put the bottle Mila had thrown on the ground and rolled it towards the jar candle representing fire. It tipped the candle just enough for the wax to put the flame out. James bowed his head like a magician, folded his wings around himself, and disappeared. The other shadow followed him.

"Shit." January walked over to the candle and picked it up. A wildness moved inside him like he'd seldom felt before. He looked at it more closely. The green jar candle was exactly the same as the one in his vision. It was homemade in a beautiful, intricately carved holder. He turned it over gently, reading the label. It said *Candle-Lit: Enlightenment.*

"Where does this candle come from?"

Melissa looked over his shoulder. "Candle-lit. A witch called Emily Rollins makes them. She's setting up a new shop in Larkshead."

"Are there others?"

Mila rolled her eyes and placed her hand on her hip. "We've just lost a demon and two shadow curses. This is not the time to shop."

Melissa moved to the corner of the store and brought two other candles to him. Although equally beautiful, they held none of the power the green one did. He scanned the room carefully.

"Phoebe said she was taking stock down here when she found the book. Was she burning this candle?"

Melissa thought hard but shook her head. "I'm not sure. I think so."

"I need to get to Larkshead and find this witch, Emily."

"Why?"

"I think she's the one that Awakened Phoebe. I think

she might be responsible for the unsanctioned Awakenings here in Boston."

Two days later, January was in Larkshead waiting for a werewolf called Noah Hernandez. His search for Emily Rollins revealed not only her location but the fact that her werewolf life-mate was hunting Phoebe. He was leaning against a wall in the early evening sun a few stores down from The Ace of Cups, the store that sold the candles to Phoebe's shop. He watched a golden-haired witch called Emily Rollins stock shelves.

She wasn't just a witch, though. January knew an angel when he saw one, but that wasn't quite right either. On the edges of her movements, he spotted something else. Whatever else she was, Emily Rollins carried Unseelie's blood. She laughed with colleagues, wrapped candles in paper and bags for Christmas, and when one of the less human-shaped Enlightened came up to her, she would stare for just a few more seconds than was necessary. Then, her smile would come to her lips as if she saw nothing unusual.

Her reactions were puzzling. If she was pretending to be Unenlightened, her slight acknowledgment of each of the Enlightened made no sense. If she was Unenlightened, her determination to ignore what she was clearly seeing would take an incredible amount of willpower. The only conclusion he could make was that Emily Rollins had to be one of the newly Enlightened, like Phoebe.

The werewolf in question came around the corner. He wasn't as large as some werewolves January had seen, but there was power in him. A quickness in his movements that spoke of Fey's blood. He was handsome, clean-cut, rugged, and clearly ready for a fight. Approaching January with caution, they both watched daylight tangle through the witch's disheveled hair. She hulked a box onto her hip, stumbling back under the weight, and he heard her laugh at something the small sea wolf said to her.

Noah followed January's gaze; his face was the picture of determination to keep his newly bonded life-mate safe.

"Do you know what it's like to lose a wife?" January asked the question, bringing the man's deepest fear to light. He needed Noah to understand what was at risk for both of them. "I was born in a time where my word was God's, and yet nothing I could promise, nothing I could do, could save my first wife." He looked Noah straight in the eye and then looked back at the witch. She looked towards them with a frown, sensing her mate's distress.

"If you touch her-"

"Spare me your threats. If I lose Phoebe, then I will seek the death you promise in the quickest way I can find it. That woman," he indicated to Emily with a flick of his chin, "will never see her death coming. When I have drained the life out of your mate, and you hold her for the last time against your body, knowing there is no way to get her back, then you may tell me how to proceed with mine. Until then, wolf, stay away from Phoebe."

He pushed away from the wall, but Noah grabbed his shoulder. "Phoebe has a right to know the truth about the choice she's making."

January shrugged Noah's hand off and straightened his jacket. "And have you given your own life-mate that choice? Did you lay all her options out in front of her or only the ones that led back to you?"

"Emily is Unenlightened."

It could be true, but a slight quiver in Noah's voice said he wasn't sure. "If you believe that, then she is a more talented liar then I gave her credit for."

Noah clenched his fists. January braced himself. Newly bonded werewolves were almost as protective as vampires. Almost.

"What are you talking about?"

January leaned forward, remembering Phoebe's fear in the circle. The warded book of witchcraft for vampires, the candle marked Enlightenment that happened to arrive on Lammas, and even the shadow-cursed souls all seemed connected to a single magic wielder. James said it was the Unseelie Queen, but she was too old and too powerful to need to be subtle. If she'd wanted himself or Phoebe dead, they would be. That meant it had to be someone who had a reason to be afraid of him.

"Every time an Enlightened person stands in front of her, she freezes for a split second. If you are looking for the first Unguided in your area, she's been right in front of you the whole time. But she doesn't come from this area, does she? She moves around, sells candles worldwide tainted with a single magical suggestion."

"Emily isn't that kind of witch. She would never put another person in danger."

"Wouldn't she? Can you prove it to the National Recovery Unit? To Carl Wedgewood? Phoebe says she read a spell from a book in her Boston shop and popped through the Veil all on her own, but I bet if you checked your life-mate's sales lists, one of the shops listed would be The Craft Shop. The shop that Phoebe works in."

It made perfect sense, but January knew there was something missing, something he was overlooked because he was too close to the situation.

"Then how do you know it's not Phoebe who taints and sells the candles?"

"Because it isn't all of the candles that are tainted. Just one type. I bet you already suspect what it's called."

Noah shook his head, but January could see the doubt forming in the young werewolf's eyes. He looked back at his life-mate. "You're wrong."

"Am I? Then, allow James to ask her about her candle

sales. For that matter, let him ask her about the weather. If she doesn't react, I'm wrong, and she is innocent. If I'm right, your life-mate has method and opportunity. It won't take a Recovery Unit long to discover her motives."

The werewolf bared his teeth, his fists clenching. Unlike Alex, he had complete control of his form.

"James is no longer welcome in this territory. He's dangerous, especially for Phoebe. You can't trust him."

January frowned. Did the wolf know about the shadow curse? "What did you hear about James?"

"That he's Unseelie and that he's in love with you. But you knew that already, didn't you? Did you know that when you asked him to swear to protect Phoebe?"

It wasn't news, exactly. James made it clear that he'd welcome January back into his life, but he believed they'd passed the point of actual desire. "I knew he loved me once but was no longer in love with me. That was why he offered to protect Phoebe-"

Noah shook his head. "He will kill her if he finds her. He is killing Unguided witches."

January pushed away from the wolf and walked away. James himself had told them he'd been assigned to track the Unguided witches, but was he killing them? It was possible. He felt sick. Noah jogged after him.

"I don't want to hurt Phoebe or take her from you. Please. I just want her to talk to my sister, Selene."

January spun around so fast that Noah almost ran straight into him. Only his Fey reflexes kept them apart. "Why?"

"Because Selene oversees tracking of the outbreaks in this area. She might be able to prove that neither Phoebe nor Emily is the source."

Noah looked back at Emily, but he didn't sound sure. Proving someone's innocence was a lot harder than proving someone's guilt. January, of all people, knew the truth of that statement. Emily Rollins might really be as angelic as she looked, but he doubted it.

"But she might also prove that they are the source." January smiled, showing Noah his fangs. It was a warning. "No one ever believes that they're a villain in the story."

Noah flinched.

"Now you see my problem," January said, trying to coax a little understanding from Noah.

Surely, he understood that if Emily or Phoebe were connected to even one unsanctioned Awakening, the consequences were unthinkable.

"Phoebe was through the Veil before she read her incantation. Whether or not she's responsible for the Boston outbreak, I won't allow her to be punished for it."

It was the truth. He tried to appeal to the werewolf the best way he knew how—a bargain.

"While my life-mate lives an uneventful life, you and Emily have nothing to fear from me. I expect the same courtesy. In the meantime, if I were you, I'd have a very serious talk with Emily Rollins."

With his position made clear, he bowed to the werewolf respectfully and began to make his way home.

THE WITCH'S LADDER

Alex's daily runs were getting longer and longer. So long, Phoebe sometimes worried he wasn't coming back and still, his energy was edgy. His form would waver while they cooked or sometimes when they watched television. Closing his eyes and clamping his teeth, he would try desperately to hold his human shape. Yet she knew that on his runs he tried to take his werewolf shape on purpose and nothing happened.

Phoebe sat with Bramble in a circle of Earth, Air, Fire, and Water. The air was thick with the smell of evergreen and mulled wine. In the background, instrumental Christmas music hummed from the smart speakers while Alex looked out at the newly fallen snow. He was dressed to impress. The meeting tonight between himself and Selene, his new guide, had been the subject of every conversation they'd had recently. He'd talked himself into and out of going so many times that Phoebe was half tempted to go on his behalf. Now he simply waited.

She touched the sweet grass and sage to the green candle in the middle of the circle. She moved the smoking herbs in a slow circle three times until the rings settled around both her and Bramble. From a small pouch in the middle of the circle, she sprinkled a few pinches of rosemary into one of the candles. Bramble picked up a black chord with nine knots, a witch's ladder, and brought it to her. The edges of the chord dangled and dragged beside him. He managed to look both adorable and dignified. Dropping the black-knotted chord into her hand, he returned to the opposite side of the circle and tucked his long fluffy tale around him.

Phoebe felt Air, her element, moving over her skin, dancing through the candles to make them flicker, moving the smoke in ever-widening circles. She took a deep breath and touched the silver oak leaf on her neck.

"Unknown, unseen, though they be. They shall be revealed to me. All the elements, you I ask. Let our enemy be unmasked."

She held the chord up to the candlelight holding in her mind the idea of the situation untangling itself. Her, January, and Bramble re-united. Alex was happy as both a wolf and a human. All of them are safe and happy. The shadow was exposed to light. She began untying the knots.

"By knot of one, the spell's begun. By knot of two, it cometh true. By knot of three, so shall it be. By knot of four, it is strengthened more. By knot of five, so may it thrive. By knot of six, all problems are fixed. By knot of seven, by hands of heaven. By knot of eight, by hands of Fate. By knot of nine, the thing is mine. By Air and Earth. Water and Fire. Re-unite us with our heart's desire."

Phoebe smoothed the chord and placed it in front of her. The candles flickered again more forcefully now as Phoebe's element collected the blessing of each element. It fluttered Bramble's hair and she could feel the pressure moving around her. She stood and walked carefully to the front door with Bramble on her heels to release the spell into the world. The air danced over her skin and as she opened the door to step out into the fresh snow, she repeated the spell for the last time adding: As I will it, so shall it be.

The air fluttered around her kicking up snow as it dashed down the stairs and into the darkness. She stepped over Bramble to get back into the house. He sat on the doorstep, his body tense, his tail swishing.

"Danger," he said staring out into the darkness.

The wind whipped back to her. *Danger Danger Danger.* She squinted into the darkness and saw a tall figure coming towards the cabin. For a moment she hoped that it was January but Bramble's low growl told her otherwise. Alex was suddenly beside her with his fists clenched.

From the snow emerged the demon, James. Phoebe waited quietly. Her spell was in place. If James meant her harm, he wouldn't be able to see her. As soon as he came into the circle of the front porch light, he lifted his head and smiled at her.

"Phoebe! Alex!" Thank the Goddess I've found you."

She stepped back into the house and James's eyes followed her. She wanted to believe that he meant her no harm but the wind murmured warnings.

"It's okay," she murmured but neither Alex nor Bramble looked convinced.

He stood at the threshold a moment flapping his wings to dislodge the snow. "Can I come inside?"

Alex shoved his hands in his pockets and stepped out of the doorway. "Come on inside." Phoebe picked Bramble up and headed to the living room. James stepped through the doorway and followed her. They settled down on the couches, James on one side and then on the other.

"How did you find us?" Alex asked the expression on his face clearly suspicious.

"I got an alert from the Recovery Center," James said

folding himself into the seat. "January asked me to keep an eye on you because he couldn't. It's taken me 3 weeks to locate you. In fact, if Alex hadn't visited the Alpha in this territory and she hadn't assigned him a guide, I would have given up."

"When did January ask?"

"Just after Phoebe was first attacked at the restaurant. He wanted me to do some digging around." James shifted forward and then back again trying to get comfortable.

But he didn't sound sure. He rubbed the sides of his head.

"I've had a splitting headache since I got here. I don't think the fresh air agrees with me."

He laughed and Alex stood up. "I'll get you something for it. Can you take Aspirin?"

"I'd rather take whiskey and a rest."

Alex grinned. "We have that too. Warm up and then tell us what's going on."

He left the room to fetch a whiskey. James's gaze followed Alex out the door and then came back to Phoebe.

"What is going on…" James rolled the phrase in his mouth like he'd never heard the question before. His wings fluttered and he rubbed his temples again. Bramble hunkered down looking up at Phoebe with a frown. "The Unseelie are killing newly Awakened witches. Witches are waking up all over the place for no reason. I'm having trouble keeping up." The voice that came from James's mouth seemed to split in two. The sound made all of the hair on Phoebe's arms stand up.

Alex returned with the whiskey but Phoebe motioned for him to stay back.

"You're having trouble keeping up with the newly Awakened witches or you're having trouble killing them?" She stood slowly and put Bramble down on the couch. James looked up but his gaze followed Bramble, not her.

"Yes," James said but this time the double voice sounded amused.

"James?" Alex said softly moving forward to hand him the whiskey. "When did you pick up the shadow?"

James took the whiskey, licked his lips, and then slung it down. He shivered and the power coming off him made the lights in the house blink. Phoebe motioned Bramble to get clear.

"About a month. It's getting stronger." He handed the glass back to Alex. "She's here. I can't see her, but I can smell her. That is, I can smell his blood in her veins."

He looked straight at her, his eyes turning from gold to fathomless black. He lunged forward covering the distance between himself in Phoebe in one move. Grabbing a hold of her shirt and then her arms, he pulled her forward until he had both. "I swore I'd protect his life-mate. It should have been me. I gave my word." His eyes shut and his hands closed like vices on her arms. "I must protect the Veil."

He was burning her, and although there was no evidence of fire, the places he touched her felt like they were burning. Phoebe screamed in surprise and Alex leapt forward. The demon shrugged him off like he was batting away a fly.

"You can't unravel the curse. The Unseelie won't let you."

Phoebe wanted to teleport but she didn't want to leave Bramble and Alex. "James. I don't know what you're talking about!"

"Emily Rollins. You're working with her to bring down the veil. The candles. I can prove it." He forced her to her knees and the feeling of fire flared down her arms. She screamed in pain. Then, without warning, the burning stopped. She could feel Bramble against her thigh. The cat growled low and fierce stepping forward to slice the demon across the shins with his little claws. James kicked at the cat but Phoebe pushed herself towards him pushing him off balance and catching the full brunt of the kick.

"Run, Bramble! Hide," Phoebe cried.

"Protect," Bramble growled coming forward again. Before he could get there Alex had an arm wrapped around James's throat squeezing for all he was worth.

"Phoebe," he yelled and she felt herself dissolving. Just as her body disappeared, she saw Bramble run into her room.

January slid his phone in his pocket checking the small hotel room for anything he might have forgotten. The Mermaid's Song offered a cozy little room for a good price. It was close enough to keep an eye on Emily Rollins and her life-mate, Noah Hernandez. Noah's warning about James scared him.

He didn't quite trust himself yet but he trusted himself more than he now trusted James. For better or for worse, he knew it was time to find Phoebe and Alex and bring them home. With the same reverence he'd had the first time he'd asked for a companion, he begged the world to give him a second chance.

A flash of golden light in the room surprised him but not as much as seeing Phoebe huddled in a ball on the floor. For a moment, he was so stunned he couldn't move. Rushing to her side, he put his hands on her shoulders to see if she was hurt. She screamed fighting blindly against his touch.

"Phoebe, it's me. It's January."

She turned and looked up, her eyes wild and full of tears. Recognition took her only moments and then she threw her arms around him burying her face in his throat. He knelt beside her wrapping her in his arms and murmuring soothing sounds. The feeling of her warm and alive in his arms, her scent washing through his lungs, he held her tight needing to just know she was real.

She pushed back, her hands moving over his face and hair, her eyes searching his as if she also couldn't believe he was real. "January? Can you see me?"

"I see you, Cariad." He brushed her fiery hair from her eyes and kissed her and then just rested his forehead against hers.

She pushed away gently. "James. He's attacking Alex and Bramble. We have to go now."

January stood helping Phoebe to her feet. "Can you teleport us both?"

She shook her head. "I'm not even sure how I got here. I can't control it."

He hugged her again. "It's okay. We'll drive. My car is downstairs, we're already in Larkshead."

They ran, hand in hand downstairs. He let go of her long enough for them both to get in the car but even that separation felt like too much for him. He put one hand on her thigh and followed her instructions to the cabin. The drive took a little over 20 minutes and as the snow-heavy trees flew past them January broke every speed and traffic law ever invented. When they slid into the cabin driveway, the house was dark and the snow had already begun to erase what looked like the footprints of two people and at least two werewolves.

January handed Phoebe his coat from the backseat. "We don't know who is here and who isn't. Let's go slow and quiet."

He opened the car door and walked to the front of the car. Phoebe came to his side putting her hand in his. He could see her. The desire to turn her into a vampire was still there, but it was a soft teasing suggestion rather than a compulsion. They moved forward together scanning the porch and the woods for any sign of movement but the forest was eerily quiet.

On the porch, January motioned for her to stay behind him as he inched the door open. The light in the kitchen was still on. The fire crackled in the fireplace and the couch and one of the side tables were knocked over. Other than that, everything appeared to be quiet.

"Bramble?" Phoebe came around January and into the front room. "Bramble baby, where are you?"

From a bedroom door, January caught sight of Bramble peeking into the living room with his belly close to the floor. When he saw Phoebe his ears perked up and he came into the room. But not all the way in. He had one wary eye in January. Phoebe let go of his hand rushing forward to scoop Bramble up and cradle him close.

She kissed the top of his head again and again. "Are you okay? My poor sweet boy. Where's Alex and the demon?"

Bramble bumped his head against hers and turned a questioning look to January. "Safe?"

January felt ashamed. Bramble had never been afraid of him before. "I'm not going to hurt her or you. The shadow is gone. I'm not sure about the compulsion, but if I feel even the slightest impulse, I will leave immediately."

Bramble twitched his whiskers back and forth. "Demon hurt. Woofs come. Scare demon. Take Alex. Alex…" he trailed off trying to find the right word but when he couldn't he placed his forehead against Phoebe's. She gasped and then cradled him close.

"What's happening?" January asked, stepping forward.

"He's sharing what he saw. He doesn't know the words. It's incredible. It's like seeing through his eyes. Alex is between forms. Wavering. Two werewolfs, one male and one female. They are helping Alex out the door."

January moved slowly towards them putting his arms around both of them. His family. They would go get Alex.

Everything was right as long as he had them. "They will take him to the local Recovery Center until he can control the shift. We'll find out where they've taken him."

Bramble stopped what he was doing and placed a paw on January's hand.

"Bramble take."

A jolt of power went through him and the last of the shadows and suggestions was shaken from his mind. He saw Enir. heard her order him to bring Phoebe across by Samhain. It was only now on the other side of Thanksgiving drawing towards Yule. The compulsion was still there but it was only a faint echo in his mind. The closer they got to Samhain, the more the order would affect him. Breathing a deep sigh of relief, he gently stroked Bramble's little ears.

"You are a gift beyond compare, a magnificent one."

"Sleep now," Bramble said with a yawn so big his whiskers shook. January realized that he was tired beyond anything he'd felt. They were safe for now. The Recovery Center would make sure that Alex was cared for, Phoebe and Bramble were where he could protect them, and they could protect him. Enir's suggestion would wait until they could find her.

Phoebe looked at him with a soft sweet smile. "I'll reinstate the ward so James can't come back."

"I'll text Olivia, Mila, Melissa, and Alex and let them know we are together and safe."

They moved together, picking up the signs of scuffle, and placing the wards back where they belonged. January rebuilt the fire and tucked Bramble into a cocoon of blankets. They shared frequent looks and touches, each moving through their tasks with an awareness that when the tasks were done, they would finally be able to hold each other. Looking at her he suddenly wondered if she would come to him. He had broken her trust.

She moved with confidence but she was thinner and paler than he'd ever seen her before. When he offered to wait for her so she could eat, she cast a frowning look at the kitchen and shook her head. His heart felt like it was breaking. Whether she wanted it or not, the conversion had begun. He would need to encourage her to take his blood tonight so that she could begin healing. Mila made sure they were both well-fed in case he encountered James on his own. She turned the lock on the door and a flash of purple light surrounded the property. The ward was complete.

He could wait no longer.

"I want to take you to bed, Phoebe. If you need-" he started to apologize, to tell her he'd wait to regain her trust but she gave him a soft sexy smile.

"I'm ready." She held her hand out to him.

Moving towards her because he felt powerless to do anything else, he picked her up and carried her towards the bedroom. She wrapped her arms around his neck and lay her head on his shoulder. The bed was smaller than his, covered with a patchwork quilt. He pulled back the blankets and lay her in the middle of the bed undressing himself and then her slowly. Rather than beginning a sensual assault, he lay down facing her and pulled the quilt over both of them.

She gave him a confused look. "You don't want to make love?"

"I always want to make love to you, but I've discovered in your long absence that unless you're with me, I don't sleep."

"Alex said you weren't sleeping." She caressed his face studying him like she'd done the first time she'd seen him, like he was something magical.

"Tell me you love me." The request felt like it was torn from his chest. "I couldn't see your face the first time you said it. I want to see you say it now and remember this as our first time."

She placed her cheek in his palm. "I love you."

He brushed her curls out of her face and kissed her passionately then pressed his forehead against hers. "You will never disappear from my side again. Promise me, Cariad."

"You've called me that before. What does Cariad mean?"

He gave her a gentle charming smile. "In my mother tongue, it means love."

She pushed back from him to look him in the eye. "How do I say I love you back?"

He sighed pulling one of her red curls hard. "It's too many gentle syllables for your barbarian tongue." She gasped in outrage and he laughed. "But you can try and convince me to teach you."

Her grin was positively devilish. "Can you be bribed?"

"Always."

AUGUSTA RECOVERY CENTER

Phoebe opened her eyes in the late afternoon sun being slowly crushed by the weight of love. Well, by the weight of January and Bramble who were both laying mostly on top of her. Her body was pleasantly sore from lovemaking, her arm was asleep because January was laying on it with a leg thrown across her, Bramble was close enough to breathe her breath directly from her nostrils, she needed to pee, and she was starving.

Even though comfort was easily within her grasp, she didn't want to wake them. In the quiet, she could make-believe they were on vacation somewhere with nothing else to do today but enjoy each other. Could they just take a day off? No shadows, no threats, no fear. Maybe they could take a walk in the woods or attend the Christmas Tree lighting taking place tomorrow. What would a normal day in their life together look like?

January's phone buzzed from the bedside table, and he picked up his head to glare at it over his shoulder. Bramble was using January's head to stay balanced on her chest and without it, he rolled straight off her onto the bed. Landing with a thump he rolled onto his belly surprised. January moved away groping blindly for the phone and put it to his ear. She used the moment to give Bramble a sympathetic pat and excuse herself to the bathroom.

Coming back into the room she saw that January was gathering their clothes, his expression grim.

"What's happened?"

"That was Mila. Unofficially the Mabon Council is building a case to prove that I am responsible for your Awakening. Olivia and Melissa looked for the book after you left and couldn't find it. Without it, I am the only obvious link."

She crossed the room to him reaching out to hug him. "No worries. Bramble and I have the book. We'll take it down and they can do their thing and see the last spell cast with it was my spell."

He kissed her forehead holding her close. "We'll have to leave immediately if we want to see Alex before we head home."

"Okay." She sighed looking around at the little cabin room that had become almost a home for her.

He ran his finger along her jaw. "We will straighten our affairs with the Mabon Council in Boston and be back the day after tomorrow."

Staying here would be so easy but her real life wouldn't wait for her any longer. "I would love to, but I have an apartment and a job that I've been away from for almost a month."

He placed his chin on the top of her head. "Then they won't mind if we take another week. I took the liberty of buying your apartment while you were gone and cleaning out your fridge. Your plants are with your brother until you get back and Olivia is discovering just what her life is going to look like when you finally get your own store."

"You bought my apartment?" She stepped out of his embrace not sure if she was pleased or disturbed.

He leaned down to scoop her bra up off the floor and hand it to her. "I drove you from your home and work. The least I could do was make sure your life was there when you got back."

She tried to hold back her laugh, she really did, but the ridiculousness of that statement was too much. Dashing away the tears in her eyes she tried and failed to shrug on her bra.

"Why is that funny?" Brows together he picked his underwear and jeans up off the floor and put them on.

She heaved a breath and then another. "My life hasn't been in that apartment since the moment I appeared in your circle."

Now he looked really worried.

"We can spend more time at your place if you want?"

She leaned forward and kissed him and then continued to dress. "It wouldn't make a difference. I did a little study on vampire culture while you were away." She pulled her oak leaf necklace out from under her top and ran her fingers through her hair. "Companions live in the same house for the first couple of centuries."

A range of expressions crossed his face in quick succession. Confusion, wonder, and then hope. "They do."

She walked straight up to him running her hands over his bare chest. "Are we not companions now?"

"We are." He caught her hands and threaded his fingers through hers.

"And to your people, that's the same as marriage, right."

"It is, but I haven't met your parents."

He said it so earnestly that she didn't dare laugh again. "I love you. My parents will love you. They aren't going to be bothered if we live together without a big ceremony."

He frowned. "You don't want to marry me in the ways of your people."

It was a blunt statement full of disappointment. She

studied his face a moment noting the hurt in his gaze. "Of course I do. I just thought you wouldn't want all the pomp and circumstance again."

He pulled her toward the kitchen scooping his shirt and sweater up as they made their way. "When I was married the first time, there were no such customs or traditions for the poor. Angharad and I were neighbors. When my parents died, I was old enough to take a wife and Angharad was old enough to be one. I arranged the matter with Angharad's father over their dining table and then we were married. We wore the best clothes we had and exchanged vows but there were no rings or feasts. I want that with you." He knelt down in front of her holding her hand—wild-haired and topless. "Phoebe, will you observe the customs of your people and marry me? A handfasting at the stone circle with friends and family as witnesses?"

She cupped his face with both hands and kissed him softly. "Yes. I would love to marry you. But you might change your minds about ceremonies after Christmas with the Pierces."

In the kitchen, Phoebe's appetite went from starving to nothing. She put her hand over her stomach trying not to alert January but it was pointless. He looked down at her hand and into her eyes with sympathy.

"I'm sorry Cariad. I know you don't want to, but if you can't make yourself eat, then you'll need to take blood."

Phoebe nodded and turned to search the cabinets. Nothing looked remotely appetizing. Taking a blueberry muffin out of its container, she peeled the paper holder off the bottom and pinched a piece off popping it into her mouth before she could change her mind. She heard rather than saw Bramble trot into the kitchen.

"Can't help eat. Not magic."

January rubbed Phoebe's back gently. "Keep trying. I'll be right back."

The food wasn't repulsive, but it wasn't good. Whether that was because it was a store-bought muffin or Phoebe was now craving blood, she wasn't sure. She made coffee wondering what January was up to. When he returned, he had what looked like two soda cans.

"Mila brought them from Japan. She calls them emergency rations. They take a minute to heat, but they aren't bad."

The black cans looked like ordinary soda cans but with a string on the side. January pulled both strings. "Have it with the muffin. Don't overthink it."

Phoebe wrinkled her nose. "I would rather you feed me."

A sexy smile crossed his lips as he handed her a can. "Me too but that way leads back to bed and we are running short on time. I'll make it up to you."

Taking a deep breath, she downed as much of the drink as she could in big gulps. It was thick and tasteless rather than repulsive. The warmth reminded her of thick broth. Broth reminded her of… She pulled the can away from her mouth and tried not to throw up. January was at her side with his arms around her.

"You will finish your drink and your muffin and remember both of them as delicious."

Phoebe allowed the compulsion to flow over and through her. Her stomach settled down and she found herself starving again. The muffin and blood drink were followed by a second muffin, an egg on buttered toast, and some coffee. Bramble and January cheered her on. For the first time since before the Ball, Phoebe felt like a human again. The thought amused her.

"I have years of this to look forward to?"

He looked down at the cans with a sigh. "I'm afraid so.

The conversion has started but the transformation takes time. It will get easier."

Phoebe put the dishes in the sink. "It better. My mom is not going to be happy if neither of us is eating. I've just about got her convinced that your liquid diet helps you with stomach problems."

By the time January packed Alex's things, Phoebe and Bramble had already loaded their things into his car. He placed Alex's things in the car that Alex had taken from the drive when he'd come to rescue Phoebe. If the Recovery Center wasn't ready to release him, then they would leave the car and his things there so that he could get home. That he might choose a different home while he was here flit-tered across January's mind, but he didn't examine it too closely.

He tossed Phoebe the keys. "Were headed to the Augusta Recovery Center. It's a little over 2 hours from here. We won't have long with Alex because we have another two and a half hours to get to Boston."

"Got it."

She looked back at the cabin for a long moment as if she were trying to memorize every detail before she left. He looked at it again understanding that this was a sanc-tuary for Phoebe as well.

"We should come back for Yule. See if there is anything in that Christmas Market that will impress your parents."

She arched a brow, her grin so cat-like Bramble would be proud. "Who says I'm inviting you to my parents' house for Christmas?"

Now it was his turn to grin. "You don't have to. Josh invited me." He got into the car and started it before Phoebe could close her mouth.

. . .

The Augusta Recovery Center was much more like a private hospital than the Boston one was. The long pale corridors, impressionist art, and sterile clean surfaces lacked the strong scent of disinfectant, but there was no doubt that this was a hospital. The door guard was a werewolf dressed all in black with no name tag, just a badge that said Dark Wolf Security.

The guard stood as they approached the door and although he was not a large man, his presence filled the corridor. "Who are you here to see?"

"Alex Kimbos," January said handing the guard his ID. "I'm his guide."

The guard's half-interested expression turned serious. "You'll need to check with reception, but I don't think he's going anywhere soon. He should have been brought here when he started having trouble."

January took his ID back with a nod. "I know. I was overindulgent. He didn't want to come, and I love him too much to force him."

Phoebe stepped closer gently brushing her shoulder against his.

The guard's frown softened, and he reached forward to pat January on the shoulder. "He's a stubborn cuss but he's going to be okay. Noah Hernandez will get him straightened out in no time. You'll see."

Phoebe frowned. "I thought Selene Hernandez was his guide here?"

The guard laughed. "Selene? She's a damn good scientist but a rotten guide. Noah gets the tough cases." He turned to January. "Reception is halfway up the hall and to your left. You'll need to sign in." He pulled a metal rod from his pocket and held it out to Phoebe. She took it from him running it over her palm like Finn had done in Boston and then did the same to January.

When she handed the rod back, the guard looked at her appreciatively. "Good luck."

As they strolled up the corridor hand-in-hand Phoebe had the impression that January was looking out for someone. He checked over his shoulder more than once, his gaze searching the face of each person he passed.

"Who are you looking for?"

"Noah Hernandez. We had a…discussion before I found you that was less than friendly. I want to make sure I'm not sneaking up on him or his life-mate."

"How do you know what his life-mate looks like?"

"I saw her at the shop you buy candles from."

"Emily Rollins? Noah Hernandez werewolf tamer is married to Emily Rollins?"

"I'm not sure she knows it yet, but yes, she is. Werewolf bonding is involuntary."

They reached the desk with Phoebe still sputtering. The receptionist glanced up, her bright smile turning into a questioning frown.

"Can I help you?"

"I'm-

"Phoebe Pierce?"

The sound of Noah Hernandez's voice echoed down the hall and everyone within hearing distance turned and looked at the werewolf. He was standing beside a giant of a man in one of the doorways. January swept Phoebe behind him baring his teeth in warning.

"Get out of my way and stop being ridiculous," Phoebe said coming out from around him with an irritated growl. She walked up to Noah without so much as a glance over her shoulder. "I'm sorry, have we met?"

The man was tall, powerfully built, his stance clearly stating that he would fight if he had to but in his golden gaze there was kindness. He was looking at her like she was something he'd lost and expected never to find.

A small, beautiful woman pushed her way between the werewolves to look at January. "Holy shit, that's a vampire. Unicorns, vampires, and werewolves. Today just keeps getting better and better."

The nursing attendant stood up from behind the desk. "Mr. Landis, please take your wife back to her room. Mr. Hernandez, take your conversation outside, you're disturbing my ward."

January didn't greet Noah or give Phoebe a chance to speak. He pulled her quickly into his arms and before she could chastise him again, they both vanished.

THE CIRCLE IS CAST

January, Phoebe, Bramble, and the green book appeared in the Mabon Council meeting room. In front of them, stood Lana, Cherry Blossom, and Jerry holding hands and chanting with their eyes closed. January stepped away from Phoebe just before Lana opened her eyes, looked straight at them, and said, "Rigor."

His arms clamped to his side and all but his head went completely rigid.

"What is the meaning of this?" he demanded.

Around the table sat Olivia, Enir, and two women January didn't recognize. They were like opposite sides of a coin, one painfully beautiful and the other so plain that as soon as you saw her, her image slipped from your mind.

Lana approached them, carrying a metal rod. "We need to make sure that we have the right people."

Before she could get close to them January heard Bramble's grumbling growl come from the floor and then felt the familiar's soft warm body press against his leg. The spell that held him immobile drained from his body and disappeared.

Bramble turned and hissed at Lana. "Bad. Apologize."

The look of shock on Lana's face almost made the experience worth it. He'd bet money that she hadn't had one of her spells reversed since she was the Maiden of the council. He walked toward her, took the metal rod from her hand, and gave it to Phoebe. She held it a moment meeting Lana's eyes and then placed it on the table in front of Jerry.

"Quite right," Cherry Blossom said. "I apologize for both the summons and the binding spell." She gave Lana a disappointed look. "We felt the summons was necessary given the situation." Cherry Blossom bowed her head. "May I introduce Isla Wildwood, representative of the Unseelie Queen."

The beautiful woman nodded her head, but her eyes were fixed on Phoebe.

"And Sophia Featherfoot, representative of the Seelie Queen." Sophia glanced at them, but her eyes were on Bramble. Phoebe picked the familiar up from the floor holding him to her chest. With his paws on her shoulder and his puffy tail twitching back and forth in irritation, there was no doubt in anyone's mind that Bramble meant business.

Lana laid her hand over her heart. "I apologize. This morning's incident unsettled me."

January glared at her running his hands briefly over Bramble and Phoebe to assure himself they were okay. "Why did you summon us? We already spoke to you. We were on our way."

"We didn't speak to you," Jerry said, apologetically. "We caught someone, a shapeshifter pretending to be Mila, making the phone call to you this morning. When we detained them for questioning, they…" Jerry shuddered taking a deep breath.

"Pulled themselves apart," January supplied remembering Marina and Enir's look-alike.

"You've seen it before?" Lana asked rubbing her forehead. She looked tired. They all did.

"Mila's house applicant, Marina, attacked Phoebe at the Sailor's Catch in September. When her maker demanded she tell us why she did it, the shadow and the blood compulsion must have been set against each other and..." He let them fill in the rest.

Jerry shuddered again. "It is a blood compulsion, but not the type you're thinking. The shadow agents have a self-destruct that is triggered when they are compelled to tell the truth."

Cherry Blossom motioned for them all to take a seat. "Please. We need your help."

Enir flipped her long hair over her shoulder. From her sharp red nails to her immaculate dress suit, she looked every bit the vampire house elder that she was. "For their help, the council will financially compensate the House of Norn for the inconvenience. If January, Phoebe, or Bramble should be injured or die while giving this assistance, or as a direct result of this assistance, then compensation will be an open vow to serve the House of Norn for the lifespan of the three combined."

"That is ludicrous. An open vow? No one would agree to that," Lana huffed flattening her ears to her head.

Enir shrugged and pushed her chair back from the table. "Then we don't help. If you aren't confident enough to make the pledge, then there is greater danger or less competence than I've been led to believe. You are asking me to risk my favorite, my newest house member, and her familiar." She motioned for Phoebe and January to follow her. "I'm not doing it for free."

"Wait," Cherry Blossom said holding up her hand. "My colleagues can do as they wish, but I'm willing to make the vow. Without them, we have no way of untangling this mess."

"Start again from the beginning," Phoebe said coming around the table and taking a seat with Melissa and Olivia. Bramble followed her to her chosen seat, and she pulled a chair out for January. Enir got up from where she was sitting to sit in the chair Phoebe pulled out.

"Thank you pet. I'm still mad at you for ruining my Samhain Party." She took the green book from Phoebe and set it on the table.

January picked up the metal rod from in front of Jerry and walked straight to Enir holding it out for her to take. "Be mad at yourself. If you'd given us a little time, you could have had your party and celebrated our joining with us. I'm mad at you for ruining my engagement proposal."

Enir wrinkled her nose at him taking the rod and holding it. "You're slow at commitment and I hate waiting. You'll just have to host the ball again, and I want a new dress."

Jerry cleared his throat. "Phoebe, is that the green book you read the spell from?"

"You could read this book?" Enir asked sharply.

Phoebe flipped the book open showing Enir the white pages. "I did read from it, but I can't see the spells anymore."

Enir put her hand on the blank page. Instantly the pages transformed into beautifully decorated spells.

January glared at her. "I knew it. You're Nesta. You planned this all along. You used the book to force Phoebe through the Veil."

Enir snapped the book closed. "Love brought Phoebe through. Not forced. I didn't know she worked for the shop, and I paid dearly to guarantee this book was warded. It was a gift for you." She pushed the book toward him. "For Samhain."

Jerry tried to regain control of the conversation. "Our investigation into Phoebe's Awakening says the primary source of the Awakenings in the Boston area in the last six months is related directly to The Craft Shop."

Olivia stood up angrily. "That's ridiculous."

"But true." Jerry looked at Phoebe carefully. "In light of the suggestion that Phoebe was already Awakened on the date that January summoned her to his circle, we interviewed some of the most recently Awakened. A majority say that they were in or purchased something from The Craft Shop."

"Were those purchases candles?" January asked.

Jerry looked down at a report on his desk. "Some of them, but not enough to connect the Awakenings to the candles. Do you have a theory?"

"There is a green-scented candle made by a witch in Larkshead called Emily Rollins. Phoebe buys the candles from her and sells them from The Craft Shop. Sometimes these candles are lit while the shoppers are in the store. I believe one of them, a candle called Enlightenment, is the source of the outbreaks."

"Let's put that at the top of our investigation list," said Lana looking relieved. "Otherwise, we will have no choice but to hold Phoebe, Melissa, and Olivia responsible for the Unguided outbreak here."

"A witch hunt, how droll." Enir folded her hands in front of her. "You just said some of the Awakenings were connected to the shop, not all. That means neither the lit candle nor The Craft Shop are fully responsible for all the Awakenings. In fact, it suggests that both are the victims rather than the perpetrators of the Awakenings. I suggest you hunt that perpetrator down first because if you come for a member of my household without undeniable evidence they are involved in this outbreak, I will make sure that your pretty little city and this council burn to the ground. Now, skip to the part where you need our help."

Cherry Blossom frowned. "We want to issue a warrant

to arrest January for the unsanctioned Awakening of Phoebe. It will be a death warrant. Phoebe and Bramble will be remanded to the Boston Recovery Center for observation. We believe that should prompt the original attacker to attempt to either obtain her or end her life."

"A trap!" Enir clapped her hands together. "Superb. Then what?"

"No," January said simply. "I won't be separated from Phoebe again, especially not to put her in danger."

Lana continued, "We will hope that Phoebe's attacker can lead us to the person responsible for the attacks on the rest of the Unguided witches."

Jerry looked at Phoebe pleadingly. "You said James tried to pick you up for the first council meeting. He's missing. He's been organizing the theft of information on the Unguided from the Recovery Centers. He delivers the names to both the Seelie and the Unseelie Queen via a court representative. For some reason, we can't locate him or the representatives he's using."

"He's shadow-cursed," January said putting the green book in his lap. "I don't know how long he's been cursed but myself, Olivia, Melissa, and Mila witnessed it."

Isla spoke, her voice both soft and powerful. "Impossible. Shadow cursing is forbidden. The method for doing it is older than this council and well-guarded. My Queen would never tolerate it."

Sophia joined in, her voice so beautiful and sweet that Phoebe found herself leaning forward to hear her. "The Seelie and Unseelie court have agreed that it is forbidden. My Queen would also never allow it."

The two women looked at each other before Sophia continued, "We wouldn't risk another war."

"My deepest respect to you and your Queens, but it is happening." January met the gaze of each woman. One of them was lying. Normally it could be assumed that it was the Unseelie Court but not if Isla Wildwood was representing them. She didn't lie, even when that lie would help her.

"We can concur," said Cherry Blossom. "The shapeshifter that died this morning was also shadow-cursed. If you would be so kind as to inform your Queens that someone is breaking their truce. Any assistance in discovering who is doing it would be well compensated."

Both women bowed their heads in tandem. Sophia began to rise but Isla stopped her. "We can help as far as this. The information about the Unguided witches is being brought to both Queens by me. I deliver the names."

Sophia placed her hand on Isla's shoulder. "Both courts are looking for the source of the unsanctioned Awakenings."

Jerry nodded but looked uncomfortable. "James said the Unseelie Queen was responsible for the attacks. He said she's killing witches to protect the Veil."

Isla arched a brow. "That is a serious accusation. My Queen does nothing that does not directly benefit her. It would be better for her to recruit Unguided witches than risk killing them."

"Even if five of those Unguided witches might bring down the whole Veil?" Olivia asked crossing her arms over her chest.

Sophia snickered. "Bring down the Veil? That is a fairy-tale told to scare Fey children. The Veil has been in existence since 43 AD. It exists in every part of the globe. One thousand fully trained witches couldn't bring it down much less five untrained witches. Come Isla. Let's leave the mortals to their stories." She held her hand out for Isla to follow.

Isla grasped Sophia's hand. "Perhaps there is something we can do to clear the air?"

Sophia placed a light kiss on the top of Isla's hand. "Speak, sister. I'm listening."

"These people say the shadow cursed have to self-destruct if they are compelled to tell the truth. Is there not a Seelie spell that can compel both Enlightened and Unenlightened to tell the truth."

Sophia frowned, sitting back down. "There is."

"If your Queen would consent to allow us to use the spell, we could use the witches here to call the elements and amplify it. Then we could be sure the shadow cursed were dead."

Jerry looked sick. "We can't. That would destroy the shadows but it would also instantly kill all of the people who are shadow cursed."

Sophia shook her head. "We can't have people tearing themselves apart on the street. My Queen would never consent to that."

"If she won't destroy them then she can't prove her innocence," Isla said pulling her hand away. "I will have to report that to my Queen."

"Summon shadows here, all shadows, not people. Phoebe help. Does truth spell here? Ask shadows." Bramble yawned and lay down on the table with his paws crossed.

Sophia folded her hands in her lap looking at Isla. "Your Queen has a blood spell that can summon the shadows. If you believe she is innocent, ask her for the blood and for the spell."

Jerry looked at Cherry Blossom. "If we can summon only the shadows and compel them to speak the truth, we can ask them who summoned them first. Then we would have the truth, and they would destroy themselves."

Lana nodded. "Sophia, Isla, can you give us the spells? You and Isla will need to leave the room when the spell is cast. If we're wrong and we can't hold the shadows with the circle and sigils, then they will come for us. The last thing I want is to have the two most senior advisors of the Unseelie and Seelie Court infected with a shadow curse."

"You need insurance. A holding vessel. A who rather than a what. Nothing is more tempting to a Shadow than the promise of a willing body." Sophia looked around the room.

"Maybe not," January said, looking excited. "When Marina was dead, the shadow looked for someone to enter, but I managed to put it in a bottle. I believe I could do it again."

Sophia looked at Isla. "We can protect ourselves. If we leave, we won't know who is lying."

Isla smiled a cold, hard smile. "I agree. We will both help. Give us until tomorrow to inform our Queens and gather what is needed for the truth spell."

James woke up with scratches on his body, blood on his hands, a deep and vicious bite mark on his arm, and almost completely frozen to the rocky shore. The shadow-curse was winning. More and more of his time was missing from his memory and for that, he was grateful. When he slept at night, he wouldn't remember the faces and the names of the Unguided his body betrayed. It wouldn't be long until his soul was displaced from this body completely and he would be able to leave it behind. He hung on for one reason only: to save January's life.

The news that January had been arrested and would be destroyed tonight had come to him accidentally. Death was not a punishment dealt out often, and the Enlightened were disturbed. January had a reputation for being cold but under that was also the knowledge that he was fair, generous with his resources and time, and that he'd rescued Alex Kimbos from death. It was hard to believe that he would be killed not only for the unsanctioned

Awakening of Phoebe Pierce but also for attacking her with the intent to force her conversion.

The need to prove January's innocence gave the small sliver of his body and mind that still responded to his commands a purpose. He bathed the bite and then his body in the seawater more to irritate the shadow inside him than because he needed to. No amount of washing would take the blood from his hands now. He had failed to get Emily Rollins to confess, and the shadow had almost caused him to kill her, but he could go back to Boston with the information he'd stolen from Augusta to prove that Emily and her candles were responsible for unsanctioned Awakenings connected to The Craft Shop. That included the Awakening of Phoebe Pierce. As for attacking her, James would show them the shadow curse. January must have also been cursed. It was the only explanation as to why he would attack the woman who was supposed to be his companion.

Willing his skin to warm, he brushed the remains of the salt off his body and headed inland. There was no path to happiness left for him now. Once this was done, he would surrender his body to the shadow and be free.

There was so much that January needed to do, but all he really wanted was to take Phoebe home. In a tearful call to Josh, Phoebe made him promise that if she became a shadow, he would take care of their parents, marry Jerry, and show up for holidays on time. January gave her some privacy.

Enir sat in the study with the green book in her lap. A black dress gave her a ghostly appearance. The book was open to the spell Phoebe had cast to come into the circle. When she saw him in the doorway, she waved him to her side.

"Are you planning a spell of your own?" he asked, sitting beside her.

She caressed the book with both hands. "I always was. I bought this book from the Seelie Court at great expense so we could cast this spell together."

"You're still looking for Nesta?"

She nodded, watching her own fingers trace the words of the spell. "Yes. She promised me that if she died, she would come back and find me. If she can't find me, then I will go to her."

January gathered her hands to get her attention. "Phoebe and I will help you cast it before we go back to the Recovery Center tonight."

Heaving a ragged sigh, Enir put her arms around him crushing the book between them. "Can I not have you both, my favorite mistake? Have I not paid enough for what I did?"

January returned her hug. "You did what anyone would have done under those circumstances. I forgive you."

She pushed away from him dashing tears from her eyes and setting the book on the table. "That is kind of you to say but you don't know the whole of the story. You don't really think it was all an accident, my favorite? Nesta wasn't on the field feeding at random. We were looking for you."

January moved back the book slipping to the ground between them. He searched her face to see if this was another of her games, but her blue eyes met his with conviction. "Why?"

"To make amends for Angharad. We didn't know she was sick. She was on her own in the woods gathering firewood. So beautiful. We fed lightly, but there were two of us. Nesta wanted to stay and nurse her until you returned, but the villagers were already looking at us with suspicion. We left her."

January got up from the couch, his mind completely rejecting the story. "She would have told me."

Enir smiled sadly. "She couldn't tell you. I gave her blood to help her mend and to forbid her from telling anyone. It was a dangerous time then. We sent word to summon you home, but it was too late. Her body rejected my blood. When you returned to the battlefront after her death, we promised each other that if you lived, we would take care of you."

"You were looking for me. That's why you weren't watching out for Nesta while she fed."

Enir picked the book up from the floor and set it beside her without meeting his gaze. "She was upset with me. I gave her a little space. When you killed her, I was distraught. I meant to kill you. I left you for dead next to a stream, and I went to bury my wife. When I pushed the soil over her beautiful body, that's when I realized what I'd done. You buried your wife because of me, and I buried mine because of you."

"You came back and finished the conversion." He came back to the couch to sit with her, but he couldn't look at her yet. All he could see was Angharad's frail body.

She nodded again. "It would have been kinder to let you die. I was so angry. I half hoped you wouldn't survive, and then you did. I punished you for surviving because Nesta didn't." She turned, running her fingers across his jaw. "We meant no harm."

He caught her hand and put it back into her lap. "Is that why you want to convert Phoebe so badly? You want to make amends for Angharad?"

Enir rolled her eyes, but her attempt at humor only made her look sadder. "I want you to have a chance at happiness, my favorite."

"Why tell me today?" He pushed himself off the couch

meaning to walk out the door, but he turned on her instead. "You had 800 years to tell me!"

"Because I'm trying not to be selfish. If the shadow takes you tonight, I vow that I will release you and Phoebe before you can cause harm." She stood and walked slowly to January's side, handing him the book. "If you both survive, then I beg you to either help me return to Nesta's side or to help me find the courage to cross death again and find her."

She could have ordered him to kill her at any time, but she was asking for his help. Angharad had always been a wild, headstrong woman. It was one of the reasons he loved her. He remembered the soul-destroying hunger of the old days. The endless searching for someone who was willing to share their blood and keep quiet about it.

He opened the book looking down at the spell on the page. "You're leaving an important part of this story out."

She shook her head, her eyes imploring him to believe her. "I have told you everything."

"What about the part where my wife was Enlightened? Or where she made the choice to feed you and Nesta in the woods even though she knew she was sick?"

"What difference does that make?" Enir crossed her arms over her chest. "The end result is the same."

He offered the book back to her. "The difference is she made a choice. She knew the consequences and chose to feed you anyway. She chose not to tell you she was ill. There's nothing to forgive. Angharad wasn't forced. She might have overestimated her own strength, but that isn't your fault, and it isn't Nesta's. You must forgive Nesta in order to find her."

Enir rocked back for a moment as if she'd been struck. "Forgive Nesta?"

"Nesta was a vampire. She would have heard me

coming. We both know she could have easily defended herself. She paid for Anghared's life with her own."

Her cry of denial echoed through the house. January knelt beside her with his hand on her back. "Forgive your companion. You have both suffered needlessly."

On her knees with shaking hands, Enir laid the book out in front of her. January stood up and stepped back to give her some room.

"My body standing on this plane, dissolve and become whole again. By Earth, Air, Water, Fire, bring me to my heart's desire."

Enir sat back on her heels with her hands in her lap and closed her eyes. There was a golden flash of light in the room, and then she was gone. He collected the book from the floor and put it on his shelf.

28

WITCH HUNT

When Phoebe came into the library, January was staring out the window. A cheerful fire burned in the fireplace, Bramble was snoozing on Alex's bed, and Enir had vanished. Josh had threatened, begged, and cajoled, but the best he could get from her was a promise to be careful and to protect Jerry.

She came up behind him wrapping her arms around his waist and laying her head on his back. "We have about four hours before we need to go. If we go now, we can make love in the stone circle and be back before Bramble realizes we're gone."

January laughed pulling her arms more tightly around himself. "It's December. That was definitely not part of my fantasy. We don't have to rush. There will be plenty of warm days in our future where we can do it without the threat of frost bite."

She placed a kiss between his shoulders. "You think we're going to win?"

"I know we are. When we come home tonight, we're going to call Alex and make sure he's okay, we're going to eat what ever is salvageable out of the fridge, and then we're going to see how many positions are actually possible on our tantra couch."

"Our tantra couch?" Her shoulders were shaking with laughter.

He looked over his shoulder at her with an arched brow. "Well, I'm not getting on that thing by myself."

She hugged him tight wishing there was some way to freeze time. "I love you. You're a very kinky man, but I love you."

January turned and swooped her into his arms carrying her out of the library.

She shrieked with laughter. "Where are we going?"

"I'm sure there's time to try a few positions on that couch before we have to go."

The council chamber was transformed into a ritual circle. The table was gone and in its place, there was a thick white circle made of salt on the floor. In each of the four corners, there was an offering bowl. A candle for fire, seawater, a bowl full of sandalwood incense filled the air with smoke, and in the final bowl, some soil from January's sacred circle.

In the center was a black circle and the sigil Olivia and Melissa used to trap James. In the four corners of the sigil Melissa, Isla, and Sophia sat waiting. Phoebe took her place in the East, Jerry took his place in the West, Olivia took her place in the North, and Lana stood in the South for fire. Mila stood next to January and Bramble outside the circles holding a bottle of the same blood wine she'd served to January on that Lammas night so long ago.

Mila would not be left behind. January didn't argue with her. She vowed to avenge Marina and he wouldn't stand in her way.

Cherry Blossom stood at the head of the circle with the

spell Sophia brought from the Seelie court to compel the truth and the spell brought from the Unseelie court to summon the shadow.

"Let's begin. Call the corners."

Lana knelt down and lit the candle. "I call upon the element of fire. Join us and be welcome here."

Olivia knelt down running her fingers through the dark soil in the bowl. "I call upon the element of Earth. Join us and be welcome here."

Jerry knelt and placed the tips of his fingers in the salt water. "I call upon the element of water. Come and be welcome here."

Phoebe knelt and wafted her hand through the sweet-smelling smoke. "I call upon the element of air, come and be welcome here."

Cherry Blossom raised her arms to the sky. "We are safe within the circle." She began the chant. Earth, Air, Fire, Water. They spoke together, the rhythm of their words syncing and then growing stronger. One by one, each witch who knelt, stood up holding their element between their hands. The earth trembled, the fire flared, a breeze moved around and through the circle, and the seawater hovered above the bowl in a wriggling sphere.

Cherry Blossom walked slowly around the circle welcoming each element. Then she turned to Isla and Melissa. "Call the shadows."

Mila opened the wine bottle and took a deep drink and then another. She handed the bottle to January. Isla took a black pouch from around her neck and removed a small vile and a piece of black glass no bigger than the palm of her hand. She placed the glass inside the sigil.

"Mirror of shadow soul's desire, I call to you by blood and fire, to this place, you are compelled to appear. Queen Banrigh demands you show yourself here."

She opened the vile carefully. January could smell the power of the blood from where he stood.

"The Unseelie Queen's blood." Mila took a step back from the circle as Isla poured five drops of blood on the mirror."

The lights flashed and then went off. The darkness was absolute and from the blackness came sounds of wailing and snarling. January felt like any hope of success was being drained from his body. Then he felt Mila push the bottle into his hand.

"Put them in the bottle and the bottle in the circle."

He opened it taking a large drink of the blood himself and then called.

"In our blackest hour of need. Darkness you are bound. Confined in this bottle until it breaks on hallowed ground."

There was a shriek of outrage as the blackness was sucked out of the room into the bottle. January moved as fast as he could to the sigil but stopped stunned. In the middle of the sigil, just like he'd been in The Craft Shop, was James. His face and body were gaunt with hunger, his black hair hanging in tatters on his head. Isla grabbed the bottle from his hands and before he could stop her, she placed it in the sigil with James.

The bottle burst almost instantly, each of the shadows attempting to destroy one another and take the body trapped in the circle with them. James screamed in pain and choked on blood.

January rushed forward to help him, but Isla stood in his way.

"If you break the circle, you kill us all and his sacrifice is for nothing." There were tears in her eyes and her voice was ragged.

Everyone but Sophia, January, and Isla closed their eyes to keep themselves from breaking the ward. Sophia removed a small bag from around her neck. She poured what looked like silver dust in her hand.

"From this moment. In this hour. I call upon the highest power. Rid the world of lies and fear. Only truth may remain here."

She blew the silver dust into the circle. "Tell us now, demon. Who sent the shadows? Who is bringing down the Veil?"

James screamed in pain. There was a flash of green light. It started from the center of James's chest and then flashed through the room, through the Recovery Center, through the city, and then through the world. For one heart-stopping minute, there were no lies, no deception, no Veil. James fell to his hands and knees, his body blackening and bulging in all directions trying to destroy itself before he could speak. He threw his head back, blood tears running down his face. His voice was like a thousand voices all coming from his mouth at once.

"The Veil is falling. It is almost gone.bWind is here and earth is called, water is here and fire is shaken when the truth speaker speaks, the world will Awaken."

"Who called the shadows?" Sophia demanded.

James looked at Isla and January he felt that there was a message passed between them. "Banrigh," he growled picking up the black glass from the ground. "By her blood, return to your maker." He shattered it against the ground.

A black hole opened between the shards of black glass and the shadows flowed down it like water down a drain. James collapsed bloody and was beaten inside the sigil. The shadow within him tried to drag him into the darkness but he drove his claws into the ground to stop it. With a final shriek of outrage, the last of the shadows were pulled into the darkness and the hole closed. Even though it was clear they were safe, no one cheered.

Isla looked at James in horror. She ran into the circle turning him over on his back. "What have you done?"

His raspy laughter broke January's heart. "I sent those bastards back to where they came from."

Sophia entered the sigil and placed her hands on him. A mellow orange light spilled from her palms. The wounds on James healed and his body plumped with health. "The truce is broken. I will inform my Queen. James, we are in your debt. How can we repay you?"

"Allow me to disappear. No courts, no questions."

Sophia nodded. "I will see that it is done."

Cherry Blossom raised her voice. "We end this here. Earth, Air, Fire, Water. Thank you for your blessings tonight. We thank you for joining us. Depart with our blessings."

"Blessed be," They all whispered.

In the darkness of the Unseelie Court Queen Banrigh screamed in agony. The restlessness amongst the Unenlightened grew every day. The Recovery Centers could barely cope with the number of people shut down by the Green Flash. Those who had seen through the Veil only to have it dropped over their eyes again were both vigilant and afraid.

29

SAMHAIN BLESSINGS

January waited for Phoebe in the center of the White Stone Circle beside Cherry Blossom. The circle was decorated with orange and black ribbons, fire caldrons, jack-o-lanterns and fancy gourds of every shape and size, and enough orange, white and yellow chrysanthemums to transform the forest into a fairyland.

From deep in the forest, music played signaling the start of the ceremony. Bramble marched forward on the silver lined path towards the stone circle, head and tail held high, an orange ribbon tied around his neck. Behind him followed Melissa, Olivia, and Jerry dressed in suits and long gowns of red.

Beside him stood Josh, Alex, and Brindle in fine linen tunics and trousers. The moon filtered through the branches and decorated the brightly covered autumn leaves with complex patterns. The music grew louder, and on the path emerged Phoebe's parents, Ellie and Adam Pierce, walking hand in hand into the circle to stand with Cherry Blossom.

Phoebe bought them an Enlightenment candle for Yule and true to their colorful nature, Phoebe's parents accepted their daughter was a witch, their soon to be son-in-law was a vampire, their other soon to be son-in-law was a witch, and that their family now had two talking cats. The Enlightened world was new and exciting to them and the only thing that seemed to shock them was that they hadn't been Enlightened before.

January had not only survived the Pierce family Christmas, he dived in head-first. From the gifts that needed to be made by hand, to the over-abundance of affection and advice, to the requirement to make a wish at midnight while standing out in the cold in your Pajamas, he performed each family ritual like it was the best thing he'd ever done. Alex spent most of his time getting the hang of being a werewolf at Larkshead, but he'd been convinced by the promise of a snuggle with Bramble and Brindle, lots of alcohol, and the opportunity to eat both his and January's portion of food to come to the Pierce family Christmas.

As recompense for distributing the candles that had resulted in the Unguided Awakenings in Boston, Olivia, Melissa, and Phoebe volunteered to help Selene Hernandez and Emily Rollins locate the Unguided affected by the candles. Although James had gone back to Larkshead to make amends to Emily, he'd been caught and lost in a Wild Fey spell. The search for the Unguided revealed what Enir had suggested at the council meeting. The failure of the Veil could not be fully attributed to the candles. Phoebe's guide for the newly Awakened was a great success and The Boston Recovery Center had suggested more than once that she re-consider opening her own magic store and train as a guide.

The music changed and at the edge of the woods, Phoebe emerged dressed in a heavy damask green gown covered with silver oak leaves and acorns. In a tradition almost as old as marriage itself, Phoebe wore a circlet of flowers on her head. She was the most stunning creature that January had ever seen. She came to his side with a smile as bright as the sun. They faced one another holding hands.

"We are here to witness the joining of two lives into one." Cherry Blossom's voice rang through the circle. She drew them closer placing Phoebe's left arm on top of January's right.

"Speak your vows to one another."

Phoebe looked at him with such love that January felt his eyes fill with tears. "Phoebe. You are my companion, my life-mate. You honor me today." He looked at Alex and then back at her. "I vow to you in this life and beyond to be never above you, never below you, always beside you."

"*Ionawr.*"

He looked at her surprised and grateful that she chose to say his name in his first language.

"You are my companion, my life-mate. You honor me today. I vow to you in this life and beyond to be never above you, never below you, always beside you."

Cherry Blossom took a long cloth also embroidered with oak branches, oak leaves, and acorns. The two branches stretched towards one another entangling and joining in the middle. She dropped the cloth over the middle of their joined hands and wrapped it around both of their arms.

"You are joined by choice. You remain together by choice. Like these branches, you must remember to reach for one another to be able to grow together. Let this hand-fasting cloth remind you of the vows you make today."

"I will," January said.

"I will." Phoebe echoed.

"I will." Bramble rumbled solemnly.

She unwrapped their hands and gave the handfasting cloth to Phoebe's brother to hold. "You may kiss the bride."

He didn't have to be asked twice. Sweeping Phoebe into

his arms just as he had the first time he'd seen her in the circle, he kissed her.

Whatever they faced in the future, they would face it together.

-The End-

ACKNOWLEDGMENTS

"Never above you, never below you, always beside you," was written by Walter Winchell, an American journalist, sometime in the 1940s. This was unknown to the author at the time her novels were written. There is no relationship between her novels and the works of Walter Winchell.

ABOUT THE AUTHOR

Dr. DeAnn Bell is a Kentucky-born, New Mexico-raised writer who lives permanently in Wales with her husband and cats. She is widely published in places such as Open Pen, Women's Archive Wales, Witches and Pagans, and Sage Woman. She has a Ph.D. in Creative and Critical Writing and is a professional member of the National Association of Writers in Education, The Society of Authors, and organizes the North Wales Pagan Moot Group. She loves coffee, cats, and genre-bending fiction with complex conflicts and real-world issues, especially if they have happy endings.

Printed in Great Britain
by Amazon